"Let me take you someplace, okay?" Max said

Becky couldn't manage more than a mute nod. She didn't bother to ask where they were going or how long they'd be there. As long as she was with Max, she was happy.

When he lifted her, it seemed the most natural thing in the world to wrap her arms around his neck—and her legs around his waist. He carried her through the empty lounge and over to the baby grand concealed behind the decorative metal screen. Kicking the bench aside, he sat her down atop the piano's glossy hood.

He stepped between her parted legs and bent to brush kisses along her knee. "You're beautiful. So beautiful."

Bracing herself on her palms, Becky leaned back on the cool surface and let the heat the man was stirring within her wash over her like a warm, sexy wave.

Then Max's hands were on her thighs, pushing her dress up and out of the way and Becky forgot everything else....

Dear Reader,

Strokes of Midnight is my second winter holiday
book for Harlequin's Blaze line and my first
contribution to its WRONG BED series.

Bound for New York on New Year's Eve, romance
novelist Becky Stone, aka Rebecca St. Claire,
feels certain her horoscope forecasting a new
year of "fresh starts" and "dazzling opportunities"
is about to come true. Instead, Becky learns
she has no choice but to coauthor her next
book with bestselling action-adventure novelist
Adam Maxwell if she's going to save her career.

The tall, blue-eyed hunk Becky bumps into in
Midtown seems straight out of a fairy tale. With
the stroke of midnight fast approaching, a sexy
one-night stand seems the perfect way to ring in
the New Year. Besides, it's not as if she has to ever
see him again—right?

Wrong. Her perfect stranger is Adam Maxwell, and
as writing partners they are going to be seeing
each other day—and night—for the next several
months. Can these two accidental lovers craft the
perfect plotline and still fall head over heels in
love?

Wishing you a holiday season filled with magical
moments and sexy surprises....

Hope Tarr
www.hopetarr.com

HOPE TARR
Strokes of Midnight

TORONTO • NEW YORK • LONDON
AMSTERDAM • PARIS • SYDNEY • HAMBURG
STOCKHOLM • ATHENS • TOKYO • MILAN • MADRID
PRAGUE • WARSAW • BUDAPEST • AUCKLAND

ISBN-13: 978-0-373-79368-6
ISBN-10:   0-373-79368-5

STROKES OF MIDNIGHT

www.eHarlequin.com

Printed in U.S.A.

ABOUT THE AUTHOR

Hope Tarr is an award-winning author of multiple contemporary and historical romance novels. *Strokes of Midnight* is her third book for Harlequin's Blaze line and her first contribution to its WRONG BED series. When not writing, Hope indulges her passions for feline rescue and historic preservation.

To enter Hope's monthly contest, visit her online at www.hopetarr.com.

Books by Hope Tarr

HARLEQUIN BLAZE
293—IT'S A WONDERFULLY SEXY LIFE
317—THE HAUNTING

To my friends, Barbara Casana and Susan Shaver, for seeing me through yet another of life's not so little challenges with wit, wisdom and laughter.

Also, to my wonderful editor, Brenda Chin, for her keen insights and patience in helping me bring Max and Becky's story to life on the printed page.

Prologue

Train bound for New York City
December 31st, 10:30 a.m. (give or take)

"SO, HAVE you started celebrating your big book deal yet? I expected to hear champagne corks popping in the background." Sharon's voice, sounding as excited as Becky felt, faded in and out amidst the cell phone static.

Holding the phone more snugly against her ear, Becky Stone, soon-to-be bestselling romance novelist Rebecca St. Claire, didn't bother to strip the smile from her voice. "It might be New Year's Eve, but I'd better hold off on the celebrating at least until we make Manhattan."

In another few hours, Becky expected she'd be kicking up her four-inch high heels and celebrating in earnest— and not because of the holiday. The day before, her editor, Pat, had called to say she had important news to share, news with far-reaching ramifications for Becky's career, and could Becky make it up to Manhattan in the next few days so they could chat over lunch? The busy New York editor generally preferred communicating by e-mail. An actual phone call requesting an in-person meeting meant something big must have happened or was about to. Becky had immediately booked a first-class seat on an express train that would get her from Washington, D.C.'s Union Station to New York's Penn Station in less than three hours. Thinking of her fellow New York-bound holiday travelers packed like sardines into the coach and business-class cars, the splurge struck her as money well spent.

Pat's impromptu call could only mean one thing. Becky's latest Angelina Talbot novel must have sold out its print run, or close to it. The genre-bending mystery erotica series seemed to have struck a chord with her female readers that her previous historical romances had somehow missed. Who knew? But maybe the book had even made one of the bestseller lists—if not the *New York Times* then certainly *USA Today*. Why else would Pat make such a huge deal about meeting face-to-face right before the biggest party night of the year?

Becky's year-end horoscope for Libras predicting a fabulous new year chockfull of "fresh starts" and "dazzling opportunities" in her houses of career and love wasn't only coming true—she had hit some sort of astrological jackpot.

Sharon's voice pulled Becky back into the present. "Don't go too overboard on the shoe shopping, at least not until the ink dries on that megabucks multibook deal. Oh, and call me as soon as your victory lunch wraps. I want to hear all about it."

"I will." The increasing static had Becky looking out the window to the tunnel they were coming up on. "We're about to go under the Hudson River. I'd better sign off before I lose you. Thanks for calling to wish me luck. Love you, girlfriend."

"Love you, too, Becks, and Happy New Year."

Becky opened her mouth to return the holiday felicitation but the cell cut out. She clicked the phone closed and dropped it into her Kate Spade tote bag, exchanging it for her latest Angelina Talbot release. Smoothing a loving hand over the paperback's glossy-finish cover, she had to admit the art department folks had pulled out all the stops on this one. The sleek, raven-haired cover model embodied her British bombshell heroine down to her chic, body-conscious black minidress, smoking pistol and shiny black do-me stilettos. The footwear was an attitude statement, not a necessity. Becky might only stand a piddling five foot one inches sans her beloved designer high heels, but her fictional creation towered at five foot ten, tall enough to look other women and most men in the eye with or without shoes on. Along with the height she'd always coveted, Becky had blessed Angelina with a Mensa member's mind, a Playboy Bunny's libido and a Victoria's Secret model's killer curves. Talk about a complete package.

But the best part of the cover was the review from *Publishers Weekly.* Printed below the gold-embossed title, the coveted blurb proclaimed Becky "a fresh, innovative voice" and "an up-and-coming talent to watch."

An up-and-coming talent to watch… Becky slipped the book back into her bag and eased into her extrawide seat with a satisfied sigh. Stretching out her legs, she cast a fond downward glance to her Manolo Blahnik chocolate-brown Napa-leather knee boots. Growing up the middle child in a family of five in Dundalk, Maryland, designer shoes had seemed about as obtainable as Cinderella's glass slippers. Even her Barbie dolls had gone barefoot. Now she was wearing Manolo Blahniks while traveling first class. Some dreams at least did come true.

Things definitely looked brighter than they had at

Christmas the week before. She'd celebrated the eve of the holiday home alone with her tiger-striped tabby cat, Daisy Bud, Thai takeout (for her) and a can of albacore tuna (for the cat). In honor of the so-called season of hope, she'd made a wish list of all the things she wanted to do—make that *would* do—in the coming year. Become bestselling author. Take trip to Ireland. Go on motorcycle ride. Go to animal shelter and find feline friend for cat. Save up down payment for house. Meet man of dreams and fall in love...

Since her ex-boyfriend, Elliot, had dumped her for a twentysomething twit the year before, she'd been pretty cautious—okay, scared shitless—about getting involved again. Romantic intimacy played great on paper, but in real life it was damned hard to achieve. In her case, she'd been so sure the former federal agent turned media commentator was The One. After two decades of dating, starting with locking lips and orthodontics retainers with her ninth-grade boyfriend in the back of the Uptown Theater, she'd thought she was a pretty good judge of the male psyche, but her ex had played her as only an A-list player could. Looking back, the red flags popped like a neon-lit roadmap—his spurts of phone calls followed by sudden silences, his plans with her that never seemed to make it beyond the talking phase, the fact that the only address she had for him was an e-mail one. And yet she'd stayed with him, believed in him, even taken his advice to quit her day job. Talk about piss-poor judgment. Forget trusting a man again. When it came to love, how could she ever trust herself?

"Next stop, New York Penn Station."

The conductor's voice blaring over the intercom had her turning her head to look out the window just as the train emerged from the tunnel, bringing the Manhattan skyline into view like the Emerald City—distant but within reach, not unlike her dreams. Lying boyfriends and tepid book sales and money worries in general were all a part of her past. For once, *this* once, luck—and the Universe—seemed to be lining up squarely on her side.

Still thirteen and a half hours to a new year, and already it was shaping up to be 365 days of "fresh starts and dazzling opportunities"—and Becky was more than ready to let the good times roll.

1

"Turnabout is fair play, Falco, or hadn't you heard? Now where are the bloody plans?"

Dressed in dominatrix black leather down to her spiked heels, Angelina trained the subcompact Beretta on the silver-haired man lying in the center of the mussed bed. Red silk scarves lashed his wrists to the bedposts, and sweat from the long, rough ride she'd just given him rolled down his taut neck and leanly muscled torso.

The year before, the double agent had seduced her and then stolen the missile plans from her flat while she lay wrapped in silken sheets and the afterglow of his expert lovemaking. To add insult to injury, he had then turned over the plans to a twenty-two-year-old blonde for a ridiculously small sum. Rumor had it the plans were once again for sale on the black market—and that Falco knew exactly who the latest purchaser was.

Falco's deep-set dark eyes met hers from across the room. "Angelina, love, you wouldn't shoot me, not after that incredible shag we just shared. Now be a good girl and let me loose."

His cocky self-assurance made her palms itch to

slap his handsome lying face—again. "Don't flatter yourself. I would have shot you when I first spotted you at the embassy ball earlier tonight, only my gown was vintage Valentino and I hated to ruin it with the splatter."

"THE BOOK tanked, Becky. I'm sorry."

Pat punctuated her pronouncement by upending the bottle of ketchup over her burger. The bright red glob landing atop the plump, midrare patty might as well have been Becky's career lifeblood.

Eyes watering, Becky took a moment to recover from the sip of champagne she'd just aspirated. Hearing the word *tanked* in the context of her hoped-for bestseller was like watching the New Year's ball drop over Times Square—and then detonate. "I'm uh…sorry, I must have misheard you. It sounded like you said—"

"Tanked, bit the dust, bought the big one—take your pick." Pat slapped the top of her bun back on, picked up the burger and sank her teeth in for a sloppy bite. "Publishing is a tough business and, as the saying goes, 'them's the breaks.'"

Oh, God. Becky felt as though the Grinch had stolen her Christmas, not just the tree but all the trimmings, including her favorite Christmas carols and her goodwill toward men. "B-but…the sales on the launch book were solid and the reviews on this book were all—"

"Raves," Pat finished for her, ketchup dribbling down the side of her mouth. The senior editor slid her side plate of crispy thin fries toward Becky. "Try a *pomme frite*. They're delish with this Dijon mayonnaise."

Becky resisted the urge to slap a hand over her forehead, which had begun pounding like a bad hip-hop beat. As if a strip of deep-fried potato with a fancy French name could possibly make her feel better. "Thanks, but I'll pass."

Pat picked up a fry and stabbed it into the space between them. "Know what differentiates my star authors from midlist schmucks? It's not talent, though sure, talent helps. It's not looks, though those don't hurt, either. It's moxie, balls, perseverance—take your pick. Today's bestsellers, Becky, are all writers who've persevered, who've done whatever it took to claw their way back to the top of the industry heap. You have to reinvent yourself. Who was that silent film actress who said 'failure isn't the falling down but the staying down.' It's time to make like the Nike ads and just do it."

The slogan-packed pep talk had Becky feeling more panicked than inspired. "Okay, I'll reinvent myself, but how? I mean, I thought that's what I was doing by blending romantic erotica with a mystery element."

Pat nodded, her sprayed-in-place platinum hair reminiscent of Meryl Streep's in *The Devil Wore Prada*. "And it was high-concept, very high-concept—for its time."

For…its…time. The gale force of those three chilling words knocked Becky back against the booth seat. The point was, she was dated, she was done. Pat might as well pull a miniature bugle out of her Fendi shoulder bag, play some taps and make it official.

"The problem is the mainstream market for genre fiction has been shrinking steadily. It's only the established star authors who've managed to hold on to their spots. Midlist up-and-comers like you are getting squeezed out. You came on the scene a few years too late to break in. Under the circumstances, I can't offer you another multibook contract. The fact is, I can't offer you a contract at all."

So much for those forecasted fresh starts and dazzling opportunities. With no regular paycheck to fall back on, she'd been counting on her advance to pay the bills for the coming year. "But I thought you said—"

"That was before the feedback from the reader poll we ran from our Web site rolled in. Readers are burned out on Angelina's bed-hopping lifestyle."

Feeling queasy, Becky pushed her salad entrée away. "But I thought her willingness to put herself out there sexually was what they liked about her?"

Pat passed a bright-pink thumbnail over her front teeth and shook her head. "Not anymore they don't. They want to see her meet her match and settle down with a sexy male counterpart."

Becky couldn't believe what she was hearing. "Are you saying readers want Angelina to be *monogamous?*"

Pat frowned, the deep crease in her brow hinting it must be time for her next Botox treatment. Ordinarily the fifty-something's face was as tight as a twenty-year-old's and as immobile as a mannequin's. "Don't say it like it's a four-letter word. Monogamy is very hip right now. Even if it's serial monogamy, readers like to see one guy and one girl at a time."

Becky laid a hand alongside her temple where the pounding had segued into thousands of tiny needles jabbing away. "But Angelina doesn't stay in any one place long enough to form long-term relationships, romantic or otherwise. That's the glamour of her job as a crime-solving secret agent. She's always on the go."

"And she can still be on the go, only instead of just designer luggage she'll travel with a sexy partner." Pat dusted crumbs from her fingers and leaned in as though to share a confidence. "Angelina needs a man who's not just another pretty face but who's her match in every way. A man's man but not a Neanderthal, an American version of James Bond sans the tuxedo and the shaken-not-stirred martini, a guy's guy who's also sexy, gutsy, smart and sophisticated—but not so sophisticated he comes off as a wimp."

Relief flooded Becky. Her editor hadn't written her off. Pat was still on her side, still in there pitching for her. Her career wasn't dead. She was just experiencing one of those annoying setbacks most writers cycled through at some point in their careers. Like a bad menstrual period or a zit that took extra-extra long to clear, eventually this, too, would pass.

"Gotcha!" Buzzing on adrenaline, she nodded profusely and slipped to the edge of her seat. "I'll get to work on writing him ASAP. You'll have the revised proposal early next week."

Was it her admittedly overactive imagination at work or did Pat suddenly look the tiniest bit uncomfortable? "That's the best part. You don't have to create him. He's, uh…already created."

Becky was feeling more confused by the minute. "Already created? But how…"

Dropping her gaze, Pat played with the lone fry left on her plate. "Ever read any of Adam Maxwell's 'Drake's Adventures' books?"

The sucker punch hit Becky dead-on, a direct shot to the solar plexus that again had her choking on her champagne. "Adam Maxwell. *The* Adam Maxwell! If you're suggesting what I think you are, my answer is no, no way. Not on your life—or mine."

Of all the writers to propose teaming her with, Adam

Maxwell was the very worst Pat could have come up with. The reclusive author rarely ventured forth from his home in New Hampshire's White Mountains, but Becky couldn't fault him for that. Introversion was a forgivable failing, particularly among writers. When you spent the majority of your waking hours creating splendid, larger-than-life fictional characters, finding real flesh-and-blood human beings to measure up was no small feat. Occupation aside, Maxwell was a native New Englander and New Englanders had a reputation for keeping to themselves. No, if Adam Maxwell had stuck with banging out his bestsellers from behind bolted cabin doors, Becky would have no beef with him.

It was the outlandish things he said when he did venture out into the public eye that set her blood boiling. In the interview he'd given just after his second book hit the bestseller lists, he'd shown himself to be a chauvinistic jerk. A year later, his remark likening romance novels to "housewife porn" still stuck in Becky's craw. Ever since reading that quote in the *New Yorker,* she and her fellow romance writer buddies had voted Maxwell the still-living white male novelist they could feel good about hating. Who was he to judge another writer's work, anyway? He penned action-adventure novels. It's not like he was friggin' Hemingway.

Pat dropped the fry and looked up. "I love your writing, Becky, you know I do, but with these disappointing numbers, I can't sell you upstairs. Teaming you with Adam Maxwell would be a way to keep you in the game, maybe even boost you into the bestseller league. What do you say?"

Their pretty blond server sidled up, saving Becky from having to answer. "Can I bring you any coffee or dessert?"

Becky opened her mouth to ask what decadent desserts

they might have on the menu—in some cultures, chocolate was considered medicine, after all—but Pat cut her off,
handing over her credit card. "Go ahead and run this, and
please put a move on—or *vite vite* as they say in Paris."

"Whatever." The girl rolled her eyes and sped away as
only a tall girl wearing comfortably flat shoes could.

Pat turned back to the table, gaze dropping to the Dolce
& Gabbana lizard-embossed print bangle watch cuffing
her right wrist. "Sorry, doll, but I really have to dash. I have
a meeting across town with another author and catching a
cab this time of day is going to be murder."

Fighting the sinking sense she'd just had the publishing equivalent of the Last Supper, or in this case, Last
Lunch, Becky nodded. "That's okay. I need to think things
over anyway."

The waitress returned in record time. Pat signed,
snapped the vinyl bill holder shut and dropped the receipt
into her purse. "The office will be closed tomorrow for the
holiday but call me on my cell before you head back to
D.C." Pulling on her hot-pink trench coat, she slid out of
the booth. "Remember, there's a jungle filled with hungry
young writers salivating for the chance to snag your spot
and be the next Rebecca St. Claire."

Elbows sinking onto the table, Becky watched the older
woman head out the door, the warning words ringing in her
ears like a blast of New Year's noisemakers. She was a
good writer, a *damned* good writer, but in a business as
fickle as publishing no one was so good they couldn't be
replaced.

The waitress returned to clear the table and pick up the
check. She glanced over at Becky's untouched lunch. "You
want a box for that?"

"No, thanks." Becky felt certain the smell of lime vinaigrette and grilled shrimp would forever be paired in her memory with the gut-wrenching feeling of failure.

Handing over the salad, she caught herself studying the girl's fresh face, mane of shiny, straight, blond hair and model svelte body—and felt the sinking sense of insecurity she'd spent the past year and a small fortune in self-help books trying to get over.

Shoving the vinyl folder into her change apron, the server asked, "Can I get you anything else?"

Becky hesitated. She did want something else, and in this case it wasn't a cellulite-free ass, straight blond hair or even the extra vertical inches that made it okay to wear sensible flats instead of nosebleed-high heels. If faced with a similar state of emergency, her fictional heroine, Angelina Talbot wouldn't hesitate to soothe herself with her signature cocktail.

"As a matter of fact, I'd like a double Bombay Sapphire martini, straight up with an olive, not a twist. Oh, and make it shaken, not stirred."

She might not be a British bombshell sniffing out kidnappers and murderous foreign agents, but it had turned out to be one roller-coaster ride of a day.

"TEAMING ME with a romance writer is your idea of a career jump start? You've got to be joking." Adam Maxwell—Max—stared at his editor, her latest editorial "suggestion" spearing the space between them like a stingray's barbed whiptail.

"It's no joke, Max." Seated across from him in the Hotel Chelsea's Serena Bar and Lounge, Pat reached for her drink, the Serena specialty cocktail known as the Pink

Bitch. Under the circumstances, the beverage struck Max as remarkably apropos. "My instincts are telling me that pairing your Drake Dundee with Rebecca St. Claire's Angelina Talbot may just be the marketing move that takes both your careers to the next level."

Glancing at the glass in his hand, Max half wondered if the single sip of Macallan single-malt Scotch he'd taken might have aversely affected his hearing. "Sometimes the next level is down."

Pat leaned over and picked at the appetizer plate of hummus, pita bread triangles and spiced olives sitting on the circular chrome cocktail table between them. Popping an olive into her mouth, she said, "I want you to do this book with Rebecca St. Claire. Think of it as a creative experiment. One book is all I'm asking."

Max shook his head. "I don't care if it's one book or a hundred and one books, the answer is still no. There's a reason I've never had a writing partner—I've never wanted one. I'm a solo act—period."

That wasn't entirely true. When Elaina was alive and still reasonably well, they'd sit up nights over an open bottle of wine or freshly brewed pot of coffee and brainstorm. Playing the "what if" game, she'd called it. Trust his wife to turn plotting a book into recreation rather than work.

He'd lost her to cancer the year before on New Year's Day, and he still hadn't gotten used to cooking dinner for one or sleeping alone or coming home to an empty house. If it wasn't for writing, he wasn't sure how he would have gotten through the past twelve months. Creating a fictional universe of colorful, noisy characters made it easier to block out the deafening silence. Once he'd forced himself to start working again, he'd quickly finished the book he'd set aside and then fired off two more in rapid succession. His adventuring Aussie hero, Drake Dundee, was too busy blazing new trails and tracking new treasure to stop long enough to feel much beyond an explorer's thrill of discovery. Bringing a fictional love interest—and a real-life romance writer—into the picture promised to seriously mess with Max's formula, not to mention his head.

Pat leaned back in her seat, the lifting of one pencil-shaded brow bringing to mind Cruella De Vil. "A sixty-percent sell-through would be considered respectable for a first book, but for a veteran author, it's pretty disappointing. Either we come up with a plan to bring your sales back up or you can expect to see your print run on the next book slashed to smithereens, and the marketing budget right along with it."

So Pat wanted to play hardball, did she? The prospect of losing control over both Drake's destiny, as well as the real life he'd spent the past year pulling back together had him lashing out.

"I've worked too damned hard building up the Adam Maxwell brand to blow it because the sales numbers for one book came in on the low end."

Drake had started off his adventures married to a tall, lovely Greek-American cryptologist, Isabel. The character was a thinly veiled version of Elaina. After her death, Max had killed off Isabel. A curare-laced arrow hit her in the left breast, the spot where Elaina's first cancerous lump was found. Giving Drake a new love interest would be a betrayal of his wife's memory. It was out of the question.

Pat picked up a pita point and dipped it in the hummus. Nibbling the edge, she said, "The Angelina Talbot books are genre benders, a blending of romantic erotica and mystery. Folding the romance and mystery elements into an action-adventure scenario could boost sales for both series. Who knows what the commercial potential might be? And I'm not just talking books. It's not unheard of for a movie screenplay to be based on a blockbuster novel."

Pat must be under some big-time pressure from her boss to sign him up because she was really putting on the razzle-dazzle. Feeling as though he was on the receiving end of an exploded bag of New Year's confetti—annoying, unnecessary and damned messy to clean up—Max shook his head. "Being a novelist and writing the best damned book I possibly can has always been a big enough dream for me."

Sticking a liver-spotted hand inside her suitcase-size pink purse, Pat pulled out a mass market paperback and handed it over. "Before you decide, give Beck—give Rebecca's work a read. This is her latest. It's gotten rave reviews, including *Publishers Weekly* and a nice write-up in the *Chicago Tribune,* too."

Max glanced at the book, not bothering to hide his distaste. The campy cover featured a slender, dark-haired female wearing a low-cut black dress, her perfect breasts standing out in silhouette along with the smoking pistol she pointed. A cone of light framed in rifle crosshairs suggested an unseen target. Talk about clichéd.

"I don't care if the woman's books are the best goddamned things to come off the printing press since Gutenberg invented it, my answer of no still stands."

Pat frowned. "I wouldn't be so sure about that. You have a multibook contract with us and, as you may or may not recall, the final book of that contract is written as 'blind,' meaning it's anything we want it to be—and we want it to be this."

Like the fictional Drake, in real life Max didn't take kindly to threats, veiled or otherwise. "I won't do the co-write. If that means we part our professional ways, then so be it. Yours isn't the only publishing house in New York and ever since 9/11, action-adventure is a huge share of the fiction market. If need be, I'll take my chances."

"We have a contract, Max, a legally binding document. Maybe you should have a talk with your agent before you burn any bridges."

Max slammed the paperback on the table and shot to his feet. He shoved a hand into his wallet and threw a wad of money down on the table. Pissed off as he was, he wasn't about to stick a woman with the bar tab even if that woman did represent the global publishing enterprise hell-bent on destroying his brand and his career.

Pat stood, as well. "Max, don't leave like this. We need to talk things over."

Max had had just about all the talking he could stomach for one afternoon. It was high time he tore a page from Drake's book, or rather *his* books, and took action instead.

"I'm going to have that little talk with my agent you rec-ommended. You can expect to hear from him by close of business today—along with my lawyer."

HALFWAY through her martini, Becky was beginning to feel a little maudlin, as well as a little numb. Some fabulous start to the new year—not! Just that morning she'd felt as though she was standing on top of the world and now she felt as though she'd plummeted to, if not exactly rock bottom then certainly some substrata of inner earth.

Maybe I have bad restaurant karma.

The final episode with Elliot had taken place in a restaurant, too. She and Sharon were sitting down to dinner at Coppi Vignorelli in Becky's Northwest, D.C. neighborhood of Woodley Park. Within steps of Becky's apartment, the Italian bistro was her and Elliot's special place when he came into town. They'd just started in on their pasta when Elliot had strolled into the dining room, the distinctive metal studding on his deconstructed Mark Nason Italian "strummer" loafers catching Becky's eye like a lighthouse beacon.

Her heart leapt and then landed, the thrill of seeing him clashing with confusion over why he hadn't told her he was coming into town. She was pretty sure he was supposed to be in L.A. that week and New York the next. Given his bicoastal lifestyle, they only saw each other once a month, but Becky was too head over heels to press for more, especially now that he'd started talking about her moving in with him. In the picture he painted, she'd spend her days lounging poolside with her laptop in L.A. or soaking up the artistic vibe of some hip Manhattan coffee bar. He'd even urged her to quit her regular nine-to-five job. She'd hesitated at first, but he'd seemed so sincere that she'd finally set aside her misgivings and given her notice. Evaluating federally funded literacy programs was a paycheck, not a dream job, the kind of steady career that justified her master's degree and the thousands of dollars she'd racked up in student loans. For Elliot, though, money obviously wasn't a consideration. Other than his running shoes she'd never seen him wear anything actually manufactured in America.

Ignoring the uneasy feeling settling into her stomach, she nudged Sharon. "Hey, that's Elliot, the guy I've been telling you about. I can't believe he's here. He must have missed seeing me when he walked in. Come on, I'll introduce you." She started up from the seat.

Sharon's hand clamped over hers, anchoring her to the booth. Face wearing a funny look, she leaned in and whispered, "Becky, don't look over there right now but he's… he's with someone."

Becky sank back into her seat, the few bites of rigatoni she'd taken threatening to come up. Following Sharon's nod, she saw his dinner date bounce over to their table, all white-toothed smile and sun-bronzed skin and long, shiny blond hair. Wearing a tight black tank top and a pair of skinny jeans with zippers at the ankles, she looked twenty-two, twenty-three tops.

But even worse than seeing her lover with a woman almost young enough to be his daughter—forget the *almost,* he *was* pushing forty-five—was the moment when Becky looked over and caught his eye. Instead of sending her an apologetic smile or a guilty wave, some recognition that she was alive, that she was there, he met her gaze head-on—and looked straight through her. Straight through her as if she didn't exist, as if she were made of see-through glass, with no more sentience than the wooden booths or the framed photographs lining the walls.

She reached beneath the table and found Sharon's hand. "Oh…God…this hurts. This *really* hurts." She squeezed as hard and tight as she could, as though Sharon was her anchor to everything that could still be counted on to be honest and safe and real.

Sharon squeezed back, whispering commiserating words—"Oh, Becky, I'm so sorry," and, "This is brutal, the worst," and finally, "I'm getting the check and getting you the hell out of here."

Feeling frantic, Becky shook her head. "No, we can't. I mean, *I* can't. I'm not going to give him the satisfaction."

And she hadn't. For the next thirty minutes or so she'd sat pushing pasta around on her plate and keeping up a show of cheerful chatter while bit by bit her heart withered and shriveled and finally died on the vine of her happily-ever-after dreams.

On the bright side, the Dark Night of the Soul had sparked a career epiphany. The next morning when she'd crawled out of bed, dredging up an evening's worth of Oreo cookie crumbs and wadded-up tissues, she knew she couldn't stomach writing period pieces about twentysomething heroines any longer. She'd called Pat and told her she had an idea kicking around in her brain for a contemporary novel that pushed the boundaries of traditional romance fiction. By the time she'd finished pitching the proposal her editor had given her a verbal green light and sworn that if the draft was even half as good as the pitch, there'd be a contract coming her way for a whole series.

Enter her alter ego, Angelina Talbot. Unlike Becky, Angelina could eat chocolate trifle without getting fat and knock back double martinis without getting toasted—and have sex with men without falling in love. Sales for the launch book had been brisk, the word-of-mouth buzz spreading like a California brush fire. Even with Elliot out of the picture, that first fat royalty check made quitting her job seem like an okay decision after all. But more than financial security, it was having created a thirtysomething heroine readers obviously loved that had helped her shake off the bad vibe from the Elliot episode—sort of.

She'd based the character of Falco, Angelina's nemesis and former lover, almost entirely on Elliot. Forget "entirely," Falco *was* Elliot down to his wavy silver hair, sexy full mouth and lean, hard, to-die-for body. She kept promising herself she'd kill him off soon but two books into the series she still hadn't been able to let him go.

But cluttering her head with a fictional character who was the alter ego of her ex was a small problem compared to the decision looming. Did she team with the publishing industry's answer to Bill O'Reilly and sign herself up for months of literary head butting or did she turn down the deal and hope another publisher would pick her up before she maxed out her credit cards and drained her small savings?

Torn, Becky reached for her drink, then realized the tip of her nose had gone numb. She popped the last fat green olive into her mouth and slid the glass away. For sure, sitting around in an empty restaurant moping over her martini wasn't bringing her any closer to those "fresh starts" and "dazzling opportunities" her horoscope had forecast, let alone to an answer to her Big Decision. Before she sank any lower into the self-pity slough, she needed to channel the Zen of her personal happy place—and in Becky's case, that meant Manhattan's Fifth Avenue shopping corridor.

She slipped on her coat, shouldered her tote and rose from the restaurant seat. Spending money was the very last thing a potentially out-of-work writer should do but then again they didn't call it retail *therapy* for nothing. This was no time to scrimp. Her career and her character's very existence were in danger of fading away. If she and Angelina couldn't go out in a blaze of glory, at least they could go out in a splash of high style.

2

Drake's Code: Never turn your back on a friend.
Never turn your back on an enemy.
Never take shit from either.

AFTER LEAVING Pat in the bar, Max stopped in at his rooftop suite to pick up his winter coat. Slow elevator notwithstanding, he still made it from his hotel to Harry Goldblatt's midtown Manhattan office in record time. Hot as he was around the collar from his meeting with Pat, the windy walk down the Avenue of the Americas did little to cool him off. Harry had represented him since pulling his first novel out of the slush. If Max could count on anyone to cover his back, it was his agent.

The first suspicion that something was wrong hit him when the purple-haired receptionist didn't seem at all surprised to see him. Like an off-Broadway actress stumbling through badly memorized lines, she looked up from her *People* and suggested he take a seat until Mr. Goldblatt got off from "a very important call." The fifteen-minute wait along with the "very important call" cinched it in Max's mind. He was being set up. While he sat sipping canned soda and gnashing his teeth, Harry was inside his office selling Max out.

He slammed the can on the glass-topped coffee table, blew by the receptionist's desk, and stormed into his agent's corner office without knocking. "Goddamn it Harry, I don't know what you're up to, but I need to talk to you—*now.*"

The receptionist hurried inside after him. Tugging her leather miniskirt down over chunky thighs, she faced the slope-shouldered sixtysomething seated behind the big chrome desk. "Mr. Goldblatt, I'm so sorry. I told him you were on the phone but—"

Covering the receiver with his hand, Harry gestured for her to go. "That's all right, Janice, I can handle this." One eye on Max, he returned to his call. "Yes, Patricia, he's here. I'll have to call you back. *Ciao,* baby." Replacing the cordless in its cradle, he smiled and said, "Why, Maxie, this is a surprise."

Eyeing the copy of the St. Claire woman's book lying on Harry's desk blotter, Max exploded. "Like hell it is. I don't know what scheme you and Pat have cooked up, but I've spent too damned many years building my brand to let some smut writer come in as coauthor."

Harry fingered his few threads of silvered hair. He'd given up the comb-over a few years back and since seeing Jack Nicholson's cue-ball head on the televised Oscars, he'd been seriously considering shaving the whole damn thing. "Max, I'm sensing some anger on your part. Have a seat and let's discuss this like rational human beings." He gestured to the pair of leather chairs set before the desk.

"There's nothing to discuss. It's not happening, do you hear me?"

"Loud and clear, Maxie, but I'm starting to ask myself if maybe all the listening isn't going one-way. All Patricia is asking is that you give the coauthorship a chance. One book with Rebecca St. Claire—is that really so much to ask?"

Max didn't hesitate. "Hell, yes! My readers are predominantly men. Men are visual. If we want raunch, we rent a movie or buy a magazine, but never a novel. Besides, Drake isn't some pretty-boy cover model with a waxed chest and a spray-on tan. He's a real guy, a man's man."

Harry let out a sigh. Pushing sixty-two, he'd been in the industry forty years. Knowing when to coddle an author and when to get tough was part science and part art. Max's bullshit barometer was a lot lower than most of Harry's top-selling clients. He didn't need ego-stroking from his agent, his editor or anyone else. Like his fictional bounty hunter, Drake, he was a man's man who appreciated it when you played it straight.

And yet everyone, including Max, had a weak spot.

"It's time for a reality check, Maxie, and the reality is the sales numbers on your last royalty statement don't look so good."

Max shrugged, though he felt far from nonchalant. A few years back he'd sold his family's regional newspaper business for a minor mint, but writing novels was his first love, his dream job ever since he could remember. The income earned from his books was a secondary reward to the joy of sharing his stories with readers around the globe.

"Everybody's numbers are down. It's a tough market. Unless you're Michael Crichton or Dean Koontz, you're bound to take a hit."

Harry mustered a sympathetic look, but Max detected a certain smugness lurking beneath. "It's a shrinking market, no doubt about it, and it's shrinking more all the time. First Generation X, then Generation Y and now Generation Echo and each cohort of kids reads less than the one before it. By the time you reach my age, you'll be writing your books as blurbs and posting them on a Myspace page, the attention spans will be that goddamn short."

Max stuffed his hands in his coat pocket if only to keep them from his agent's throat. "Come to the point."

"Gladly. My point is this—our entertainment-glutted society has created a survival-of-the-fittest publishing market. Only the toughest authors survive. These days toughness means tenacity and tenacity, Maxie, means flexibility. Look at this collaboration as your golden opportunity to grow your readership. Women are the number-one consumers in this country. Whether the product is a book or a car tire, they drive the purchase decisions, not men."

The old buzzard was playing him, no doubt about it. Determined to stand his ground, Max shot back with, "I didn't become a writer to churn out trash I wouldn't read myself."

Harry bobbed a vigorous nod. "Of course, of course, *quality* is our watchword, but this Rebecca St. Claire is supposed to be very good." To Max's chagrin, Harry picked up the paperback and tapped a finger to the quote on the cover. "Her latest received a very favorable review from *Publishers Weekly.* Pat tells me she has quite a following. Why not look at collaboration as an opportunity not only to broaden your readership but give Drake a little action between the sheets for a change? The poor bastard's been living like a monk for the past two books now."

The remark hit home. Drake wasn't the only one who'd been living like a monk. Over the past year, well-meaning friends had foisted one woman after another on him, begging him to start dating, start *living* again. The trouble was, Max wasn't interested in dating. His ten-year marriage hadn't been perfect, no marriage was, but it had been damn close to it. It might not be macho to admit it, but Max had *liked* being married. Still, he couldn't see himself taking that step with just anyone, and Elaina was one hell of a tough act to follow. At thirty-nine, he'd more or less resigned himself to living out the second half of his life solo. If he wasn't exactly a confirmed bachelor, he was well on his way to becoming a confirmed curmudgeon.

Harry clucked his tongue. "Your personal life is affecting your writing and not in a good way. Killing off Drake's wife at the beginning of the second book wasn't the smartest marketing move."

Writing Isabel out of the story hadn't been about marketing. It had been about survival—Max's. When Elaina lost her battle with cancer, the second "Drake's Adventures" book had existed only as a rough draft. It had taken Max months before he'd been able to look at it again. When he had, he'd known there was no way he could carry his wife's fictional persona into future books, just as in real life there was no way he could imagine another woman ever filling her shoes.

Harry's voice pulled him back to the present. "I hate to bring this up, I know it is a sensitive subject, but the clause in your last contract—a clause you willingly signed off on—states that the last novel is a blind book, meaning the publisher, not you, calls the shots on content. If they want you to write a comic strip or pulp fiction, you are legally bound to do so. It could always be worse."

His hopes sinking like the *Titanic,* Max doubted it.

Pressing his advantage, Harry added, "If it doesn't work out, I give you my personal guarantee I'll find a way to break the contract."

Max folded his arms across his chest, adrenaline firing his blood like rocket fuel. "In that case, find a way now."

"It's not that easy."

Max stabbed his index finger into the air. "If it were easy, I wouldn't be forking over fifteen percent for your commission. There has to be some loophole, and I expect you to find it."

Harry pressed a hand over his heart. "Now after all we've been through together, that hurts me, Maxie. When I discovered you, you were lucky if you could—"

Max held up a silencing hand, in no mood to hear yet again how Harry had pulled his unsolicited manuscript from the slush pile of submissions and generously overlooked his shaky sentence construction and typo-riddled prose to focus on the star quality blazing beneath. Certainly Max was grateful for all Harry had done to build him into a name, but loyalty had its limits. If the coauthored book with the St. Claire woman tanked, Harry wouldn't hesitate to toss him out like a week-old deli sandwich discovered at the back of the office fridge.

Harry waved a hand. "Okay, okay, you win. I'll get our literary attorney to look into it but I'm making no promises. In the meantime, do me a favor and at least make it look like you're complying. Pat tells me Rebecca St. Claire is in town overnight. Why not invite her out for drinks, or better yet, buy her dinner? It is New Year's Eve after all and something tells me you don't exactly have big plans."

Max's biggest plan for the evening was to catch a drink and light dinner at his hotel and turn in early. If he did stay up to see the ball drop over Times Square, it would be on a television screen. Still, he shook his head. "No way."

Pretending not to hear him, Harry held out the paperback. "Here, take her book with you. Skim a couple of chapters and be sure to tell her how much you admire her work, yada yada. Remember, Maxie, in life you win more flies with honey than vinegar."

Though Max hadn't ever met her, Rebecca St. Claire was already turning out to be a fly in the ointment and a pain in his ass. He grabbed the novel out of Harry's hand. "You're full of good advice. Too bad none of it's free." Jamming the book in his coat pocket, he made a mental note to leave it for the hotel maid along with the tip when he checked out in the morning.

Harry took off his glasses and scoured his forehead with the back of his hand. "You don't pay me to lie to you. You pay me to tell it like it is. You're not going to win this one, Maxie. This time you really don't have a choice."

The last time Max had been told he was powerless to turn a bad situation around he'd been sitting in the oncologist's office with Elaina. Despite a scathing protocol of high-dose chemotherapy, a strict macrobiotic diet and the best doctors money could buy, his wife's cancer had not only come back but had spread. There was nothing anyone, including him, could do beyond making her last months as pain-free as possible.

Remembering how helpless he'd felt then, how angry at everyone and everything, he punched a fist into the empty air. "No choice, huh?" Fisting his hands at his sides, he stormed to the door, shaking his head. "We'll see about that, Harry. We'll just see."

CHOICES, choices. Standing in stocking feet in the shoe department of Saks, Becky did her best to ignore the captive salesman's foot-tapping and throat-clearing. No doubt he was impatient to clock out for the night and get started celebrating the new year, but she had a big decision to make, and she couldn't afford any distractions. Should she take the fun and flirty Manolo Blahnik black leather ballet pumps with the adorable little bow on the vamp, or the ultrasvelte Jimmy Choo red satin sling backs topped off with stunning black and red crystal-encrusted brooches? The Jimmys cost almost twice as much as the Manolos, but then they were special-occasion shoes, which meant they'd last a lot longer. On the other hand, the pumps were a lot more practical. Solid black, they could easily double as day and evening wear, so she'd really be getting two pairs of shoes for the price of one—way too sweet a deal for a savvy shopper such as herself to pass on.

It was a case of apples and oranges—or more appropriately, Cristal and Dom Perignon. Each shoe was so stylishly distinctive and yet so seductively hip, it was impossible to pick. For someone with Becky's sweet tooth for designer foot candy, there was only one conceivable course of action.

She dug out her wallet, surrendered her credit card, and uttered the words she would undoubtedly live to regret. "I'll take them both."

What the hell, I'll be the best-shod woman in the shelter.

On her way out of the store, she picked up a Roberto Cavalli beaded bracelet bag from the accessories department and a red lipstick from the Clinique counter, both to go with the shoes. Wrists rimmed in shopping bag handles, she stepped out onto the Avenue. Across the street, the bronze doors of St. Patrick's Cathedral offered a portal to a calmer state of mind. She hesitated, thinking about going in, but shuffling through the sanctuary with shopping bags didn't strike her as particularly respectful. Instead she made her way over to Forty-ninth Street. Skirting Rocke-feller Center, she headed toward the Avenue of the Americas. Given the number of large hotels in close prox-imity, she should have better luck catching a cab there.

Several whizzed by, either already occupied or with their roof lights turned off. By the time she came up on the New York Hilton, the pointed toes of her boots were rubbing her feet raw and the wind had picked up, pulling the pins from her hair and sending rogue strands stream-ing over her face. Seeing a taxi that looked as if it might be slowing down, she shot a hand up into the air, hoping to catch the driver's attention before he headed for the hotel pull-up.

She was in luck. The cab skidded to a stop a half block up the street, tourists pouring out of the rear passenger door. Arms raised, she raced to catch it before someone else beat her to the punch.

"Taxi. Taxi! Hey, wait up…oomph!"

She hit the pavement hard, bags flying. Pulling herself up on bruised elbows, she blinked. Damn, but she was smack dab in the middle of a moveable feast of footwear, everything from top-tier designer shoes like the ones in her bags to sock-clad feet stuck into leather sandals so limp and scuffed they might have been left over from the sev-enties. Wow, a lot of people had really bad foot-care habits.

"You walked right into me. Are you all right?" The deep New England-accented male voice apparently went with the pair of pebbled-leather penny loafers parked in front of her. The classic shoes badly needed a good polishing.

"I…I think so. Oh…shit." Eying a pair of muddy Nikes coming on at a brisk clip, she grabbed the tissue-wrapped Cavalli purse and tossed it back in the bag.

Mr. Loafers swooped down beside her. "Here, let me help you."

Becky looked up and caught her breath, feeling as though the wind had been knocked out of her a second time. Blond and blue-eyed, her hunky Good Samaritan was probably in his mid- to late-thirties—and certifiably hot. Stealing a glance at his broad shoulders, she was pretty sure his khaki-colored trench coat was Burberry, not London Fog.

"That's all right. I think I've got—"

A breath-stealing whip of wind ripped through, and Becky felt the snap of cold air on her crotch. *Uh-oh.* Looking down, she saw her caramel-colored knit dress was bunched at her waist, her peach-colored Victoria's Secret panties on display for all to see. *Oh...my...God.* She snapped her legs closed, yanked down her dress, and grabbed hold of his arm as if it was a lifeline.

Taken by surprise, Max brought the woman to her feet, amazed at how tiny she was, how light. Even wearing high-heeled boots, she barely reached his breastbone.

Brushing herself off, she glanced down at their feet. "Oh, look, you dropped your book." Before he could stop her, she picked up Rebecca St. Claire's paperback and handed it to him. "You read romance novels?"

Max knew his burning cheeks had nothing to do with the wind. "Not really. Not yet, anyway. A...friend passed it on and said it was worth having a look at. I'm not sure whether I will or not."

She pushed back her hair and looked up at him, and Max forgot all about the damn book. He felt the breath leave his lungs as though *he'd* just hit the pavement. Talk about a knockout. In one sweeping glance, he took in her wide-set brown eyes, porcelain-perfect skin and delicate features—delicate except for her full pink lips. An image of her head of maple-colored curls buried between his thighs, those luscious lips slipping over his cock, burst into his thoughts and he felt his erection rising like a sail caught in a stiff breeze.

"Well, you should give it a try. You might be surprised. You might even enjoy it." Was it his writer's imagination at work or had her expressive brown eyes narrowed ever so slightly?

Pocketing the book, he said, "Thanks, maybe I will." Taking up her packages in one hand, he laid the other on her elbow and steered her away from the busy sidewalk to a public bench fronting a snow-covered patch of urban park. Setting the packages on the seat, he turned back to her. "You fell pretty hard. Are you sure you didn't hurt yourself?"

"Mostly my pride." She reached behind to brush off her bottom. "I didn't think this day could get any worse, but this brings it to a whole new level."

So she'd had a shitty day, too. That was interesting. Running his gaze over her, he decided she definitely wasn't a tourist—too well-dressed and too obviously at home in the city. He could see her if not in Tribeca or Soho then certainly in one of the trendy up-and-coming neighborhoods in Brooklyn or the Bronx. Wherever she was going, she'd squeezed in a little shopping before heading there. He shifted his eyes to the two heavy Saks bags. Make that a *lot* of shopping.

"Sometimes the next level really is down," Max said, thinking of the book in his coat pocket.

She nodded. "You can say that again." She turned her attention to rearranging her jumbled purchases, maple-syrup curls blowing about her face.

Max knew he should probably be on his way, but curiosity kept him hanging around. Gaze gliding over her, he found himself wondering what she wore beneath her three-quarter-length camel-colored coat—aside from peach panties, that is. The coat's belted waist suggested a trim torso and softly curved hips, but beyond her small size it was hard to get a sense of her body beneath the outerwear.

For whatever reason, he found himself confiding, "I haven't had the best of days myself."

Her brown eyes stole a quick sidelong glance at his face. "If you don't mind my asking, what sign are you?"

Feeling himself harden—thank God for overcoats—Max wondered what the hell was going on with him. Since his first book had hit the bestseller lists, he'd come into contact with any number of women, from attractive news reporters to bikini-clad Playboy Bunnies, the latter when his book was excerpted in the magazine. Despite numerous opportunities, he hadn't had sex in more than a year, closer to two. His need for release was something he'd gotten used to taking care of himself when Elaina was ill. After she'd passed, going to bed with another woman hadn't even entered his thoughts.

So why was he so completely turned-on by a shopaholic stranger?

Catching her curious stare, he realized he hadn't answered her question. At times like this, he'd give a lot for Drake's smooth-talking tongue. "Taurus."

"The sign of the bull." She gave a sage nod. "That makes sense." Sexy lips pursed, she studied him as though he was a *New York Times* crossword puzzle she'd just begun figuring out. "What does your horoscope say?"

He hesitated. "My horoscope? I…I don't know. I never

read it." He considered astrology to be a bunch of New Age crap but since he'd probably pissed off his quota of people for one day, he held back from saying so.

Expressive brown eyes settled on his face, bringing a funny fluttery feeling to Max's stomach—and a warm sensation over the vicinity of his heart. "Well, I read mine every day online, the monthly and daily forecasts and then the end-of-year predictions. I suppose you could say it's my guilty pleasure, only I don't really feel guilty about it." Slender shoulders lifted in a hint of a shrug. "I figure it's free, so why not? I'm a Libra—you know, the scales, the eternal search for balance and justice and…well, partnership." When she came to *partnership,* her breezy tone seemed to falter. "January is supposed to be bringing me fresh starts and dazzling opportunities in my houses of career and love. Transportation is another area apparently not going so well for me." She shifted to look around his shoulder. "I guess I lost out on that cab, huh?"

Bedazzled, it took Max a moment to absorb that last bit of information. He looked back over his shoulder, past a cluster of young people, tourists judging from their I Love New York baseball caps, sweatshirts and windbreakers, to the empty curb. "Looks like it." Turning back to her, he realized he was fresh out of excuses to linger. "Well, I guess I should be getting on—"

"Oh, no. No!" She stuck a hand inside the open shopping bag and brought out a tissue-wrapped red satin high-heeled shoe.

Staring at the shoe and then back at her stricken face, Max asked, "What's wrong?"

"I'm missing a shoe. The mate must have rolled out when I fell." She unfurled the shoe from the paper and held it up for him to see, the sparkly beaded medallion on the top winking in the waning winter light. "What am I going to do? I can't take them back like this, and I can't go around wearing one shoe."

"I don't know about that. It worked for Cinderella." He couldn't remember the last time he'd cracked a joke, but even if his attempt was pretty lame, it still felt good, damn good.

"Very funny." Her frown told him she found it anything but. "If you knew how much these cost me, you wouldn't be laughing, either."

He made a show of sobering. "Designer stuff, huh?"

She answered with a guilty nod. "Yeah, I really splurged."

Max might not be much of a talker but like his creation, Drake, he was a man of action. "In that case, Cinderella, hold the carriage horses. I'll be right back."

Leaving her standing by the bench, he went to scavenge the sidewalk where she'd fallen. It was a long shot but then it didn't hurt to try. After peering beneath a hot pretzel cart, the sneakers of a twentysomething kid handing out free passes to a nearby comedy club, and the paws of a trio of leashed French poodles, he was close to giving up when he spotted a flutter of white in the curbside gutter. At first he thought it must be one of the city's ubiquitous pigeons but bending closer, he saw it was tissue paper—tissue paper with a slender red heel sticking out.

He scooped up the shoe in the nick of time, seconds before the wheel of an oncoming taxi sent frozen mud splashing up. Brushing it off on his coat, he brought it over to her, proudly presenting it like his dog, Scout, dropping his retrieved rawhide in a guest's lap. "If the shoe fits…"

Her smile rapturous, she took it from him. "Thank you, thank you! Look, it didn't even get messed up. The sales clerk wrapped it really well and then used the Saks sticker seal to hold the tissue in place. I love Saks, and I absolutely *love* these shoes." Holding the shoe to her heart, she looked up at him with shining eyes.

Max felt as though his six-foot-three frame had just shot to a full ten feet. Eyeing the four-inch heel, he shook his head. "You really walk in those things?" Balancing on stilts like those might send her the podiatrist sooner rather than later.

She shrugged. "I'm used to it." She laid the shoe in the box beside its mate with loving care, replaced the lid, and picked up her packages. "Well, uh, thanks for all your help."

Max realized he wasn't ready to let her walk out of his life, not yet anyway. Stalling until he could come up with some way to ask her name without seeming like a stalker, he said, "Red shoes always remind me of that Brothers Grimm fairy tale."

"Excuse me?"

Shit. Judging from her startled look she didn't think he was a stalker but instead a stalker with a foot fetish. *Great going Maxwell*—not!

"You know, the children's story about the match girl who covets the pair of fancy red slippers. Once she puts them on, though, they take over and won't let her stop dancing, and she ends up begging a woodsman to cut off her feet to be free."

Though she'd never been much into shoes or fashion, period, Elaina's classic copy of the children's book had been one of her cherished childhood possessions. He still had it on his bookshelves somewhere, unable to part with it when he'd boxed up the rest of her stuff. Still, that didn't explain what he was doing standing around in the middle of midtown spouting a story by the mid-nineteenth century's answer to Stephen King. Back in his hometown of Hadley, New Hampshire, he scarcely said hello to people he'd known all his life.

"And I thought I had a bad shoe habit." Instead of freaking out, she shook her head and smiled. "I think you mean Hans Christian Andersen, though."

Caught up in that delightful smile, it took a moment for her comment to sink in. "Sorry?"

"Hans Christian Andersen wrote 'The Red Shoes,' not the Brothers Grimm."

Max thought for a moment. Damned if she wasn't right. "I stand corrected." Sexy, sophisticated and smart, she was appealing to him more by the minute—minutes that were rapidly slipping by.

"I do know my shoes if you hadn't already guessed." She shot him a wink, and he saw her eyes had little flecks of gold rimming the pupils. "Well, thanks again for all your help." She stepped around him, shopping bags swinging. "Sorry again for running into you."

Cinderella brushed by and started up the street, brisk strides carrying her quickly away. Max hesitated, asking himself what his alter ego would do were he standing in Max's loafers in the middle of Manhattan instead of in his cowboy boots in the Australian Outback. The answer was a given.

Drake would go after the girl.

"Hey, wait up."

Threading through the foot traffic, Max dodged several baby strollers, a homeless man's shopping cart and a trio of Japanese tourists pausing for a photo op.

He caught up with her just before the next crosswalk.

She stopped and turned around, looking puzzled. "Did I leave behind more shoes?"

Feeling like a high-school kid stumbling through his first ask out, he caught his breath and shook his head. "I was thinking maybe we could share a cab. Better yet, why not let me buy you a cup of coffee? We could go inside somewhere and warm up and…" He let the rest of the clumsy sentence die.

She hesitated, biting her full bottom lip, her pretty top teeth coming into view, then the tip of her tongue darting out to moisten the plump pink flesh. Watching the machinations of that amazing mouth, he felt telltale heat pooling in his groin.

The streetlight changed and a wave of pedestrians poured into the crosswalk and headed toward them. Max felt the spell break—and the moment slip away.

"I can't," she finally said, dashing all his hopes with those two regrettable words. Though she shook her head, he was pretty sure he saw real regret in her eyes. "I really have to be…getting back. It was nice meeting you." Again that hint of hesitation that had him hoping. "Have a happy New Year."

Feeling like a dolt, Max watched her walk away, sexy hips swaying. Of course she had to be on her way. It was New Year's Eve, after all, the biggest date night of the year after Valentine's. Women who looked, spoke and *moved* like that didn't stay home alone on New Year's Eve.

He thought of the lucky guy who'd be kissing her come midnight, the one for whom she'd be wearing those sexy red shoes, and felt a jolt of jealousy. Mentally putting himself in the man's place, he imagined the sexy little black dress she'd slip into to go with the stilettos. By the time the fantasy progressed to the dress lying in a puddle on the floor, her clothing winnowed to a pair of black garters banding the slender white thighs he'd ogled earlier, and of course those red shoes, his semierection had rocketed to a full-throttle hard-on.

"Hey, buddy, watch where you're goin'."

Max looked into the scowling face of the falafel vendor whose cart he'd apparently just stumbled into. "Sorry."

He walked back to his hotel in a sort of semiconscious daze. By the time he reached The Chelsea's neon-lit marquee, it was dark outside. He couldn't remember how he'd gotten there or what he might have passed along the way. It didn't matter. Despite being turned down, he was in a "New York State of Mind," not to mention one hell of a good mood.

Humming the Billy Joel song beneath his breath, he stepped inside the lobby elevator. The doors closed, the scent of rosemary and mint filling his nose. At first he thought it must be air freshener but after a few more whiffs he realized it clung to his clothes. It was *her* scent, so fresh and wholesome and altogether clean he couldn't think of it as perfume. With her maple-colored curls, warm brown eyes and the light brown coat wrapping her petite figure, she reminded him of a tightly rolled caramel confection, sweet but not too sweet, satisfyingly rich, sumptuously delicious. There was no chance of sampling her now, but those magical few moments on Sixth Avenue had certainly sweetened his outlook on the year ahead. For the first time in a long time, he felt alive.

Alive—he'd almost forgotten what a good feeling that could be.

The elevator doors closed, the polished metal reflecting Max's smile.

3

Drake walked into the outback bar, ordered a Foster's lager, and slid onto the stool. Restless after concluding his latest adventure, he took a long pull of the beer and glanced across the wood-paneled room hoping for some distraction. A long, tall drink of water with waist-length black hair, a body-hugging black dress and red do-me pumps stepped inside the door. Crikey, what a beaut. But more than the woman's stunning face and killer body, it was her confident carriage as she made her way over to the bar that brought the blood pounding through his veins. She reminded him of the sleek thoroughbred filly not yet broken to the saddle stabled back on his ranch. She'd let you ride her but only bareback—and only on her terms.

Ever ready to rise to a challenge, Drake slid back his stool, got up and rounded the bar. "Goodday, love." He sidled over to the woman, head filling with wild images of all the ways he might go about taming her. Looking into her slanted green eyes, he lifted his beer bottle and gently slid the glass rim over the seam of her full, luscious lips. "Fancy a drink?"

BECKY CAUGHT a cab at Forty-sixth Street, not far from where she'd left the handsome, helpful stranger. Maybe it was just wishful thinking, but she swore she felt the burn of those blue eyes following her all the way up the boulevard.

Climbing inside the taxi's stale-smelling interior, she said, "The Hotel Chelsea, please. That's 222 West Twenty-third between—"

"Between Seventh and Eighth, yeah, I know." The cabbie pulled out into traffic, cutting off an oncoming car and flipping the driver the bird.

Becky settled herself and her packages on the cracked vinyl seat, asking herself why on earth she'd just turned down the hottest man to cross her path in…well, forever. There'd been nothing remotely creepy about him, no bad vibe or warning facial tick. Just the opposite—he'd had charming manners and a sexy smile and the absolute longest eyelashes she'd ever seen on a man. He'd even stuck around to help her up and then gone on a quest for her missing slipper like a modern-day Prince Charming. Come to think of it, he *had* called her Cinderella.

And she'd liked his classic clothes, or more to the point, the totally casual, totally sexy way he wore them, as though he'd thrown on whatever and ended up looking fabulous by sheer accident. Even his lame attempt to impress her with his knowledge of classic children's literature struck her as endearingly sweet.

It was his eyes she kept coming back to, though. They were cerulean-blue, Jude-Law-blue, Prince-Charming-blue, but beyond that so soulful and so sad she'd had to dole out the time she spent looking into them for fear that, like the classic Cure song, "Just Like Heaven," she might fall in and drown deep inside of him.

Had she accepted his coffee invitation, they would have found a Starbucks or some other perfectly acceptable public place, shed their coats and settled in with white porcelain mugs and maybe a shared snack. Afterward they would have split a cab or parted ways on the street, exchanged phone numbers or not depending on how the conversation and chemistry had flowed. It could have been just a lovely interlude or one of those "fresh starts" and "dazzling opportunities" her horoscope had predicted, a prelude to the kind of happily-ever-after ending she used to love writing for her Regency romance heroines but had yet to find for herself. Either way, it would have meant breaking what she'd come to think of as her five-years-and-running curse, by having a date on New Year's Eve.

"Damn, I really blew it this time."

She caught the driver staring at her in the rearview mirror. "You say somethin'?"

"I was just uh…talking to myself. It's a writer thing," she added because a) it really was, for this writer at least and b) she didn't want him to think he was ferrying around a psycho.

He shrugged and turned his attention back to the bumper-to-bumper traffic. In a city the size of New York, apparently talking to oneself was a normal level of crazy.

Thoughts circling back to her latest lost opportunity, she admitted she hadn't turned her sexy stranger down because she was worried about getting robbed or raped or otherwise jeopardizing her physical safety. She'd played it safe, too safe, because deep down she was afraid of trusting her heart and getting badly hurt—again.

The driver skidded to a stop in front of her hotel. "That'll be $7.50."

She handed him a ten, retrieved her purse and shopping bags, and stepped out onto the street. Standing curbside, she looked up to the modest redbrick hotel, the neon sign for Hotel Chelsea welcoming her like an old friend's smile. Formerly home to the likes of Bob Dylan, Janis Joplin and Leonard Cohen, the campy old hotel had hosted its share of suicides, drug overdoses and artistic spats. But even sans its colorful past and celebrity cache, Becky still would have wanted to stay there. With its smaller, more intimate scale and comfortably worn interior, the Chelsea always made her feel welcomed and at home in a way the big, impersonal chains never quite could.

She bypassed the front desk and cut through the art gallerylike lobby on the lookout for celebrities. Half the fun of staying at the Chelsea was never knowing who you might see, be it a Hollywood legend like Peter O'Toole who had a suite named after him, or an under-thirty brat packer like Christina Ricci, or…a handsome blue-eyed stranger with a penchant for classic clothes and classic fairy tales?

Get real, Becky. How many times could she expect the universe to drop a tall, broad-shouldered hunk into her path? In this case, she hadn't just let "dazzling opportunity" pass her by. She'd turned tail and run from it.

Wishing she could rewrite the episode on the street as easily as a scene in her book, she stepped inside the elevator and pressed the button for the third floor. Room 324 was spare and smallish but at only $200 a night, it was a bargain by Manhattan standards. She hung up her coat in the tiny closet and offloaded her shopping bags onto the bed. Sitting down on the side of the mattress, she bent to take off her boots, belatedly realizing her butt was feeling pretty tender.

Crossing her right leg over her left, she massaged her cramped arch and took stock of her blisters. Since quitting her consulting job, her power lunches with Pat provided one of her few chances to step into the shoes—literally— of a glamorous romance heroine like Angelina. Pat telling her to call her on a holiday, even one largely devoted to football and loafing around the house, still amounted to a huge deal. Depending on what answer Becky gave her editor, today's lunch might be their last.

Switching legs, she rubbed her left foot back to life and considered what to do with her evening. Usually after an afternoon immersed in the Manhattan mayhem, including a soul-satisfying shopping spree, she was content to order room service and hunker down to write, but tonight was New Year's Eve. Even if it had been a regular night, until she decided what to do about her career, writing anything would be tantamount to spinning her wheels.

Picking herself up off the bed, she shuffled into the small bathroom, switched on the light, and took stock of the damage in the chipped wall mirror. *God, I'm a mess.* Worse than a mess, she looked like hell, or at least like a bat recently flown out of it. Her hair was down around her shoulders with one side sticking out like porcupine bristles, and her lipstick had worn off, along with most of her mascara. To add insult to injury, when she slipped off her dress and underwear, she saw that her right butt cheek was sore with good reason. It looked like a hippie's tie-dyed T-shirt, a mottling of black, green and blue bruises.

She turned around to face her reflection and gave her naked self a good long look. Barring her bruised backside and sad lack of a tropical tan, for thirty-four—okay, almost thirty-five—hers was not a bad body. Forget the thirty-four-almost-thirty-five part. Not a bad body *period*. Sure, it would be nice to be a little taller—okay, a *lot* taller—but then again that was why some gay European fashion designer, bless his soul, had invented the stiletto. And yes, she supposed if she were the shallow type, she might wish her breasts were a bit bigger—okay, a *lot* bigger—but thanks to the invention of various bras with words like *miracle* and *wonder* in the name, she could at least fake filling up her A-cup. On the upside, her waist was small, her hips were trim, and when it wasn't swollen from kissing the sidewalk, her butt was tight enough that other women in her aerobics class still laid claim to hating her. If that wasn't positive confirmation, what was?

She turned back to the counter with a sigh and looked for the small travel-size hair brush that would fit into the new Cavalli purse. In no mood to hunt, she upended her toiletry bag. A year's worth of beauty supplies spilled out—along with three shiny gold foil packets.

Condoms. She must have had them in her bag for over a year, packed and ready to go for that L.A. trip that had never materialized. She started to toss them in the trash but something stopped her. How long did condoms stay…*fresh* anyway? She picked up one of the packets and read the expiration date. Sturdy little devils, they didn't expire for another whole year—a year supposedly chockfull of fresh starts and dazzling opportunities, at that.

Becky hesitated. Maybe it was her horoscope-inspired optimism or just her ingrained dislike of wastefulness from growing up in a big family, but instead of dropping perfectly good prophylactics into the garbage, she dropped them into her evening purse instead.

Manhattan was a magical place. She'd always thought

so and after that day's midtown encounter, she was more convinced of it than ever. When you were in a city that never slept, you never knew who you might…*bump* into. From now on there would be no more hiding behind her laptop screen and definitely no more tossing sexy blue-eyed strangers back into the single sea (no wedding ring— she'd checked), at least not without first testing the waters. It was New Year's Eve, after all, the holiday for embracing the boundless possibility of 365 days of yet-to-be-written-upon blank pages.

If there were fresh starts and dazzling opportunities to be found out there, by God, Becky was going to find them.

MAX'S GOOD MOOD lasted until he got back to his rooftop suite and saw the phone's message light blinking. There was a voice message from Pat and another from Harry, no big surprises there. Both said about the same thing, the wording close enough to make him wonder if his editor and agent weren't practicing a little collaboration of their own.

Harry's voice mail was slightly more detailed. "As I may have mentioned earlier, Rebecca St. Claire is in town for just the one night. As a gesture of good will, why not meet her for drinks or better yet, dinner? Flies and honey, Maxie, flies and honey. Her number is…"

Max caught the 202 area code but let the other seven digits slide by. There was only one woman he was interested in meeting, and he'd let her get away with her glass slipper without leaving behind so much as a business card or a cell phone number. Disgusted with himself for not trying harder, he punched the delete key and headed into the bathroom for a shower—a cold one.

Ten minutes later he stepped out, wrapped a towel around his waist, and walked up to the vanity mirror. He ran the back of his hand over the five o'clock shadow on his cheek, debating whether to shave or let it go until morning. Other than shaving, he couldn't remember the last time he'd given his face more than a passing glance. Studying it now, he searched for anything that might have scared off his skittish Cinderella. Sure there were some lines on his forehead and creases at the corners of his eyes and a few grays in his beard, but she didn't strike him as someone looking for a twentysomething boy toy. The way she'd lifted her eyes and met his without looking away, he'd gotten the distinct impression she liked what she was seeing.

He dressed in jeans, a collared shirt and a sports jacket, and then spent the next hour checking e-mail and channel-surfing—and negating the benefit of the ice-cold shower he'd taken by conjuring steamy images of peach-colored panties and red high-heeled shoes and slender legs that would look absolutely killer in black garters and silk stockings until the spacious suite might as well have been the close confines of a sauna.

Around eight he couldn't take it any longer. Leaving his room, he took the hallway elevator down to the basement-level lounge, which he was coming to think of as the scene of the crime. Normally his overnights in New York ended with him sitting in his hotel's lounge for hours, noshing on appetizers and sipping Scotch and writing amidst a backdrop buzz of noise. Entering the quiet, nearly empty bar, he felt a sense of letdown. A campy old hotel must not count as a New Year's Eve hot spot. If he was honest with himself, he'd admit he set up the meeting with Pat for New Year's Eve because he hadn't wanted to spend the first-year anniversary of Elaina's death home alone. To get through the night, he needed bodies around him, and it didn't really matter that he'd be looking on from the side-lines rather than joining in. Crazy as it was, he almost wished he'd saved Harry's message with Rebecca St. Claire's phone number just so he wouldn't have to eat alone. But that was desperation talking. It wasn't the romance novelist with whom he was interested in ringing in the new year but his sexy shoe-shopping Cinderella.

The bartender recognized him from that afternoon and poured a generous measure of Macallan Scotch over a single ice cube without having to be told. Max took a sip of his drink and looked around. "When I checked in this morning, the desk clerk mentioned something about a piano in the lounge."

The bartender nodded toward the back of the room. "We just got it in today."

Max hesitated. The only keys he'd touched over the past year were on his computer keyboard. Like his flirting skills, he expected his piano-playing would be embarrass-ingly rusty. Still, a few bars of "Stormy Weather" might settle his mind, and it wasn't like there was a big crowd to hiss and boo. If nothing else, playing would fill the empty silence.

"Mind if I play?"

The bartender shrugged. "Help yourself."

Max pushed back his stool and got up. Scratch "Stormy Weather." Thinking back to his midtown encounter, he decided he was more in a "New York State of Mind."

ALL DRESSED UP with nowhere to go, Becky stood in the hotel lobby, her black cashmere coat draped over one bare arm.

Like Dorothy in *The Wizard of Oz,* she wished she could click her ruby heels three times and be, if not transported back home to D.C., then certainly somewhere other than alone in an almost-empty hotel lobby on New Year's Eve.

Their lack of magical properties aside, the red satin slippers were hands-down hot, and the black and red crystal detailing made her feel a lot more like a cosmopolitan Cinderella than a jumper-wearing Dorothy. The shoes also went beautifully with the Valentino black tie-waist cocktail dress she'd brought from home "just in case." She'd bought the dress when she'd still been seeing Elliot, and he'd been doing a lot of talking about all the great places he was going to take her once she moved out to L.A. with him. This was the first time she'd had it on her body since she'd tried it on in the Neiman Marcus fitting room. Fortunately it still fit—perfectly, as a matter of fact. The side zipper had rolled up without a hitch and the deep V neckline and banded Empire waist actually gave her the illusion of having boobs. Her hair had turned out pretty good, too. Instead of pinning the wild curls into her normal tight twist or bun, she'd let them fall loosely around her shoulders.

Too bad her hunky Prince Charming wasn't here to see her. He might not recognize the bedraggled klutz who'd barreled into him—and yet, even then he'd somehow seen past her wrecked hair, mussed makeup and torn pantyhose and asked her out anyway. Mentally kicking herself yet again for turning him down, she wandered over to the concierge's desk to look over the tourist pamphlets for some clue of where to go.

"Do you need dinner reservations?"

Becky snapped up her head from the brochure for Madame Tussaud's she was pretending to read. "Excuse me?"

The dark-suited concierge looked at her expectantly, phone in hand. "How many are in your party?"

Becky froze. She opened her mouth to answer "Party of one," but the words stuck in her throat. Somehow dining alone on New Year's Eve didn't measure up to the fresh start or dazzling opportunity she was looking for, not with a heart full of sinking hopes—and an evening bag full of condoms.

She shook her head, brain unfreezing—and racing toward meltdown. "I'm, uh…waiting for someone. She…I mean *he* should be along any time. Yep, any second now, he should be walking through that door…" Remembering her writer's stagecraft, she played it big by peering out into the lobby entrance. "Darn, he's late again. I think I'll have a glass of wine downstairs while I er…wait…for him." *Smooth, Becky, really smooth*—not!

He put the phone back in its cradle and nodded. "What does he look like?"

"Look like?" The echoed question came out somewhere between a squawk and a squeak.

He nodded. "I'll flag him when he comes in and tell him to meet you in the lounge."

Oh, shit. Just when she'd given up complaining about the sorry state of the service industry, she got an overachiever. "He's uh…" A mental picture of her sexy stranger flashed into her brain, and she relaxed. "Well, he's very good-looking. Tall—definitely over six feet—short blond hair, a high forehead but not too high. Oh, and he has the most beautiful blue eyes."

The concierge stared at her, a smirk on his face. He was probably thinking she needed to go back upstairs and stick herself beneath a cold shower—and he was probably right. "I'll send him down when he comes in, miss."

"Great, thanks."

She shoved the brochure back on the rack and dashed to the elevator. Taking it down to the basement level, she asked herself why she'd made such a big deal of being alone. It wasn't like being single was some kind of social disease. Angelina wouldn't think twice about going out solo. Just the opposite, the brainy British bombshell would totally groove on being the center of attention, especially if it was male. She'd sidle up to the bar and order her signature dirty Bombay Sapphire martini while holding the eye of every man in the room. Maybe it was time Becky channeled some of her character's chutzpah in real life.

Piano music greeted her as she stepped off the elevator. She'd been in the Serena a couple of times before but she didn't remember there being live music. Looking around, she decided it was too bad there weren't many live customers to enjoy it. A few lounge tables were occupied, but otherwise the place was deserted. Brad Pitt, George Clooney and Matthew McConaughey must all be making the New Year's scene elsewhere along with the other million-and-a-half Manhattanites. So much for those dazzling new opportunities....

Determined to channel her inner Angelina, Becky strolled up to the bar, folded her coat over an empty stool, and slipped onto the seat, careful of her bruised bottom. Catching the bartender's eye, she said, "You have a pianist, but I don't see the piano."

He looked up from the glass he was dunking in the double sink and nodded toward the back of the room. "Behind that metal screen."

"Well, it's a nice touch. Live music always adds something." God, she was babbling like a lonely little old lady on a subway bench—so much for playing it Angelina cool.

He set the clean glass on the shelf and wiped his hands on a towel before turning to face her. "The guy playing is a guest in the hotel. Since it's a slow night, I told him to go ahead and play if he felt like it."

"Well, he's very good. That's 'New York State of Mind,' isn't it?" She knew full well it was, but already the silence was getting on her last nerve.

He blew out a breath. "Yeah, I guess. What can I get you?"

"I'm not sure. What do you recommend?"

Shit, she'd just sat down and already she'd blown it. Angelina would never under any circumstances solicit a man's opinion about a cocktail or anything else. Among her many stellar qualities, the Brit was a woman who knew her own mind—and owned her feminine power. She would have captured the bartender in the thrall of her sexy, slanted green-eyed gaze and ordered her signature Bombay Sapphire martini dirty—make that *extra* dirty.

The bartender rolled his eyes and shoved a drink menu at her, his reaction reminding her that in Manhattan an out-of-towner chatting up the waitstaff made the list of Seven Deadly Sins. "I can make anything you want, but these are our specialty drinks."

"Thanks, I'll take a look." Face warm, she opened the menu and made a show of studying it.

She ended up ordering one of the house martinis, a raspberry Cosmo with a float of champagne dubbed the Flirtini. Champagne was the official beverage of New Year's Eve and, like the red shoes on her feet, the cocktail's name seemed symbolic of the sexier, bolder self she was resolving to bring out of the closet.

"New York State of Mind" segued into "Stormy Weather." Sipping her drink, Becky considered making a request when the music ended midsong. She hadn't realized how much company the unseen pianist was providing until he stopped. Feeling all alone again, she was about to call over the scowling bartender to place an appetizer order when a warm hand settled on her shoulder.

"Mind if I join you...Cinderella?"

4

Three hours and several rounds of drinks later, Drake leaned in to the beautiful Brit and lifted a strand of long black hair from her neck. Covering the delicate shell of her ear with his mouth, he said, "Love, I'm mad for you. Come back to my room and let me make love to you. What do you say?"

For one of the few times in her thirty-odd years, Angelina hesitated. The Aussie bloke was definitely rough around the edges, not at all what she thought of as her type, but then again there was something about his deep blue eyes, strapping body and blunt speech that warmed her from the inside out. Unlike Falco, he didn't mince words—or play games. Regardless, she needed him to complete her mission. But first she had to determine whether or not he was trustworthy.

Capturing his blue-eyed gaze, she slid her hand down his hard-muscled torso to the telltale bulge below his silver and turquoise belt buckle. Cupping him with an expert touch, she moistened her lips and tipped her face up to his until their lips all but brushed. "I'll go back with you to your room, but mind I have two rules. No regrets—and no names."

THE SEXY New England baritone sent Becky swiveling in her seat—and swimming in twin pools of deep blue eyes. Her sexy stranger, her Prince Charming from midtown, stood at the bar beside her. Becky couldn't believe her eyes. She blinked, expecting him to disappear, a wishful daydream, a few seconds' tricked-out fantasy. When he didn't, she half wondered if the bartender had spiked her drink with something a lot stronger than alcohol. Two chance meetings in the same day in a city the size of New York couldn't be a coincidence—could it?

Finding her voice, she asked, "Was that you playing?"

He nodded. "Yeah, I'm pretty rusty."

"I thought you sounded great, very professional. I was just about to make a request." She sent him her best take on a sultry Angelina-like smile.

His gaze never left hers, the intensity of his stare doing funny, fluttery things to her stomach. "I'll do anything you want," he said and somehow she didn't think he was talking about playing—at least not the piano. "What did you have in mind?"

A moment ago, Becky had had several songs in mind but the heat in his eyes had her forgetting every single one. Even if she had remembered, the look on his face assured her he wasn't really referring to song titles. Surprised at his forwardness—until asking her out for coffee, he'd seemed a little shy on the street—she answered honestly, "I...I don't remember."

Rather than press her, he glanced over to the next stool. "May I?"

"Oh, God, yes...I mean, please." She shifted over to make room for him.

"Thanks." He set his drink on the bar and settled in

beside her. "The coffee here isn't much, so you're going to have to let me buy you a cocktail instead." He glanced at her half-finished martini. "What is it you're drinking?"

Becky hesitated. "I'm having the, uh…Flirtini." *Geez, what a name for a drink.* She felt her face warming and reminded herself that the Angelinas of the world never ever blushed.

"Flirtini, huh?" His smile widened. "I'll take that over a Pink Bitch any day."

She pulled back. "Excuse me?"

"The Pink Bitch. It's another of their house drinks."

"Oh, right. I think I saw it on the menu." *Lame, Becky, so lame.*

He hailed the bartender and ordered them another round. Turning back to her, he held out his hand. "I'm Max, by the way."

Becky glanced down, the fluttery feeling in her lower abdomen morphing into a steady thrumming. Sliding her hand into his broad-backed one, imagining all the wonderful things his long, thick fingers might do to her, she felt his warmth soaking through to her skin, sending her sex-starved brain spinning salacious fantasies like Rumpelstiltskin spinning gold.

"And your name is…or should I stick to calling you Cinderella?"

Becky hesitated. Had the universe just sent her a golden, maybe even a dazzling opportunity to escape being boring Becky for one sexy night? For a second or two she actually considered answering "Angelina" but held back, thinking that would be definitely over the top. On the off chance he'd taken her advice and skimmed her book, he might start to wonder at the coincidence.

Speaking of coincidences, how weird was it that his name was Max? Here she'd been fretting all afternoon over the coauthorship deal with Adam Maxwell, and it turned out her midtown Prince Charming had a similar name.

"Cinderella it is, then." His voice pulled her back to the present, reminding her she'd yet to answer.

Looking over his shoulder, Becky noticed the single roses in bud vases decorating the lounge tables. "I'm Rose." Actually Rose was her mother's name, which, while a little freaky, should make it easy to remember.

He gave back her hand, but his eyes still held hers. "That's a pretty name for a pretty lady." He glanced down at her legs, and Becky resisted the urge to yank down her shorter-than-usual skirt. "I see you're wearing the shoes."

"Yes, well, after all that trouble, I figured I might as well take them out for a test drive. It is New Year's Eve after all."

"Yes, it is," he answered, and a shadow passed over his face. "You must be on your way out, then?" She thought she detected disappointment lacing his tone but couldn't trust herself to tell.

"I was but…my plans changed at the last minute." That part was no less than the truth. She hadn't planned on meeting him in the first place and certainly not again. Her planets must be aligning in a major way.

"You're a guest at the hotel, too?"

Becky might not be Angelina Talbot, but even she wasn't so out of touch she didn't recognize the question as code for "your room or mine?" Remembering the condoms in her purse, she met his gaze head-on and asked herself, *Can I really do this?* followed by, *Why the hell not?* Unlike

Angelina, she'd never had sex with a stranger, but there was a first time for everything. She'd never coauthored an action-adventure novel with a chauvinist pig, either, and it was shaping up to look as though she'd be doing that soon, too.

"You don't have to answer that, by the way."

His teasing tone set her once more at ease. She nodded, drawn to the warmth of his eyes and his smile. "I always stay here when I'm in town. The big chains just don't do it for me."

"Me, either. They're too impersonal, too noisy and too damned big."

Becky nodded. Not only was he tall, well-built and gorgeous but it seemed he was a kindred spirit when it came to travel, too. "I feel the same way. Whenever I walk into the lobby of the Hilton in midtown, I feel like I'm being sucked into some kind of sound vortex."

He threw back his head and chuckled and Becky couldn't help wondering if his closely cropped hair felt as silken as it looked. If the night stayed on its current sexy course, she just might be finding out sooner than later.

Swiping the back of his hand across his eyes, he said, "That's quite a vivid imagination you've got. You ever do any writing?"

Becky hesitated. Biting her bottom lip, she wondered how many more lies she'd be telling before the night was over. "Some."

Their drinks arrived, saving her from having to say more. Max lifted his glass of Macallan Scotch. "To those fresh starts and dazzling opportunities your horoscope predicted."

Becky had only mentioned her horoscope in passing. She touched her glass to his, surprised and pleased he'd apparently paid such close attention during their short sidewalk conversation. "I have a feeling this may be my year after all."

The evening flew by. Max quickly showed himself to be charming, courteous and funny, as well as amazingly well-traveled. Other than the bartender, soon they were the only two people left in the bar, but Becky was beginning to feel as though they were the only two people in the world. She couldn't remember the last time she'd felt so comfortable with a man—or so incredibly turned-on. She was starting to regret not giving him her real name. Once again she'd been a coward and played it safe.

"Travel has always been a passion of mine," Max was saying. "I've been to thirty countries in all, but Australia and New Zealand are the ones I keep going back to." He opened his mouth as if to say more but instead reached for a pita triangle from the hummus platter, one of several appetizers he'd ordered for them to share.

Becky held in a sigh. Angelina's globetrotting had grown out of her creator's frustrated travel bug. Growing up, she had dreamed of traveling the world, but an annual beach trip to Ocean City, Maryland, was about as far afield as her family ventured. Come to think of it, that probably explained why she'd started out writing historical romances set in England. Once she'd made the career switch to contemporary books, she'd gotten her Anglophile fix by making Angelina a Brit. In real life, though, her international travels were limited to a few trips to Canada. She wasn't sure why but the older she got, the easier it was to get stuck in place. Whether it was bills to be paid or a sick parent who needed her or back-to-back book deadlines, there was always some obstacle to breaking away.

Part of the fallout from the bad lunchtime news was she'd be tabling any vacation plans yet again.

"Do you travel a lot for work?" she asked. As a program consultant, her trips to evaluate federally funded literacy projects had all been domestic and largely limited to the west and midwest. Paris, Texas, was a far cultural cry from its namesake city.

He hesitated and she wondered if she hadn't over-stepped her bounds. Stranger sex relied on knowing nothing or next to nothing about the other person.

Reaching for his drink, he answered, "I'm a travel writer."

A writer! No wonder they'd seemed to have so much in common. Talk about a coincidence-packed day, not to mention a small world. Then again they were in Manhat-tan, the publishing epicenter of the U.S., perhaps the world.

"What do you do?" he asked.

Taken off guard—so few men thought to ask a woman about *her* career—she almost blurted out she was a writer, too but caught herself in time. This was her chance to escape being Becky for one night. She wasn't ashamed of writing romance fiction by any means, but she also wasn't up for mounting a defense of the genre—or getting into a discussion of such libido-busting subjects as declining book sales and competing entertainment markets.

"I'm a program consultant."

Not really a lie. That had been her day job until a year ago. As the middle kid in a blue-collar family, she'd felt an obligation to get a degree in a field that was practical rather than creative. Her bachelor's in sociology and her master's in statistics had put her in line for any number of decent-paying if boring government positions. Though she'd been good at her job, that was one shoe that had never really fit.

He tossed back the last sip of Scotch and set the glass aside. "That sounds interesting. What kind of programs do you consult on?"

She waved a hand in the air. "Oh, it's boring. I'd much rather hear about what it's like to be a writer. I'll bet anything you're in town for meetings with your editor or agent."

He smiled but this time the expression didn't reach his eyes. "Actually I had meetings with them both." Judging from the frown furrowing his forehead, neither meeting had gone particularly well. "I head home tomorrow morning."

He was leaving in the morning. How great was this! Talk about a made-to-order one-night stand.

"What about you?" The smile he shot her was so blindingly sexy she almost slipped off the stool for her second tumble of the day.

Becky decided there was no harm in telling him her general geographic location. Washington was almost as easy to get lost in as New York. "I live in Washington— the city, not the state. I'm leaving tomorrow, too."

She caught him staring at her hand, which she'd apparently been waving like a flag, and folded it over the other one in her lap. "They're plain, I know."

As much as she loved to shop until she dropped, she'd never gotten into manicures. Clear nail polish was about as wild and crazy as she got.

Beneath the bar, his fingers closed around hers. "They're beautiful, subtly elegant just like the rest of you."

He lifted her right hand to his mouth and pressed a kiss

to the palm. Becky drew in a breath, the feel of Max's lips sending ripples of heat running through her. Talk about romantic! She'd always had a thing for men's hands, but she'd never thought of her own as an erogenous zone. Boy, had she been wrong!

Above them on the wall-mounted flat-screen TV, the Times Square countdown to the new year began. "Ten, nine, eight..."

The bartender sidled up and slid two glasses of complimentary champagne and noise makers toward them.

"...Seven, six, five, four..."

Becky turned to Max. Gaze going to his sexy mouth, she acknowledged that her New Year's Eve curse had been broken in a big, big way.

"Three, two, one...Happy New Year!"

Becky couldn't say who was the first to reach out, but the next thing she knew she and Max were locked in each other's arms, mouths crushed together and tongues twining, his fingers threading through her hair.

The blare of a noise blower had them pulling apart. The bartender drew the paper horn from his smirking lips. "It's last call. We're closing early due to renovations. Can I get you anything else?"

Stroking his thumb over the sensitive spot inside Becky's thumb, blood-warmed like the rest of her, Max glanced at her half-finished drink. "Would you like anything else?"

Feeling heat pooling into her panties, Becky shook her head. "Nothing more for me, thanks." At least there was nothing more she wanted from the bar. She hadn't finished her second Flirtini or touched her free champagne. If she was going to have sex with Max, she wanted to remember it.

He turned back to the bartender. "Just the check, thanks."

She pulled her hand away to reach for her purse. New Year's Eve or not, she didn't want him to think she was the type of woman who hooked up with men for free drinks.

Max's hand settled atop hers. "You're my guest." Before she could protest, he leaned over and brushed his mouth over hers, a soft, sweet caress that stole her words and her breath. Pulling back, he smiled over at her. "I'm old school when it comes to who pays."

Becky ran her tongue along her bottom lip, savoring the faint, buttery taste of the Scotch he'd drunk. "Old school is okay…if you're sure."

"Oh, I'm sure," he said, and Becky didn't think he was talking about the bill.

The check came. Max added the gratuity and signed the slip. The tip must have been generous even by Manhattan standards because when the bartender looked up, he was smiling for the first time that night.

"Appreciate it. You have a good night." He glanced to Becky and then Max. "Feel free to hang out as long as you want." He backed away and disappeared through a side door that probably led to a stockroom or outside exit.

Max smiled over at Becky. "Do you realize we've been talking for more than three hours?"

She hadn't realized that, but then, ever since Max had sat down beside her, she hadn't been aware of anything beyond him, including the time. "Three hours might as well be three minutes when I'm with you. I don't want the night to end."

God, had she really just said that? For a split second she thought Angelina had taken control of her voice, but no, not only the voice but the sentiment came from her, albeit a brazen side of her nature she'd never dared reveal beyond her books.

His blue eyes melting into her brown ones, he admitted, "I don't want it to, either. Maybe it doesn't have to. I know we just met, but I very much want to make love to you. Would that be okay?"

Taking her cue from the ever-seductive, ultra-self-confident Angelina, she leaned in, close enough that a tendril of her hair brushed his cheek. "I think that would be better than okay. I think that would be pretty great, in fact."

He smiled, the corners of his eyes crinkling in that sexy way she was coming to love. "Good, that's settled then." He dropped his gaze and traced the edge of her dress's deep V neckline with a single finger. "That's a really nice dress, by the way."

Beneath her bra, her breasts felt heavy and hypersensitive. "I'm, uh…glad you like it."

His voice dropped to a sexy soft whisper. "Oh, I like it all right. I like it a lot." Below the bar, his other hand settled on her knee and then slid slowly up, stopping at her thigh. His eyes widened and his smile warmed. "Are you wearing…garters?"

"Uh-huh." She'd packed the wicked underwear along with the dress without really knowing why. Basking in the glow of Max's warm-eyed admiration, she was so very glad she had.

"Thought so." His fingers played with the lacey strip, circling and then sliding beneath, sending hot chills racing along her spine—and a wet warmth soaking into her thong panties.

The main house lights dimmed, shrouding them in semidarkness. Becky opened her legs wider and leaned into Max's heat. If someone were to walk in from the lounge, his back would shield her from obvious view. Still, being touched in such an intimate way in such a public place was just the sort of wickedly erotic scenario she wouldn't think twice about writing for Angelina but would never have imagined in a million years for herself.

Max pushed back from the bar and stood. Voice husky, he laid warm hands on her waist. "Let me take you someplace, okay?"

Becky couldn't manage more than a mute nod. She had no more need for words, written or spoken. She didn't bother to ask where they were going. So long as she was with Max, he could have shot them both to the moon for all she cared.

When he lifted her, it seemed the most natural thing in the world to wrap her arms around his neck—and her legs around his waist. He carried her through the empty lounge and over to the baby grand concealed behind the decorative metal screen. Kicking the bench aside, he sat her down atop the piano's cool, glossy hood.

"Beautiful, so beautiful." For a handful of moments, he stood looking at her. Then he stepped between her parted legs and bent his head to brush kisses over the bruise on the outside of her knee.

Bracing herself on her palms, Becky forgot about her sore bottom and her former adherence to the Three-Date Rule. Instead she leaned back and let the heat of the man and the moment wash over her like a warm, sexy wave.

Max's hands were on her thighs, pushing her dress up and out of the way. He lifted his head and looked up at her with reverent eyes. "God, you're drenched."

"I know." She reached a hand to his handsome face, her fingertips trailing his gold-dusted jaw.

He grimaced. "I guess I should have shaved."

Tenderness welled up inside her. She shook her head, savoring the slightly sandpapery feel of him. "You're perfect. I wouldn't change a thing."

And he *was* perfect. More than perfect, he was a dream come true. Earlier that day on the street he'd shown her how kind he was, how caring. They'd been strangers then. They were scarcely more than strangers now, and yet in the past few hours she'd felt closer to him, more connected, than she had to her ex after months of dating.

And then there was the whole chemistry thing, which there was no point in fighting, had she been so inclined. Everything about him, absolutely everything, she found endlessly appealing, mind-numbingly sexy. Even his New England accent and the way he had of pronouncing certain words, truncating certain syllables and doing funny things with his *r*'s, brought her close to coming.

He turned his face to the side and captured the inside of her wrist in a kiss. "You're the one who's perfect. You're just like I imagined you in my fantasy only even more beautiful."

It was true. Her sexy mouth was bee-stung from his kisses, her smooth cheeks pink from the brush of his beard, and her shapely legs were spread wide, hips lifting as if begging for the touch of his hand.

"You fantasized about me?" She lifted her head to look at him, brown eyes melting over him like liquid caramel.

He nodded. "I did."

His sexy Cinderella must be packing some kind of fairy-dust mojo because he couldn't remember ever being so completely turned-on by a woman, God help him, not even his wife. Until now he'd thought raw animal lust was reserved for men like his character, Drake, not writers with archeology degrees and bifocal reading glasses, but whatever "it" was, this woman, Rose, definitely brought it out in him.

He bent and kissed the inside of each smooth thigh, then pushed the slender strip of lace panty aside and spread her between his fingers. Dewy wetness coated her nether lips, her rose-petal-pink clitoris standing out from its hood as if begging for his tongue's attention. A younger man might have taken those signs as a green light to unzip his pants and dive in. He doubted she would complain let alone ask him to stop. He hadn't exaggerated when he'd said she was drenched. More than drenched, she was dripping, more than ready to take him as deeply as he could go. But there was something to be said for the thrill of anticipation and the richer reward of pleasure prolonged. Though he knew next to nothing about her, he knew she deserved to be savored like a fine wine or better yet, a single malt Scotch, the subtle flavors of butter and oak not something you swilled but rather sat with awhile, rolling on your tongue, teasing out the subtle flavors.

He sank a finger all the way inside her. Crooking it gently, he knew the moment when he found the supersensitive spot.

Thighs quivering, Rose moaned and slid urgent fingers into his hair. She bucked her hips and tossed back her head of shiny curls and grabbed for his wrist, pressing him closer.

Harder and hotter and thicker than he'd ever been before, he edged his gaze upward, drinking in the stark beauty of her flushed face. "Easy, baby, I'll get you there."

Keeping his finger inside her, he slid his free arm beneath her hips and lifted her to his mouth. He nuzzled the nest of crisp curls, the scent of rosemary mint soap mingling with her own tangy musk. Moving lower, he stroked his tongue along her slit, and her cream spurted into his mouth.

She bucked beneath him, her voice coming out as a raspy moan. "Oh, God, oh, Max, I'm so close. Please don't stop."

"I'm not stopping, sweetheart. I could do this all night. You taste…amazing."

Writer though he was, he was at a loss for words beyond that. She did taste amazing, musky and salty and absolutely, indescribably delicious. He couldn't imagine ever getting enough of laving and licking and suckling her. It was only his mounting sense of urgency that prompted him to hurry. Though he'd yet to unzip his jeans, he knew his balls were drawn up tight and aching, his cock harder and heavier than he could ever remember it being. Like standing on the edge of a demolition site waiting for the hard-wired building to implode, it was only a matter of time. He circled her clit with the point of his tongue, a slow, thorough sweep, and seconds later she came apart in his arms.

Drinking in her orgasm, Max looked up into her wild eyes and moist mouth and felt a trickle of come slide down the side of his cock. "I need to get us out of here and up to my room. You'll come back with me, won't you?" he asked, not sure what he'd do if she were to change her mind now.

Lifting herself up on her elbows, she swallowed hard and nodded. "Yes, Max, I'll come with you. I can't think of anywhere I'd rather be."

5

Inside his room Drake watched the beautiful Brit lift one red high-heeled foot and kick aside the dress at her feet. Covered only in black garters, silk stockings and the silky curtain of her hair, she strode toward him, green eyes holding his in the semidarkness. Since his wife's death the year before, he hadn't been able to bring himself to make love to another woman, but that was about to change.

She drew up an arm's length away from him, a deliberate tease. "Tell me how much you want me. Before we go any further. I want to hear every naughty bit."

Drake was in no mood for games. He closed the gap between them, his arms going roughly about her, his fingers sinking into her tender white flesh.

He slid one callused palm downward over her taut belly and squeezed the plump Mound of Venus between her slender thighs. "Open for me, love, and I'll make both our days."

12:15 a.m. (give or take)

THEY RODE the elevator up to Max's rooftop suite. Becky was in his arms before the double doors closed.

He lifted his face from her hair and looked down. "Thank you for coming upstairs with me. I'm not sure what I would have done if you'd said no." The obvious desire in his blue eyes was a more potent aphrodisiac than any mood- or mind-altering substance hotel guests in the sixties and seventies might have used.

Head tucked beneath his chin, she slid her hands under his jacket, savoring the sensation of shirt-covered muscles rippling beneath her fingertips. "Thank you for asking."

She wasn't sure what she would have done if he hadn't asked. Invited him back to her own small room, she suspected. She'd never propositioned a man in her life, but this was her day for firsts. Certainly she couldn't imagine parting ways in the bar downstairs. The episode at the piano was a prelude, not an ending. As amazing as those moments had been, they had only whetted her appetite for more—more of him.

Never before had she felt so sexy, so completely and thoroughly desired. Knowing how much Max wanted her, seeing and feeling the proof of it in the hot glances he sent her way and the hardness crowning his thighs was an incredible turn-on. Even though she'd climaxed mere moments ago, she was already pulsing with a sweet liquid ache, an ache she knew he could more than satisfy. But more than him giving a repeat performance of the interlude downstairs, it was her eagerness to give back that had her counting ascending hotel floors with the bated breath enthusiasm of a New Year's countdown only in reverse.

Max's thoughts were apparently tracking hers. Glancing up at the lit display above their heads, he blew out a heavy breath. "Suddenly a rooftop suite doesn't seem like the good idea it did when I booked the reservation over the phone."

She smiled into the heat of his strong neck, drunk on the smell and taste of his skin, loving the way his lean, hard body fitted hers. Remembering the amazing feeling of his lips and tongue pleasuring her, the incredible turn-on of looking down and seeing his blond head buried between her thighs, and the erotically wicked feel of doing all those things atop a piano in a public place sent more warm moisture jetting. Though she was sure his suite would be many times larger and many times nicer than her small third-floor room, Becky wished they'd stopped off there instead. She didn't need a fancy backdrop to set the mood for making love. She was already in the mood and then some. All she really wanted was Max naked and inside her.

Another tortured few seconds passed and then the elevator doors opened. Becky stepped out first, her shoe's narrow high heel catching on the metal groove and sending her flying.

Max caught her elbow, saving her from falling on her face. She sent him a sideways look of apology. "Believe it or not, I'm not usually this klutzy."

He held her steady while she slipped her foot back in the shoe. "C'mon, Cinderella, we've already made it past midnight. You haven't turned into a pumpkin yet, and I don't think I can stand to stop and hunt for any more left-behind shoes."

They hurried down the hall, Max leading the way. When they came to his suite, he shoved the key card into the slot and pulled on the handle, cursing beneath his breath when the door didn't immediately open. He succeeded on the third try, and they stumbled inside.

Max fell back against the closed door, bringing her against his chest. "God, you feel so good against me."

He hooked his hand to her nape, and she tilted her face up to receive his kiss. Even wearing her Cinderella slippers, she had to stand on her toes to reach him, but it was worth it—more than worth it. His lips were warm and moist, his tongue flavored with the rich Scotch he'd drunk, as well as some other earthier flavor. It took her a handful of seconds to realize the earthiness she tasted was herself, her essence. She shouldn't be surprised. She had come in his mouth. Like making love atop a piano, that was another first for her. Thinking how gentle and generous he'd been with her, how natural it had felt to open her legs and accept his intimate kisses, to, for once, turn off her brain and live fully and completely in her body rather than vicariously through her fictional characters, she tore her mouth away and kissed his closed eyelids, the corners of his sexy mouth, and the cleft of his square chin. She kissed his lightly lined forehead, his dark blond eyebrows, and the tip of his slightly-too-long nose. She kissed the hollow of his throat, the corded muscle that ran alongside and the sculpted V of his breastbone. She kissed him because she couldn't stop kissing him, because in the small sensory sphere to which her world had been reduced, not to kiss him was unimaginable.

Remembering how impatient Elliot had been to get to the main event, she stopped and said, "I'm sorry. All this kissing, is it too much? Am I…bothering you?"

Max groaned and slid his hand into the back of her hair. "Are you crazy? I love the way you kiss me. I'm drunk on it, but I really need to get you—us—into the bedroom."

They backed across the living room, passing an ornately carved fireplace mantel and several pieces of framed artwork, shedding clothes along the way—Max's jacket,

Becky's coat, the dress she suddenly couldn't wait to get out of and no longer had to.

By the time they reached the bedroom, Becky was stripped down to her black bra and panties, lace garters and silky hose. Shirt hanging open, Max sat her down on the side of the bed, a king-size four poster, and went down on his knees.

He slipped off first her right shoe and then her left. "You have such little feet." He unsnapped her garters and rolled off her stockings, pausing to press savoring kisses along her inner thighs.

Becky glanced down. "My older sister used to say I had funny-looking feet. The second toe is longer than the big toe, see." She lifted a foot to show him. "Maybe that's why I like shoes so much. It's a great way to cover up the flaws."

"I say they're beautiful." As if bent on proving it, he took her foot between his hands and carried it to his mouth. He laid a tingling trail of kisses on her arch and ankle, and then sucked her big toe into his mouth.

Oh, my God. Just as he'd made love to her hands earlier, he was making love to her foot now. And amazingly it didn't tickle. In fact, it felt really, really good.

Hands on her upper arms, he ran his hungry gaze over her as though he couldn't get enough of looking at her. "You really do look just like you did in my fantasy."

"You actually fantasized about me?" When he'd first said so downstairs, she'd assumed he was exaggerating or just being nice.

He nodded. "After you left me standing on the street, I couldn't get you out of my head. On the walk back to the hotel, I kept imagining you wearing the red shoes and nothing else. Well, I imagined your peach panties, too." The corners of his mouth lifted in that oh so sexy smile.

"I fantasized about you, too."

The smile reached his eyes, bringing out that sexy crinkling about the corners. "You did?"

"Uh-huh. When I got back to my room, I took a really long shower."

He cocked a sandy-blond brow. "A shower, huh? A cold shower?"

She shook her head. "A really hot one. Steaming, almost scalding, in fact."

Intense blue eyes bored into hers. "What did your fantasy...involve?"

"Well, first, this..." She slid her hands inside his shirt. Feeling his firm, flushed flesh beneath her fingertips, she slid the garment over his powerful shoulders and off.

Becky sucked in her breath. She'd known even before unhooking the first shirt button out in the living room he would be strong and lean and fit, but not even her writer's imagination could have prepared her for the purely perfect beauty of Max's bare chest, the sculpted planes dusted with golden hair and flexing with muscle. She ducked her head and drew one flat, brownish-pink nipple into her mouth.

Max groaned and sank hard fingers into her hair. "God, woman, what are you doing to me?"

Outside of her books, Becky had never before been so bold. Looking up, she couldn't help smiling, a very Angelina-like smile, she was sure. "I was showing you my fantasy. If you stand up, I'll show you the rest." He hesitated and then rose to his feet. Looking up, she snagged his hungry gaze along with the tab of his zipper. "I imagined taking you as far down my mouth and my throat as you'd go. Would it be all right if I acted on that part of the fantasy, too?"

Gaze riveted on her mouth, he swallowed hard and nodded. "Believe it or not, that was part of my fantasy, too."

"Good, because it's a big part of mine. A *huge* part you might even say." She carefully rolled the zipper down over his erection.

He wasn't wearing briefs, and the backs of her fingers trailed down his bare skin. She slipped a hand inside, drawing him out. Becky sucked in her breath. She'd known he was very hard and she'd guessed by the bulge in his jeans he would also be large—make that *very* large—but she couldn't have known how perfectly shaped he would be, how beautifully formed.

"When I asked you up here, I figured I'd be doing most of the seducing."

She tilted her face to look up at him and ran the tip of her tongue along her lips. "That's not a complaint, I hope."

He let out a ragged laugh. "Not hardly."

"Good." She bent her head and lapped at the creamy bead of moisture crowning the tip. "Hmm, you do taste good, delicious in fact. Mind if I have some more?"

Eyes stark with need, he answered with a sharp shake of his head. "I don't know how much more I can take, how much longer I'll last…"

"Let's find out." She angled her face to his groin and guided him into her mouth, slowly sliding her lips over the silken length of him, savoring inch upon precious inch. "Hmm, so good," she murmured, and then relaxed her throat and drew him deeper still.

"God, I love the way you smell," he said. His hands stayed buried in her hair, fingers threading through her curls, gently pulling her head down. "What's that perfume you're wearing?"

She pulled back and stroked her hand over his balls. "I don't wear perfume. It must be my bath gel."

"Whatever it is, I'm drowning in it. I could buy it by the case."

"We can go back to my room later and take a shower with it if you like."

Smiling, he shook his head. "Now that I have you behind closed doors doing…that, I can't imagine letting you back out anytime soon."

So he meant for her to stay the night or what remained of it. When they'd left the bar, it had been just after midnight. Though she was in no danger of turning into a pumpkin— she had both slippers in close proximity—there were only so many hours left before morning, not nearly enough time to do all the things she was fantasizing about in her mind.

Anchoring her hands to his waist, she pushed the jeans down his narrow hips and then the rest of the way off. Max stepped out of the pants, sweeping them aside with an impatient foot. She slid her gaze over his body, wanting to appreciate him properly before they spiraled further out of control. He was a beautiful man, broad shouldered and narrow hipped with a washboard stomach and a tight ass that made her want to bite into it like an apple. He was muscled in all the places a man ought to be, but not too much, like someone who used his body in a very physical, very real way rather than just pumping iron at the gym.

"I'm sorry, Rose, I can't wait anymore. I need to be inside you." Hands on her shoulders, he gently pushed her back on the bed.

Becky hesitated for the first time since he'd walked up to her at the bar. "I brought condoms with me. They're in my purse on the table in the other room."

Max nodded. "I'll be right back."

Becky took advantage of the time alone to pull back the covers and slip beneath. Max returned a moment later and handed her the purse. Sitting up against the headboard, she opened it and took out the three packets.

The mattress dipped as he joined her on the bed. Holding her gaze, he went up on his knees. "You do the honors."

Becky ripped open one of the gold foil squares and took the disc of latex out, anticipation making her clumsy. She rolled the condom over him, loving how long and thick he was, how beautifully big and hard. Too bad she hadn't considered buying a larger size. Max definitely qualified as *extra* large. He stretched the standard-size prophylactic to its limit.

Finishing, she looked up at him and asked, "Does that, um…hurt you?"

"It's a little tight," he admitted, "but in the next couple of seconds, it's going to feel really good, and I'm not going to care."

He eased her onto her back and straddled her hips. Fitting himself to her, he said, "I'm a lot bigger than you are. You'll have to tell me if I hurt you."

The remark tugged at her heartstrings. Stranger or not, he really was the most tender man. "You won't hurt me."

Looking up into his warm blue eyes, Becky found herself wishing she'd told him her real name if only so she could have the pleasure of hearing him call it out when he came inside her. Though she'd lectured herself ad nauseam over the past year about trusting too much too soon, she knew in this case it was all right. Max really wouldn't hurt her.

He entered her very slowly, very gently but neither of them had counted on how wet she would be, how ready to take him all the way. He glided inside, burying himself to the root, filling and stretching her to her limit. She anchored her hands to his hard shoulders and wrapped her legs around his waist as she had downstairs, loving the way he moved his hips in slow circles and full-on thrusts, reveling in the delicious feeling of having him fully inside her.

He reached down between them and found her clitoris with the pad of his thumb. "I'm sorry, baby, but I can't wait anymore."

Drowning in his eyes, in the throbbing heat his hand was raising, Becky wrapped her arms about his damp neck, pulling him closer. "Don't wait. I don't want you to wait."

Max pulled out and thrust hard and deep. He let out a hoarse cry and came inside her.

2:30 a.m.

BECKY LAY on her back, her legs spread open and knees bent. Max knelt in the space between, resting back on his heels. They'd made love a second time since coming upstairs, a quick, feverish coupling that had left them sweaty and satisfied and lying in a twist of damp sheets. Now that the initial sexual tension between them had been sated, she was ready for a more leisurely ride.

Even fully, gloriously erect, Max didn't seem to be in any hurry, either. He had one finger buried inside her and was patiently working in a second, the milking motion of his hand sending sticky warmth sliding down her thighs.

She lifted her head from the pillow. Never before had a lover treated her with such thorough care. Feeling almost guilty and wholly decadent, she said, "You don't have to keep doing that. I mean, you must be getting tired or bored or…"

"Bored?" He looked at her and smiled. "I could play with you this way for hours. In fact, I just may." He moved the thumb of his other hand over her clitoris. Becky moaned. "Right on your clit, is that where you like it, or do you like it lower, more…here?" He slid his thumb down to her slit. "I want to know how to touch you. It's *important,*" he added, as though the fate of the free world rested on her getting off.

Becky hesitated. She'd never before had a lover so eager to please her in every way. "Lower feels nice, too, but it feels…well, it feels *really* good higher."

"I thought so." Pulling out of her, he bent and licked the hood of her clitoris, raising her turn-on to a whole new level of heat. Suddenly she came apart, the spasm striking deeper than she'd ever before experienced.

The last flutter of contraction was still rolling through when Max turned her over onto her stomach. She scrambled to her knees and spread her legs, wanting to share the last ebb of pleasure with him, her hunky blue-eyed stranger, not exactly a stranger anymore. Even though the connection they shared wasn't strong enough to survive the morning light, he was the first lover she'd ever had who'd made it possible for her to fully let go.

He went still behind her. "Baby, your back. You should have told me." Pulling out of her, he pressed a light kiss to her bruised buttocks.

Becky shivered, his lips in that spot raising all sorts of erotic thoughts. Until he'd mentioned it, she'd forgotten all about being banged up. If anything, she'd never felt more whole in her life. "I'm okay—better than okay. Just don't stop. Please."

He entered her again in one smooth thrust. She arched back to meet him, capturing him inside her, deliberately flexing her inner muscles in a way calculated to drive him over the edge.

Max's breath was a balmy breeze against her damp nape. "God, you're so tight. I love the way you fit around me."

"You feel pretty amazing yourself." She bit her lip, absorbing the blunt pressure and the delicious edgy thrill of going down on her hands and knees for him.

Reaching down between them, just above the place where they were joined, he stroked her clitoris.

Palms braced on the mattress, Becky bit her lip. "Oh, God, I'm going to come again." She'd assumed she was through with orgasms for the night.

Max's voice was a warm whisper in her ear. "Go ahead and give in. If you fall, I'll be right there to catch you."

Becky grabbed the edge of the pillow and focused on free-falling into the building climax. She had no doubt Max would make good on his promise. Her sexy Prince Charming had come to her aid two times already, in front of the hotel that afternoon and then stepping out of the elevator tonight. After all that rescuing, what would a third time matter?

Max would be there to catch her—but only until morning's first light.

3:30 a.m.

MAX ROLLED onto his side and reached for her. "Show me how you like to be touched—how you touch yourself when you're alone."

Half asleep, Becky had been having—or was it living?— the most deliciously wicked dream. Pulled from the thrall of it, she lifted her head from the pillow. "What do you mean?"

He kissed her shoulder and thinking of where those lips had recently been, she felt a shiver shoot through her. "You know what I mean." He wrapped strong fingers around her right wrist and drew her hand down to her pubis. Setting it there, he turned his head and gently bit the lobe of her ear. "Touch yourself for me."

Becky hesitated, feeling shy for the first time that night. Silly, since they'd been making love almost nonstop. It wasn't as if she was a prude. After the things she'd done with him already, what he was asking wasn't even all that risqué. Even if it was, just thinking about it was an incredible turn-on. And yet the thought of masturbating in front of him had her feeling vulnerable and naked in a new, not entirely good way. Go figure.

He looked down on her and brushed back the damp curls from her face. "Don't tell me you're going shy on me now." He picked up her hand and drifted it over her pubis. "Touch yourself for me. I want to watch you. In case you have any doubts, I'm going to love watching you. Just thinking about watching you is making me hard all over again."

Even feeling shy, the sexy demand was too tempting to pass on. She felt herself going wet all over again. Her skin had the hot, prickly feeling she normally associated with the early stage of sunburn, the telltale tenderness that told you you'd overindulged in the sun worshipping but, tough luck, it was too late to cover up now. The hot look in Max's eyes when he talked dirty to her, the sight of his broad, damp chest hovering over her, the sense that he really was going to get off on watching her helped her find her courage—and her sense of adventure.

"I've never done that before." He tossed her a skeptical look, and she clarified, "I mean, not in front of another person."

Bringing herself to orgasm shouldn't take long. She'd touched herself so many times over the past sexless year she'd jokingly suggested to Sharon she was thinking of giving classes on the subject. Five minutes when she woke up in the morning was all the time it usually took. Afterward she got up, brushed her teeth, and jumped into the shower. An orgasm might not qualify as a breakfast of champions, but it definitely took the edge off her frustration so she could focus on getting her daily pages written. But could she really masturbate in front of Max? She supposed there was only one way to find out.

Still sensitized from her recent climax courtesy of Max's very talented tongue, she slid her hand between her spread thighs and found the nub of her clitoris with her middle finger. Closing her eyes, she started the slow circular sweep she knew would bring her to a quick, golden peak. At this point, she usually reached into her mental stockpile of fantasies for one of the classic erotic scenarios guaranteed to get her off—a desert sheik, a British nobleman in period dress, a navy SEAL or FBI agent or international spy. But this time her fantasy was flesh-and-blood and right there in bed beside her, stealing the scene—and her heart, if she let him.

"Does it feel good, sweetheart?" Max's sexy whisper floated above her.

Eyes closed, she nodded, focused on the musk and heat of him surrounding her. "You know it does."

"I want to hear you say it."

"It feels good. Actually it feels great."

Performing for him was proving to be a major turn-on for her, too. Alone, she'd never gotten this wet this fast. She spread her legs wider and lifted her hips to match the increasing rhythm of her damp hand.

"Look at me. Open your eyes and look at me." Max's breath blew across the side of her damp throat, raising gooseflesh in the midst of all that heat.

She obeyed, opening her eyes and looking at him. Brown eyes met blue ones—and suddenly Becky was in over her head, drowning in deep waters.

"Tell me again how good it feels."

Becky shivered and bit the inside of her lip. The tingling was rapidly building to a full-blown ache, the first delicious spasm promising a deeply satisfying release only a breath or two away.

"Look at me." Braced above her, Max lifted one hand from the mattress and laid it along her face. "Open your eyes and look at me and jump off that cliff. I'll be there to catch you. Trust me."

Trust me. The last lover she'd trusted had done the equivalent of taking a razor and slashing her heart into bloody strips. But this was no time for cynical thinking. This was no time for thinking at all. Becky opened her eyes and looked up into Max's face, his lean jaw set tight.

She circled her finger one final time—and hurled herself over the cliff edge and into the deep blue ocean of her lover's eyes.

4:45 a.m.

LYING ON HER SIDE with her head resting on Max's shoulder, Becky traced the musculature of his chest with a single finger. "Would you believe the shoes made me do it?"

He shook his head and laughed. "Rose, right now I'd believe anything you told me."

Becky bit her lip, once again wishing she'd been honest with him about her name at least. Even though they'd be parting ways in a few hours, it would be nice in years to come to look back and think of him as a friend.

Steering the subject into safer waters, she teased, "Are you sure you're a travel writer?"

His smile dimmed. "What makes you ask that?"

She slid her palm over the queue of damp golden hair leading down his flat belly to the erection standing out from his thighs. Technically, it was morning already, but dawn was at least another hour away, and in the interim that beautiful thick cock was meant to be touched and tasted and worshipped.

"I don't know. I could almost imagine you wrote about sex for a living." She wrapped her hand around his shaft and lightly squeezed, loving how he let her fondle and play with him, pleased at how effortless it was to turn him on.

He smiled over at her. "If I do, it's only as a hobby." He ran a single finger down the side of her neck, drawing her shiver. "Are you cold? Do you want the sheet?"

"No, thanks." She shook her head, never warmer in her life. Making love to Max was a bounty for all five senses, including visual. She didn't want to cover up any part of him, particularly the part stiffening in her hand.

Settling a hand atop her thigh, he sucked in a breath. "God, I can't believe I just met you today. I feel so comfortable, as if I've known you for years."

"I know. I feel the same way." It was true. She'd never felt this relaxed with a man and at the same time so excited. She glanced over to the torn condom packets lying atop the nightstand and then back at Max. "We're officially out of condoms. Unless you have a hidden stash, we can't— what I mean is, I'm not on any kind of birth control. Sorry."

"I'm the one who's sorry." For the first time that night, Max looked less than sure of himself. "I didn't come on this trip expecting to meet anyone."

Even though what they were sharing was a one-night stand, it had turned out to be the most special night of her adult life, not to mention a truly memorable New Year's Eve. She didn't want him to think she went around picking up strange men in bars, either.

"Believe it or not, I bought those condoms a year ago. I've been carrying them around ever since. As they say, hope springs eternal."

She could tell from the expression on his face that he wasn't sure whether or not to believe her. "I can't imagine a beautiful, intelligent woman like you lacking for partners."

The unexpected compliment took Becky off guard. She clamped her mouth closed before she was tempted to deny the compliment or, worse yet, ask for confirmation. Angelina wouldn't ever turn down male admiration or second-guess it. The Brit's confidence in herself as a woman, as well as a spy, was a pivotal part of her character. Maybe it was time Becky scripted some of her fictional creation's self-assurance into her real life.

He looked over at her and confessed, "Before tonight, I hadn't had sex in almost two years."

It was Becky's turn to be skeptical. With his face lost to the shadows, she couldn't read him, and she supposed it didn't really matter. Stranger sex was, by definition, a one-time thing. In a few more hours, they'd go their separate ways and never see each other again. There would be no do-over and no repeat performance.

Earlier in the evening, the thought of seeing him for one night and then never again had provided a sexual and psychological thrill. Now, thinking of how little time they had left, she felt more than a little sad. Stranger sex or not, this night was the best of her adult life.

Why was it the good things in life always seemed to go by so quickly?

6

Angelina peeled herself from the Aussie's broad, damp chest and reached for the sheet. She'd just had the best bloody shag of her life and the brilliant part was he didn't have a clue as to who she was. Anonymity was proving to be a potent aphrodisiac, for her at least. Thinking how good he smelled, recalling how amazing he'd tasted, she leaned over and ran her lips along the corded sinew at the side of his throat, sampling the salt on his skin.

He pulled her atop him so that she straddled his narrow hips, his cock pressing into her lower belly. "Angie, you're one hell of a woman."

Angelina froze. Feeling like an acrobat whose safety net had just been taken away in the middle of a high-wire act, she stared down into her lover's blue, bedroom eyes. "How the hell do you know my name?"

BECKY OPENED her eyes the next morning to a new year and a new day. She felt like a fairy-tale princess waking from a dream—a red-hot sexy dream. Rolling onto her side, she reached for her gloriously naked Prince Charming, but the mattress beside her was empty and cold.

"Max?" She opened her eyes.

Wrapping the sheet around her, she sat up in bed. Fully awake now, she spotted the sheet of hotel stationery and single red rose on the pillow beside her.

A rose for a rose…
    Thanks for an unforgettable New Year's night.
Max.

She picked up the flower. He must have snagged it from one of the lounge tables last night or early that morning. Inhaling its fragrance, she felt her throat tighten and her eyes water. This New Year's Eve would always stand out in her mind as the sexiest, most romantic night of her life. Now that it was over, she felt like Cinderella the day *after* the ball.

She read Max's note again, searching for clues much as Angelina might decipher an encrypted piece of code, torn between gratitude that he'd bothered to leave a note at all and hurt that his goodbye was so very brief. But then, he was a travel writer, not a poet, and they'd had a one-night stand, not a love affair. What had she expected, a Shakespearean sonnet in iambic pentameter?

Sliding the silky petals down her cheek, snippets of scenes from the previous evening ran through her mind like highlights from a movie trailer. What a beautiful night, what a beautiful man, what a beautiful…*memory*. If only it might have been more than that.

But it wasn't. They'd had a one-night stand, end of story. Max was a thrilling and tender lover, the *perfect* lover, but none of that meant he had feelings for her beyond lust. What they'd shared was a moment, not a future. Despite his claim that he hadn't had sex for almost two years, for a hot-looking man who traveled for a living such encounters must be commonplace.

Holding the sheet around her, she shuffled out into the living room, the suite echoing with an empty stillness. She checked the alcove for luggage that might indicate he hadn't left quite yet, but it was empty, too, as she'd known it would be. In the bathroom, droplets of water still clung to the glass shower stall, suggesting he hadn't left all that long ago. She picked up a corner of the damp towel hanging on the bar and inhaled his musky soapy scent, the same scent clinging to her body.

Tears stung her eyes. How was it possible to miss someone you hadn't known even twenty-four hours?

Surveying her watery eyes in the mirror, Becky told herself this weepiness had to stop. It was time to start acting her age, or at least to start *living* her life like a grown-up woman, feet firmly planted in the present, not the past, even if the past was just a few hours old. She had to pull herself together and call Pat with her answer. But for sanity's sake, before she did anything else, she needed to wash off Max's scent.

The bathroom in her room was a closet compared to this. She surveyed the deep double sink and separate shower and tub and thought, *Why the hell not?* She didn't have her toiletries with her but there were complimentary travel-size bottles of shampoo and conditioner set out on the counter and a dispenser of all-purpose shower gel inside the stall.

She stepped out of the bed sheet and treated herself to a long, hot shower, almost as long as the one she'd taken the previous evening and even more needed. Along with her bruised bottom, she was sore and stiff in several other very private places. By the time she stepped out again, she was feeling better, or at least more like herself. She dried off with one of the fluffy white towels, wrapped another around her wet hair, and slid on the complimentary guest robe which, wouldn't you know it, smelled just like Max.

Max…Maxwell. Who knew, but maybe meeting Max was the universe's idea of delivering on the promise of fresh starts and dazzling opportunities in her houses of career and love in one fell swoop. She couldn't shake the feeling that the similarity in names was some kind of sign.

By the time she finished drying her hair with the blow dryer anchored to the wall, she'd made up her mind. She would coauthor the book with Adam Maxwell. She really had nothing to lose—well, nothing beyond her dignity—and the sooner she and Maxwell got down to figuring out exactly how coauthorship was going to work for them, the better it would be.

Dressed in her outfit from the night before, red shoes and beaded evening bag included, she stepped out into the hall. She felt a little sleazy leaving a hotel room that wasn't hers in rumpled cocktail clothes, but then again, this *was* the Chelsea.

Back in her own room, she plugged her cell into the wall charger and speed-dialed Pat's number. A few rings later, her editor picked up.

"Hey, Pat, it's Becky. I'm checking in as promised. Look, I've thought over the coauthorship deal, and I've decided to accept."

On the other end of the line, Pat hesitated. "That's great, Becky. There are some kinks to work out before we go to contract, but we can chat about that later."

Picking up on Pat's nervousness, Becky wanted to chat about it now. "What kind of kinks?"

"Maxwell blew a fuse when I pitched the coauthorship. I spoke to his agent last night and again this morning, and so far he's not budging."

Feeling as if the floor was caving beneath her feet, Becky held the phone away from her ear. It had never occurred to her Maxwell would reject *her*. Housewife porn comment aside, she'd assumed he must already be on board with the deal, otherwise why would Pat have approached her?

Thinking about that, her shock rapidly turned into full-blown pissed off. "Who the hell does he think he is, anyway? Does he think Drake is too good for Angelina? That tree-trunk-necked primate should count himself lucky that a sexy, sophisticated woman like Angelina would even let him put his ham-handed mitts on her, let alone agree to share her spotlight."

Becky stopped herself, realizing she'd once again spiraled into her alternative universe, an occupational hazard of writing fiction. The problem, or rather the pain-in-the-ass she had to deal with wasn't a fictional character but its real-life creator, Adam Maxwell. "I need Maxwell's phone number."

"You know I can't do that, Becky. Let me keep working this behind the scenes with the agent and our legal department. You go home to D.C. and I'll call you as soon as I know something."

Becky wasn't going home to D.C. or anywhere else, at least not yet. "If Maxwell still refuses the deal, where does that leave me?" Pat's answer was dead silence, which told Becky all she needed to know. Still, she had to hear her say it. "Unemployed, right?"

Pat sighed into Becky's ear. "I'm afraid so. What I told

you at lunch the other day hasn't changed. I can't offer you another solo contract right now."

Becky shot up from the side of the bed. "In that case, give me a fighting chance. Give me his number, his cell number, not his home. I swear to you I won't give it out to anyone."

Pat heaved a sigh. "I hope not, because if you do, I could lose my job. If he finds out, I still could."

Becky was already reaching for a pen and the hotel message pad. "He won't. You have no idea how charming I can be—or how persuasive."

In life sometimes it was easier to ask for forgiveness than permission—and Becky suspected this would turn out to be one of those times.

As soon as Becky jotted down Maxwell's number, she ended the call to Pat and programmed it into her cell. But first—even though he couldn't see her over the phone, she knew she'd feel on firmer footing if she wasn't wearing last night's rumpled clothes. She took off her dress and shoes and changed into jeans and a soft-pink angora cowl-neck sweater before packing up her things.

Sitting down on the side of the bed, she took a deep breath, highlighted his number from her address book, and hit the green send button. It rang a few times and then his voice mail kicked in, inviting her to leave a message. Oh, she'd leave a message all right.

Remembering her promise to Pat to be charming and persuasive, she left a pleasant to-the-point message and then went out of the hotel in search of coffee. Two skinny lattes and five messages later, she was steaming mad, as well as running out of time and caffeine tolerance. She glanced at her watch. Checking out would leave her barely enough time to catch a cab to Penn Station and make the eleven o'clock train to D.C.

She hesitated, asking herself how she would write the scene if it was for Angelina rather than herself. Angelina wouldn't stand by and let herself be brushed off, no matter how big a name Maxwell was in the publishing industry or anywhere else. No way would her intrepid creation give up that easily, or at all.

Becky flipped open her laptop. Balancing the computer on her lap, she logged online. A quick Internet search brought up Maxwell's Web site at *www.drakesadventures.com*. Not so surprisingly, there was no publicity photo of the reclusive author. There was a short bio, though. She skimmed the sparse few lines.

Bestselling author Adam Maxwell writes from his home surrounded by the serene backdrop of New Hampshire's White Mountains region. Like his fictional alter ego, Drake Dundee, Maxwell is an ardent traveler and outdoor enthusiast. He has traveled to more than thirty countries and four continents, experiences that lend an astonishing authenticity to his Drake's Adventures series. Look for his next Drake's Adventure novel in brick-and-mortar and online bookstores this fall.

More than thirty countries—hadn't Max said almost the same when they'd been sitting downstairs at the Serena? It was a further sign that taking the coauthorship was the right decision for her. Now all she had to do was get Maxwell to agree.

The bio's mention of the New Hampshire White Mountains was the equivalent of striking pay dirt. Another search yielded a list of the forty or so towns comprising the region. A little more digging via the Web sites of several local newspapers narrowed it down to the tiny town of Hadley. She couldn't get an address listing but no matter. In a small, rural town, a Big Famous Author like Adam Maxwell couldn't possibly fly under the radar screen.

It was time to reach inside herself for the moxy, balls and persistence her editor had touted as star author qualities at lunch yesterday. She zipped the laptop back in its case.

Adam Maxwell, you have no idea who you're dealing with.

MAX STEPPED inside the foyer to his house. Though he was glad to be done with the drive, he still braced himself before entering all that emptiness. Fortunately his golden retriever, Scout, greeted him at the door, tail wagging. Pushing eleven, the dog was getting white around the muzzle but then, so was he.

"Good boy. I missed you, too. That pet sitter treat you okay? Yeah, I know. There's no substitute for the real thing, huh?"

Parking his luggage inside the door, he bent down to pet the dog. As he did, something—Rebecca St. Claire's paperback romance—fell out of his coat pocket onto the floor. Damn, he'd meant to leave it behind for the hotel maid but had been distracted by a certain brown-eyed, brown-haired, shoe-loving temptress in his bed.

He picked up the book and tossed it onto the marble-topped foyer table next to his stacked mail, thinking his housekeeper might want to read it. He wasn't going to and by now there shouldn't be any need. Harry had had plenty of time to work his behind-the-scenes magic and find a way to break the contract, though the drive home from New York had been ominously quiet. Not only had Harry not called but no one else had, either. Taking out his cell, he saw the reason for the unusual stretch of silence. He'd been so busy that morning coming up with corny notes and pilfered roses he'd forgotten to turn his phone back on.

He turned it on now. With any luck, there'd be a message waiting from Harry to confirm the good news about the broken contract. Despite the agent's hemming and hawing, he was an ace deal maker—and Max reasoned that the flip side of that was he must also be an ace deal *breaker.*

Seven messages waited. Unlike his alter ego, Drake, Max wasn't a fan of surprises. He thumbed through the roster of recent calls. There was only one Manhattan number on the list, and it was Pat's, not Harry's. There was a message from his mother, no big surprise there, and five more messages, the latter all made from the same unfamiliar number, a 202 Washington, D.C., exchange. That was weird. Offhand he didn't think he knew anyone in D.C., except for his pretty Cinderella, and like a dolt, he hadn't written his number on the note he'd left behind.

He punched in the security code and put the phone on speaker, letting the new messages play through. "Max, it's Pat. Look, Rebecca St. Claire just called to accept the co-authorship. I know you're still not crazy about the idea, but I'm asking you one last time to reconsider. You've been with us a long time, Max. Keeping the lawyers out of this is to everybody's benefit. Call me or better yet, have Harry call me. *Ciao.*"

If Pat thought the mention of lawyers would bring him

to heel, she apparently didn't know him all that well. He saved the message and moved on.

"Mr. Maxwell, this is Becky Stone calling. Rebecca St. Claire, I suppose I should say. I wanted to let you know I've accepted the coauthorship deal our publisher offered. I'd like to set up a time for us to chat about next steps. I know it's a holiday but please call me back at this number. I look forward to hearing from you and, er…to working with you. Thanks—and Happy New Year."

By the time message four rolled around, she sounded a lot less breezy. "Hello, Mr. Maxwell. It's Rebecca St. Claire again. Per my previous message, please call me to discuss the book—our book."

By the fifth and final message, she was obviously pissed off and taking no pains to hide it. "Maxwell, this is Rebecca St. Claire—*again.* I appreciate that you're busy, and obviously screening your calls, but really, your time is no more valuable than anyone else's. Surely you can find five minutes, and the basic courtesy, to call me back—today!"

Jesus, what a pest. Max deleted her messages and clicked off the cell. More than pissed off, she sounded really desperate. Desperate or not, there was no way he was going to saddle himself with a writing partner. If she was pissed off at him, let her join the club.

But something more than simple annoyance tugged at him. Her slightly husky voice sounded familiar, as though it belonged to someone he'd talked to not all that long ago. Had they met at some publishing event? New York was a big place, so he supposed it was possible. With the exception of her last message when she'd turned kind of shrill, her voice didn't fit with his mental picture of a romance-novel writer. He hadn't bothered to see if her publicity photo was at the back of her book, but he'd always thought of romance writers as plump grand dames with blue hair, feather boas and a brace of snow-white poodles. Rebecca St. Claire sounded a lot closer to thirty than sixty. Not that it mattered.

Max walked into the dining room and over to the marble-top bar. He poured a splash of Macallan vintage thirty-year-old single malt Scotch into a Baccarat crystal tumbler and took a slow, satisfying sip, rolling the liquor on his tongue. Drink in hand, he moved to the bay window. It was too dark to see much of anything, but by tomorrow morning the window would open out to snow-covered mountains, a pine forest and, if it was as clear as it was supposed to be, a canopy of dazzling blue sky. He and Elaina had built the simple Craftsman-style house with just that view in mind.

The thought of Elaina prompted a twinge of guilt. This New Year's Day was the one-year anniversary of her death. It wasn't that he felt guilty for having sex with another woman, at least not exactly. He was only human, after all. Some men in his position would have remarried by now. If he felt guilty about anything it was that he'd gone nearly twenty-four hours without once stopping to pay tribute to her memory or find some ritual to mark her passage. A mental-health professional would likely view that as progress, a sign he was moving on, but he wasn't so sure. What he'd had with Elaina had been wonderful, a special gift. He didn't ever want to forget her.

And yet he knew if he were to walk into the Serena Lounge and see Rose sitting there, he wouldn't hesitate to do the same thing all over again. The whole encounter had the feeling of something that was fated, a meant-to-be. To run into her (literally!) in midtown was one thing, but then to find her a few hours later in his hotel was a pretty incredible coincidence. In a city the size of New York, what were the odds of that?

Once they got to his suite, he'd expected to feel awkward, maybe even a little shy, but he hadn't felt either of those things. Rose was a complete stranger and yet sex with her had felt so unbelievably good, so natural and right, it was as if they'd been lovers in another life. He and Elaina had had a good marriage in every way, but sex had been more tender than adventurous. If he were honest with himself, he'd admit his night with his sexy Cinderella was the hands-down best sex of his life.

She'd said she hadn't had sex in a while, either, and as many times as he told himself he was a sucker to believe her, he did. Not because she'd seemed awkward or unsure—she hadn't seemed either. She was good in bed, pretty damned amazing as a matter of fact. It was more the sense he got from her, a vibe she put out that he couldn't quantify but felt all the same. Their bar hookup aside, she didn't strike him as the sort of woman who slept around.

Celibacy for a woman who looked like she did had to be a choice on some level. She was altogether too sexy and too pretty and too smart to go without a lover for long. It was obvious she liked touching and being touched, kissing and being kissed far too much to be satisfied with taking care of her sexual needs exclusively on her own. Even between lovemaking, she'd kept some part of her connected to him at all times, massaging his neck, sliding gentle fingers up and down his arm, lightly scratching her nails over his back. There was one explanation, a theory really, he kept coming back to. The last man she'd been with must have hurt her badly, badly enough for her to swear off lovers for a whole year.

That he'd been the one whose kiss had brought her back to sexy life felt like an incredible honor. It really was too bad he hadn't gotten her phone number or left her his. But then if she'd wanted him to call her, she would have found some subtle way to let him know. Women were good about that sort of stuff. It was probably for the best. The cardinal code of casual sex was you didn't try to turn your one-night stand into a relationship. What happened in Manhattan would stay in Manhattan, end of story—*theirs* at least.

And yet, were she to materialize miraculously on his doorstep, he knew he'd toss caution to the wind along with just about any rule he'd ever lived by. Just remembering her—how soft her rosemary-and-mint-scented skin had felt on his fingertips, the throaty little noises she'd made when he pleased her, the salty flavor of the sweet spot between her thighs—he felt himself growing thick and hard.

In a week, or at least a few weeks, the memory should start to fade. By next New Year's she'd be a vague recollection that brought about an occasional smile but nothing more. That thought filled him with a sad sense of regret. It might not be manly to admit it, but he wasn't cut out for casual sex. He wanted a lover he could hold afterward, not one who expected him to get up and leave.

One thing was for sure. Be it weeks, months or years, he'd never again think of roses without thinking of her.

IT WAS dark outside by the time Becky drove up the pine-lined drive leading to Maxwell's residence. If it hadn't been for catching the number on the streetside mailbox, she would have missed the turn altogether. But then again, Maxwell was some kind of hermit, albeit a hermit with very vocal opinions about what kinds of books he wanted to write and, more to the point, who he *didn't* want to write them with.

After leaving the hotel, she'd taken a train from Penn Station, only instead of going home to D.C. she'd headed northeast. The five-hour-plus trip was pretty grueling, but it had also provided her with hours of uninterrupted writing time. Her previous night with Max must have gotten her creative juices flowing, as well—before reaching Boston, she'd banged out almost ten pages of Angelina's next adventure while sitting in the café car sipping really bad coffee and picking at an even worse packaged pastry snack. She had no idea how or even if the scenes she wrote would fit into her and Maxwell's joint novel, but there'd been no ignoring the words—or the spark—burning inside her. Whatever else he was—a modern-day Prince Charming, an amazing lay or just a really sweet guy, Max was one hell of a muse.

There'd been one layover in Boston. Getting off the train to stretch, she'd walked into the station bookstore and walked out with Adam Maxwell's latest Drake's Adventures book. By the time she reached her Manchester destination, the nearest stop to Hadley, she'd read several chapters, enough to get a flavor for his style. Becky doubted she was in any danger of becoming an action-adventure fan, but he definitely had a bestselling author's sense of timing and flair. His distinctive voice rang out from the printed pages, pages she caught herself turning pretty rapidly to see what happened next.

She'd picked up a rental car and driven the rest of the way. It turned out Maxwell didn't live in Hadley but rather fifteen miles north. To her knowledge, the town, if you could call it that, didn't have a name. Aside from a two-pump gas station, a truck-stop diner and an apple-cider stand, there didn't seem to be much there.

The drive dead-ended into a gravel lot. She parked and climbed out, muscles stiff from the other day's fall, all the sitting she'd logged in and, well, the previous night of vigorous sex. Her rental car wasn't the only thing running low on gas. She seriously hoped that after they got past the initial clash of wills (his and hers) and star author egos (his), Maxwell would offer to put her up in a guestroom for the night. The one ramshackle motel she'd passed on the way might as well have been the Bates Motel.

Becky looked up the slope to the house. The outdoor lights illuminated a stucco exterior in the Craftsman style, the building's long, low profile suggesting its owner would have more than one bedroom to spare. She wasn't sure what she'd been expecting, but it definitely wasn't this. To someone who rented a one-bedroom apartment, it looked huge, more mansion than house. Action-adventure novels, at least bestselling ones, must have a bigger market than she'd thought.

She left her luggage in the trunk and hiked up the snow-packed pavers, her high-heeled boots slipping in the slush. Reaching the pinnacle, she thought of how far she'd come in just twenty-four hours. She couldn't make fresh starts and dazzling opportunities materialize at will, but at least she was taking positive charge of her life. The very resourceful, very Angelina-like way she'd gone about getting Maxwell's address stood out as a particular point of pride. By some miracle, the diner was open today, and once she'd made it into "town," she'd bought herself yet another coffee and settled in to chat up her fellow customers. As she'd expected, having a bestselling author in their midst amounted to bragging rights for the entire town. Even better, Maxwell was a local boy, a native son. Inside a half hour, she was on her way again, the directions to his house on a paper napkin lying on the front passenger seat. It had been pretty simple.

Now came the hard part: convincing him to team with her.

Becky rang the doorbell and stood back to wait. Damn, it really was cold in New England. Stamping her feet to bring back the feeling, she ran through her rehearsed speech in her mind, a paraphrased version of Pat's lunch-time pep talk. The more she thought about it, the more she suspected Maxwell's last book must not have sold all that well, either. Why else would their publisher pressure him to team with another author? If only she'd thought to get her hands on his Bookscan numbers before she'd left New York, she'd have some solid ammo to hit him with if their conversation started heading south.

Speaking of heading south, she couldn't wait to get her butt back to D.C. It was cold there, too, in January but not *this* cold. Assuming Maxwell relented, she hoped the bulk of their collaboration could be accomplished by trading files over the Internet.

She punched the bell again and squinted, trying to see through the door's glass panel. Somewhere inside the house, a dog barked. She laid her ear against the door to see if she could hear anyone coming. *Get a move on, Maxwell. I'm freezing out here—*

The door opened and Becky almost fell inside. Stepping back, she looked up—and felt her breath freeze along with her body. Max stood framed in the timbered doorway, a golden retriever flanking his side. Wearing a pullover sweater and a pair of stone-washed jeans, he looked very different than he had a few hours before, or maybe it was just the look of a man in his element, in this case, his home.

Meeting his shocked eyes, which must have mirrored her own, Becky felt she wasn't drowning so much as reeling. Her sexy travel-writer lover was the bestselling action-adventure novelist she'd spent the past several hours cursing. The one-night stand she'd planned on never seeing again was standing there in front of her. And if things worked out the way Pat wanted, she'd be seeing a lot more of him.

The retriever chose that moment to go into watchdog mode, barking and snarling like a Cujo wannabe. Snapping out of his zombielike daze, Max reached down and grabbed hold of the animal's collar.

"Scout, heel. *Heel.*" The dog went down on his haunches with a whine. Straightening, Max looked her over, blue eyes bulging. "Rose, what are you doing here?"

Becky swallowed hard. Now that the first shock was wearing off, she was beginning to grasp just how bad her showing up on his doorstep was going to look. Deciding to go for broke, she said, "My name's not really Rose. It's Becky—Rebecca, actually. Rebecca St. Claire."

Pupils huge, he fell back a step. "You're the romance writer Pat wants me to team with?"

Eyeing the doorway, she calculated there was just enough space to squeeze past him. "Yep, I'm her, the one and only." Not about to miss out on the opportunity, dazzling or otherwise, to salvage her career, Becky shouldered her way inside.

7

"Crikey, you're a bloody spy?" Drake stared at Angelina, feeling as though he was seeing her for the first time. The beautiful brunette had played him like a fiddle, and he'd been too caught up in shagging her to see her for the scheming seductress she was.

Propped against the banked pillows of his hotel-room bed, Angelina folded her arms across her chest, the low-riding bedsheet showing off the high slopes of her breasts, creamy as alabaster. "To be perfectly accurate, I'm an international espionage agent in the employ of Scotland Yard specifically and the British government generally."

Drake paused in pacing the room to glare at her. "Like I said, a spy?"

Angelina nodded. "Basically, yes. You must be something of a spy yourself, otherwise how did you know my first name?"

"Easy. I bribed the bartender to have a look at your passport."

"Clever," she allowed. "Look, Drake, here's the thing. I need a guide to see me to Toro Toro."

"Toro Toro is the deep bush, beyond the black stump as we say. What business do you have there?"

Angelina blew out a breath. As much as she detested being patronized, she did really require the Aussie's help. "I have reason to believe some stolen rocket plans are being concealed in the caves there until they can be passed on to an enemy government. The dossier I have on you from Scotland Yard indicates you're the man for the job. What do you say?

Hands on his hips, Drake broke into a broad grin. "In that case, Angie, I'll lead the way."

"Is YOUR DOG friendly?" Rose, or rather Rebecca, bent down and stuck out her gloved hand for the golden to sniff. "He seems friendly now that I'm inside."

Blind in one eye, half-deaf and arthritic to boot, Scout was no real threat to anyone. In his present mood, Max felt far more likely to bite than his dog.

He slammed the front door closed and wheeled around to face her. "I don't know what your game is Rose, Rebecca, whatever the hell you're calling yourself today, but you have one hell of a nerve."

Cheeks pink and eyes glittering, she withdrew her hand and lifted outraged brown eyes to his face. "I don't have a *game,* as you call it. When you didn't return any of my calls, my *five* calls, I tracked you down on the Net. All I wanted was the chance to talk to you one-on-one. You probably won't believe me but until you opened that door, I had no idea who you were."

She was right. He didn't believe her. The amazing set of coincidences that had brought them together in New York twice in the same day hadn't been coincidences at all. She'd staked him out, set him up and then seduced him, the whole time letting him think it was all his idea. All that astrological bullshit was just another aspect of her act. What remained to be found out was whether or not Pat and Harry had put her up to it. Come to think of it, he had run into her a block from his agent's office.

Whether she'd acted solo or as part of a trio of publishing plotters didn't matter all that much to him, at least not right now. Tomorrow it would probably matter a lot but right now what mattered most—and hit him hardest—was the bloodless way she'd used him. The previous beautiful night had been just one big dirty lie.

Rather than get into the sordid details, he demanded, "Is that how you deal with unreturned phone messages—you just show up on people's doorsteps?"

She pulled off her knitted hat and shook out her brown curls. "Of course not. But in this case, you didn't really leave me much choice. Think about it. If the other night had been about buttering you up, I would have let my name slip when we got back to your room, wouldn't I?" Hat in hand, she glared at him as though he were the one in the wrong.

Max wasn't sure what to think. He raked a hand through his hair, struggling to make sense of it all. If she was telling him the truth, then life really was stranger than fiction— a lot stranger.

"Well, now that you are here, I'll tell you what I told Pat and my agent, as well. I'm a solo act. Always have been and always will be. A solo act—and by the way, I don't take kindly to stalkers."

Or users, he almost added but something in her face, a look in her eyes, held him back. Maybe it was the closet romantic in him but despite all the evidence to the contrary, he still wanted—needed—to believe that something about the previous night had been pure and real and good.

She unfolded her arms and shoved her hands in her coat pocket instead. "I'm not a stalker or a groupie, either. Until a few hours ago, I'd never even read one of your books." She paused and bit her bottom lip as though just realizing what she'd let slip. She was right about one thing. She really wasn't much good at buttering him up. "I'm a writer just like you are. I may not be at bestseller level yet, but I'm getting there."

Bingo. She might not realize it, but she'd just made his argument for him. "Great. In that case, you go write your books and I'll write mine."

She hesitated. "Unfortunately that's not an option for me at the moment."

Reading between the lines, he gathered her last book had tanked. He was sorry about that, but it was happening to a lot of authors these days. But her bad break wasn't his problem. Getting her out of his house was.

"Look, it's nothing personal. I just don't work with partners. I don't believe in them. It's not my process. Besides, the books you write are very…different from mine."

The latter was his best shot at diplomacy, never his strength. Under the circumstances he wondered why he was bothering with it at all.

"By different, you mean pornographic?" One dark eyebrow edged upward, framing the skeptical brown eye beneath.

"I didn't say that." He had, but not to her, at least not that he remembered.

"Actually you did—in your interview with the *New*

Yorker you referred to romance novelists as 'hacks' and romance novels as 'housewife porn.'"

Talk about a "gotcha" moment. The out-of-context quote had come back to haunt him more times than he cared to consider, generating mailbags of angry letters to his publisher from outraged romance writers and readers who'd also seen fit to bombard his e-mail inbox. What could he say? Elaina had been gone just a few months when his publicist at the time had pushed him to give the interview. He'd been struggling to keep it together, and he was the first to admit his judgment hadn't been the best. Looking back, it was no big surprise he'd said a great many things he regretted, most of which had wound up in print. Since then he'd made it a rule to steer clear of the media, earning himself the label of recluse.

"Look, it's late and I don't know about you, but I've had a long travel day and so far no supper. You can stay the night but first thing in the morning I expect you to get in your car and drive yourself back to wherever it is you came from."

He was within his rights to open the door and insist she leave now, but sending a lone woman—and such a small woman, at that—out into unfamiliar territory in the cold and dark on a holiday when most businesses were closed went against the grain. He had seven bedrooms spread across the house's two wings. It wasn't going to kill him to let her have one of those rooms for the night. His elderly cleaning lady would be thrilled. Changing the guest sheets when she came later in the week would give her something to do.

"I just came from New York obviously, but I live in Washington, the city, not the state. I told you last night, remember?"

Her reference to his previous night's pickup had his face

going warm. "You also told me you were a consultant and your name was Rose."

For the first time since she'd barged inside, she looked less than sure of herself. Twisting the hat in her hands, she said, "I *was* a consultant until a few months ago. And Rose is my mother's name." Her expression firmed and she lifted her gaze to his face. "What about you? You said you were a travel writer."

He hesitated, suddenly finding himself in the hot seat. How the hell had she managed that? "When I first got out of college I freelanced for Fodor."

It occurred to him she still had on her heavy outerwear. He reminded himself she was a guest in his home, albeit an uninvited one. "Here, let me take your coat."

Rose—*Rebecca* hesitated. "Thanks." She peeled off her gloves and stuffed them into her coat pockets, and he caught her hands shaking. So she was flustered, too. That he wasn't the only one had him feeling somewhat better.

He stepped behind her. Sliding the coat off her slender shoulders, he tried ignoring the familiar fragrance of rosemary and mint drifting from her hair, but it was no use. Her scent still turned him on, along with everything else about her.

Going to hang the coat in the closet, he asked, "I'm assuming you have some luggage, an overnight bag, with you?"

She paused and then admitted, "My suitcase is in the car trunk."

He closed the closet door and turned back to her. "I'll bring it in after dinner."

Startled brown eyes lifted to his. "Dinner?"

He nodded, tamping down the uncertain, fluttery feeling

she brought out in him before it might take hold. "I was just starting to cook."

She folded slender arms over her breasts. "But—but we're in the middle of a conversation…an argument actually."

"It'll keep." He signaled to Scout lying inside the door and turned to go.

The dog rose on stiff legs and followed his master through the open archway. Becky couldn't believe he apparently meant to continue on with his evening as though she'd never interrupted it.

Trailing after him, she said, "I'm not interested in having dinner until we settle this."

He didn't bother turning around. "In that case, you can keep me company while I eat."

As if on cue, her stomach rumbled, making a liar of her yet again.

Maxwell obviously heard it, too. Turning back to look at her over one broad shoulder, he smiled the sort of smug male smile that made her itch to slap it off his face—the same handsome face she hadn't been able to get enough of kissing and stroking and gazing just that morning. What a difference *less* than a day could make.

He skirted the large living room and headed down a side hallway, his old dog hobbling after him. Becky hurried to keep up, not wanting to lose him in the sprawling, super-size house. She followed him through a maze of rooms into a large timber-framed kitchen. Standing in the doorway, she felt as though she was about to enter a Williams Sonoma catalogue. The cabinetry and appliances and cookware were all top-of-the-line. A bank of tall cherry cabinets hung along one wall above and below a marble-topped counter.

Backless stools lined one side of a center cooking island with an electric cooking range and a second prep sink.

A sunken family room sloped off to the side, three steps down from the kitchen. Shaker-style furniture was arranged around a dressed-stone fireplace flanked by built-in bookshelves. Like most writers, herself included, Maxwell had a ton of books, and, in addition to those on the jam-packed shelving, there were more piles scattered about. A flannel-covered pet bed occupied one corner. The room wasn't messy by any means, but it did have a cozy, lived-in look. Becky could imagine winter nights sitting snug before the fire toasting marshmallows or sipping wine or, better yet, making love on the comfortable-looking couch.

Whoa, wait a minute. Max had started out as her sexy stranger and become, through a bizarre twist of fate, her prospective writing partner. If pursuing a romantic relationship with a one-night stand pushed the boundaries of modern-day relationship rules, certainly pursuing one with a one-night-stand-turned-colleague qualified as going over the edge.

Standing behind the island, he beckoned for her to enter. "Don't just stand there. Come in." His voice, though not angry anymore, carried a definite edge.

She walked up to the backless stools. She still didn't think he'd believed her when she'd said she'd only just found out who he was. Why he seemed hell-bent on thinking the worst of her, that she'd slept with him because of the book contract, mystified and insulted her. It also really hurt. Strangers or not, they'd shared a beautiful night together, the sexiest, most romantic of her life. Now like snow driven through by one too many cars, the memory was soiled.

"I was about to open a bottle of wine." He turned away to open a cupboard door, offering her a bird's-eye view of his broad shoulders and beautiful back. "Is red okay?" he asked.

Remembering how she'd kissed and stroked and clung to those shoulders, she swallowed hard, heat hitting her face—and pooling between her thighs. "Sure, whatever you're having."

Turning around, he handed her a full wineglass—and a folded chef's apron.

"What's this for?"

He looked at her as though she were an idiot. "To protect your clothes while we're cooking."

"We?" She slid the apron back across the counter at him. "I don't cook."

"Everybody cooks." He slid the garment back at her.

She shook her head hard. "Not me. I barely microwave."

"In that case, consider this your golden opportunity to learn. Make that your *dazzling* opportunity."

If he'd said the latter with anything approaching a smile, Becky would have gladly taken it as a joke and responded in kind. But with his eyes looking out at her frozen hard as ice chips and his sexy mouth drawn into a flat line, she knew he wasn't teasing. He was mocking her.

It had her digging in her heels. "I don't want a cooking lesson. I want a book deal and if the only way to get it is to work with you, then so be it."

Over the top of his wineglass, he shot her a frown. "Flattery really isn't your forte, is it?"

He was behaving like an arrogant ass, but then again she *was* standing in his kitchen, which happened to be in his house, which happened to be in the nexus of Nowhereville.

Driving in, she hadn't seen a streetlight or a road sign for the last ten miles. She was damned lucky he was letting her spend the night because she seriously doubted she'd have found her way back to town in the dark.

"I didn't mean it that way."

Acting as though she hadn't mentioned the book, he set down his glass. "Cooking isn't all about the end result, you know. It can't be rushed or at least it shouldn't be. It's a process like writing or dancing or…"

He broke off and turned away, ostensibly to stir the pot, but she was pretty sure she knew what he'd meant to say. Cooking was like making love.

"We're having venison stew, by the way, a departure from the traditional New Year's dinner but the market was closed. It's going to be a while though. If you're not interested in helping, then at least have a seat."

Following his gaze to the stools, Becky hesitated. The last time they'd sat on stools they'd ended up making love atop a piano and then for hours afterward in his room. She wondered if he was making that connection, too, or if the previous amazing night was so run-of-the-mill for him that the memory was fuzzy already. He'd said he hadn't had sex in almost two years, but then he'd also said he was a travel writer. That she'd also fudged some facts and, okay, *lied* about her name suddenly seemed peripheral to the point. Once again she'd put her trust in a man and once again she'd found herself on the receiving end of a nasty surprise.

He opened the double doors of the brushed-metal refrigerator and brought out a wedge of cheese and an apple. Carving off a bite-size sliver of each, he put the two together. "You may say you're not hungry but you look like you're about to fall off that stool—and if my memory serves me, you've done enough falling for one week. Here, eat." Leaning over the counter, he held the snack to her mouth.

For whatever reason, he was testing her or teasing her or maybe both. Becky hesitated and then opened for him, letting him slide the food between her lips. She couldn't miss how he stared as she swallowed. Not so very long ago she'd taken *him* in her mouth, as well as let him sample any number of her body parts in return. After sharing that kind of intimacy, it was stupid to be shy now, but she couldn't help it. Things had changed. They were strangers still, but they were no longer anonymous—or equal. Max might not know it yet but he held her fragile career, her future, in the palm of his hand.

He flicked his thumb over the corner of her mouth. "You had a crumb just…just *there*."

He took his hand away, but Becky felt the residual tingle of his touch down to her toes. "Thank you, I think."

"You're welcome, I think." The heated gaze he sent her told her he knew exactly what his nearness was doing to her. Moreover, he was savoring every uncomfortable minute of it.

She set her wineglass down with a bang. "I know what you're up to, and it's not going to work."

He placed the lid on the stewpot. "In that case, care to fill me in? What exactly am I up to?"

Becky snorted. "You think I can't resist you, that between the cheese course and the dessert course you'll send me running to the hills or at least the interstate rather than risk falling into bed with you, but you're wrong. Last night was a freak occurrence for me. I'm not normally like that."

He lifted a brow and looked at her. "Like what?"

"Like...*that*. I usually have a lot more self-control." That was an understatement. For the past year she'd lived like a nun. "What I'm trying to say is, I don't sleep around." She eyed him, weighing how much more to say. "Hooking up with a stranger, someone I've just met, I've never done that before."

"Are you saying I'm your first one-night stand?"

"Yes." Embarrassed, she dropped her gaze to the cheese he'd left out. Adam Maxwell might be a sexist pig, a prima donna author, and the closest to a nemesis she'd ever come to having, but suddenly it felt really important that he didn't think she was promiscuous.

"Believe it or not, you're mine, too. Now that we've settled that much, I'd better pay attention to the main course. If I burn it, we're going to be eating a lot more cheese."

He lifted the lid and peered into the pot. Whether the stew needed checking or whether it served as a convenient excuse to cut off the uncomfortable conversation, Becky couldn't say. She hadn't been exaggerating when she'd said she barely microwaved.

He turned back to her. "You strike me as someone who needs a job."

Heat stung her cheeks as though she were the one standing over the stove. He must have got his hands on her sell-through numbers for the last book or maybe their mutual editor had told him about canceling her contract. Talking out of school about her to another author didn't sound like something Pat would do, but having recently done some pretty out-of-character stuff herself, how could she know for certain?

She was on the verge of demanding what he'd meant

by that when he added, "Since you don't cook, you can set the table. Bowls are in that cabinet over there. Silverware's in the top drawer to your right, and the dining room's through that door."

Feeling foolish for jumping to conclusions—now which one of them was determined to think the worst?—she slid off the stool and opened the drawer he'd indicated. Neatly stacked cloth napkins, no doubt one-hundred-percent Egyptian cotton, lay folded inside, as well. Thinking of her mismatched plates and the disposable paper napkins in her tiny kitchen at home, she couldn't help being impressed.

Napkins and cutlery in hand, she walked over to the stove. "It smells good."

He looked up from shaking a canister of dried rosemary over the pot and shrugged. "I hope so. We'll see."

Becky hesitated. This was a lot harder than she thought. "About last night, I know you probably still don't believe me, or maybe you don't even care at this point, but for what it's worth, I really didn't set you up."

His blue eyes brushed over her face, and for the first time since she'd arrived, she saw a flicker of the previous day's warmth. "I believe you. I don't know why, but I do."

Two GLASSES of wine and one very full stomach later, Becky laid her cutlery down with a satisfied sigh. "You really can cook."

He glanced at her bowl. Aside from the china pattern, it was scraped clean. "For someone who wasn't hungry, you didn't do too badly."

"I guess I was hungrier than I thought. I didn't really get breakfast."

Actually she'd had breakfast, in a manner of speaking—she'd had Max. Around sunrise she'd woken up horny as hell, slipped beneath the sheet and gone down on him. He'd been sound asleep when she'd slid her wet lips over him, tight as a vise. Ravenous, she'd licked and laved and sucked him, milking him until he'd come in her mouth. She'd never known a man could be so incredibly delicious. Even now that she knew who and what he was, her mouth watered at the memory—and at the thought of doing it all over again—which was most definitely *not* going to happen.

"More wine?" He picked up the almost-empty bottle.

"No, thanks." She shook her head, which felt wobbly and heavy all at once. She'd only gotten a few hours sleep the night before and now the two glasses of wine, okay, two and a half, were hitting her bloodstream hard. She was way more relaxed than she should be, and they still hadn't settled their business.

"You should know that when it comes to the book, I'm not taking no for an answer, at least not until you hear me out."

"Are you always this bull-headed?"

She could have pointed out that stubbornness went both ways. Instead, sensing some concession on his part, she said, "Only when I'm right. I read your last book on the trip up here, and I think I've come up with a concept that might mesh our strengths."

"In that case, pitch me." He leaned back in his seat as though settling in to be entertained, perhaps even amused. "Let me have it."

Oh, Becky wanted to let him have it all right. The hubris of the man was almost beyond belief. He acted as though she was some newbie writer and he was the agent or editor interviewing her to see if she had the right stuff.

"I'm a multipublished author who has won several fiction awards. I shouldn't have to pitch you. We should be able to discuss this like colleagues. You know, back-and-forth, brainstorm."

"Suit yourself." He shrugged and reached for his wine-glass. "I'm a late sleeper, so you'll have to let yourself out in the morning. Just watch that the dog doesn't slip out past you. Scout is old but wily. Can you find your way back to the interstate or do you need me to give you a map?"

Becky threw her hands up in the air. "Okay, okay, you win. I'm thinking a sort of *Sleepless in Seattle* setup where we have Angelina and Drake connecting emotionally but not necessarily physically—not until later in the book. To make it really clean and to give the protagonists equal weight, we can alternate chapters in each character's point of view, showing them in their element, powerful and yet missing that special something only the other can provide. Interleaving the story arcs will be the biggest challenge, but it's doable." Out of breath and out of ideas, she lapsed into silence.

He folded his arms and stared back at her. "Is that all you have?"

Becky felt her shoulders falling forward in defeat. He wasn't going for it. There was nothing more she could do or say to change his mind. Because of his bestselling track record, disappointing sales on one book wasn't going to break him as it was her.

Dejected and angry all at once, she shook her head. What the hell, she had nothing more to lose at this point. "No, as a matter of fact it's not. The truth is, I need this coauthorship. I *really* need it. You might even say my career is riding on it." Suddenly holding back, for pride's sake or anything else, was no longer an option. "You know this business better than I. Midlist authors like me are only as good as our last book. Mine didn't sell so well and unless I can bring my numbers up fast, I may be a research consultant again for real. I know I've drunk too much wine, and I probably wouldn't be telling you this if I hadn't, but what I'm telling you isn't coming from the bottom of a glass. It's coming from the bottom of my heart."

She stopped for breath, looking away so he wouldn't see the tears spilling from her eyes. A year ago when she'd run into Elliot and his new girlfriend, she'd managed to hold back from crying until she'd reached her apartment. Showing weakness in public, or in this case in front of a semistranger, wasn't any more like her than having sex with him the night before had been. That horoscope had really played with her head—along with the sadness and desperation that went with starting out another year still single and alone.

Max clearing his throat had her brushing her hand across her eyes. Dropping her hand, she turned back to face him.

He pushed back from the table and stood. "We can call Pat and set up a schedule in the morning. For now, let's get you to bed." His eyes and voice held traces of the tenderness she recalled so vividly from the night before.

Sniffing, Becky couldn't believe she'd heard him correctly. Without thinking, she reached out to him, fingers slipping over his forearm. "Wait a minute, what are you saying? Are you…you'll do it?"

He hesitated, and then admitted, "Your pitch needs some fine-tuning, but it's good. Better than good—I think it has bestseller potential. I'm willing to give working together a shot, a one-week trial period. If we can manage to mesh our writing styles and our characters, you'll stay here until we get through the rough draft at least. I don't know about you but for me that means about two months. Afterward, we can handle the revisions by e-mail, but for the actual writing, I'm going to need you here."

He paused and Becky realized he was waiting for her to answer. "O-okay. I—I can do that." She wasn't sure how, but she'd figure out the details tomorrow.

Looking down on her, the momentary softness in his face solidified. "But if it doesn't work out, you'll pack your bags and leave by the end of the week *after* you join me in telling our mutual editor that we tried but the collaboration was a no-go. Do we have a deal, Ms. St. Claire?"

Becky wondered what had made him change his mind, her pitch or her crying or both, but she wasn't about to risk looking a gift horse in the mouth by asking. For the moment, at least, her career was saved.

She held out her hand and his big, broad one closed around it, sending warmth surging through her. Doing her best to shake it off, she looked up into his blue eyes and said, "Yes, Mr. Maxwell. We have a deal."

8

"How many times do I have to say I did not lie to you before," Angelina demanded. "I merely omitted the bit about my being a spy. The rest of what I told you is straight on."

Standing on the opposite side of their shared shanty, Drake shrugged. "Omitting, lying, they're flip sides of the same coin. But in the interest of saving the free world, what do you say we set aside our differences and move forward with our mission?"

Angelina arched one black brow and stared at him. Even knowing she'd set him up, he still wanted her. "*My* mission, don't you mean? You're only the hired help."

"The hired help? You need me to get you to those caves, you said so yourself." Drake shook his head. "Like it or not, love, we're in this together."

ONCE BECKY fell into bed in one of her host's many guest rooms, she'd been too excited to go to sleep right away despite being tipsy and exhausted. Still, she woke up the next morning at her usual seven o'clock. She lay in bed staring at the ceiling, ear cocked for some sound that Max might be stirring. Other than hearing what had to be the clicking of Scout's doggie toenails on the uncarpeted hallway floor, the house was silent.

She tried closing her eyes and slipping back to sleep but it was no use. Her body might be tired and stiff and her brain fried, but she was also wired, thoughts racing, anxieties on the upswing as she asked herself just what teaming with Max might mean as far as daily life went. He obviously had no further interest in sleeping with her. The bedroom he'd given her was on the opposite side of the house from his, and when he'd delivered her suitcase to her room a few minutes after getting her settled, he hadn't lingered, though she'd half hoped he might. Instead he'd spoken to her through the closed door and had left her luggage in the hallway outside.

Now that they were colleagues, his standoffishness ought to come as a huge relief—it *was* a huge relief—and yet she wasn't sure how she was going to handle spending the next weeks alone with him. He might not be attracted to her anymore, but unfortunately she was far from being able to say the same. Last night at dinner she'd caught herself stealing glances at his broad-backed hands, his strong forearms and his supersexy mouth. Even though he'd spent most of the tension-packed evening scowling at her, she'd still wanted to kiss him. Who was she fooling? She'd wanted to do a lot more than just kiss.

Another kink yet to be worked out was how she was going to manage her situation back home. Assuming the partnership worked out, she'd be gone two months. There were bills to be paid and plants to be watered, but most importantly there was her cat to be cared for. She'd boarded Daisy Bud at the vet before leaving town, but that wasn't a long-term situation. It wasn't good for a pet to be caged for weeks on end, especially one as catered-to as hers. Boarding over the long haul was also expensive. It was a lot to ask, but maybe after the trial week was up, Sharon could drive into D.C., pick up Daisy Bud, and take her back to Fredericksburg until Becky got back. Because of her rottie-mix, Minnie the demon dog, she'd have to close Daisy off in her spare bedroom, not ideal but still better than a prolonged stay at the vet's.

Becky slipped out from beneath the Shaker quilt and padded across the hooked rug to where her cell phone was charging. Amazed she'd had enough functioning brain cells the night before to remember to plug the thing in, she disconnected the phone and carried it back to the bed.

Shivering, she sat on the side, pulling the quilt over her bare legs. God, it was cold here. The New England winter weather was one of many things she'd have to get used to in the coming weeks.

Sharon answered on the third ring. "Hey, Becks, I didn't expect to hear from you so soon. How did things go in the Big Apple? How many pairs of shoes did you come back with this time?" Despite Sharon's chirpy tone, her voice sounded husky as though Becky had woken her. It was a weekday and her friend would usually be getting ready to go to work. Maybe she had a cold.

"Listen, Shar, it's a long story, but my editor wants me to coauthor a book with this other author, Adam Maxwell, and, well, let's just say I don't have a choice. I'm calling from his house in New Hampshire."

"You're staying with him at his house?" Husky tone or not, there was no missing Sharon's surprise.

"Yeah, but it's not what you're thinking." Actually it had

been exactly what her friend was thinking, only not any-more. "It's looking like I'm going to have to hunker down here for the next month at least, maybe two, while we bang out the draft." *Bang*—a Freudian slip if there ever was one. "I know it's a huge favor to ask but is there any way you could drive into D.C. this weekend and pick up Daisy Bud from the vet's and take her back to Fredericksburg with you?"

There was a long pause, and Becky chewed on her bottom lip. Thinking she might have pushed the bounds of their friendship, she started backpedaling. "Listen, don't worry about it. It's a lot to ask, and I'll figure something else out. The vet can probably recommend a pet sitter or…" She broke off when she realized Sharon was crying. "Sharon, sweetie, are you okay?"

"Not…really. Minnie…died yesterday."

"On New Year's?"

Sharon sniffled. "Uh-huh."

"Oh, no, I'm so sorry."

"I found her when I came downstairs. A heart attack in her sleep, the vet thinks. I couldn't bring myself to sign off on an autopsy to know for sure. She was getting up there, I guess, but, oh, Becky, the house is so empty without her."

Having lost her beloved cat, Gabby, a few years before, Becky could more than understand. "I know, I know. It's terrible. The worst…"

In between Sharon's snuffling, more bad news spilled out. "I called in to work a while ago to say my dog had died and I was too upset to make it in. My boss gave me shit about it and, well, to make a long story short, I quit."

"You quit?"

"It's been coming for a while, and to tell you the truth I think I need a change of scene. This detective guy I've been seeing, well, that's not going so good, either. My rental is up in a month, and I'm seriously considering relocating. The only good thing about this dump was I could have a dog, and now I really feel like I need the vibe of a big city for a while. What would you think about me apartment-sitting for you? I could forward your mail and water the plants and take care of the cat while I job-hunt and figure stuff out."

Becky hesitated but only for a fraction of a moment. "That's a great idea."

If the deal with Maxwell fell through, she'd be back to D.C. in one week rather than two months. Even if that were the case, though, she didn't mind Sharon bunking in with her. The company would probably do her good. Who knew, they might make it a permanent thing. At that point, she'd need a roommate to make the monthly rent.

They spent the next few minutes working out details, and she gave her friend Max's address. Becky clicked off on the call, pulled on her sweatpants, and padded into the room's private bathroom to brush her teeth and comb her hair. The conversation with Sharon had certainly put her current "problems" into perspective. She might not be thrilled at the prospect of coauthoring the book with Maxwell—Max— but in the big scheme of things it wasn't a tragedy. As far as their romantic interlude went, nothing had really changed there, either. It had started out as a one-night stand and that was exactly what it had turned out to be. That might not be the romantic ending she would have written for her character, but for her real-life self it was definitely for the best. At this point, she really needed to focus all her energy on salvaging her career. She couldn't afford a distraction.

Thinking of the six feet plus of blond, blue-eyed *distraction* with his butt apparently still planted in bed, she glanced at herself in the mirror and shook her head. Workout clothes and jeans were pretty much her writing uniform, but before there'd been no hunky writing partner to see her. Their sexual association might be over, but that didn't mean she wanted to walk around looking like crap in front of him. As soon as Sharon settled in, Becky would ask her to courier a few essential items from the apartment. She'd also ask Max where the closest shopping mall was and try to carve out the time to do some basic shopping, emphasis on basic. Now that she was in a place where people had to wear snow boots three-quarters of the year, she doubted she'd run across any Jimmys or Manolos to tempt her.

She tiptoed downstairs in search of coffee. At home she was used to bopping down the two city blocks to her local Starbucks whenever she pleased. The little treks were a big part of her self-reward system, but she knew from driving in the other day that there were no Starbucks or shops of any kind for miles.

After several wrong turns, she found her way to the kitchen. Sighting the coffeemaker on the marble-topped counter, her spirits brightened. Apparently Max drank coffee, too, but then of course he must. When they'd first met, he'd asked her to have coffee with him. What a long time ago that seemed.

The top bank of cherry cabinets presented a daunting prospect, hung too high for her to reach. Feeling like an interloper, she reminded herself she was searching out coffee and coffee accoutrements, not family secrets or hidden jewels. She dragged over a stool and climbed up to open the first cabinet door. Voilà, she found the cone filters on the lower shelf and brought out the box.

"I see you're making yourself at home."

Becky started. She dropped the box, scattering filters to the four corners of the slate-tiled floor.

"Easy. No more falling, remember?" Max was beside her in a minute, laying steadying hands on her waist. "If you're this jumpy without caffeine, maybe you should consider switching to decaf." Without asking, he lifted her down.

"Not on your life." Glad to have the floor beneath her feet, but shaky from the brief but intimate contact, she darted a quick glance at him. She'd never seen him in the morning, at least not with clothes on, in this case a belted blue terrycloth bathrobe that had seen better days. With his short hair mussed and sticking up at the back, he seemed almost boyish, certainly more approachable than he had the night before at dinner—and even sexier.

She caught him staring and realized he must be checking her out, too. Self-conscious, she glanced down at the drawstring of her baggy pink sweatpants. "I know it isn't exactly Victoria's Secret but what can I say, it's comfortable."

He smiled, the corners of his very blue eyes crinkling in that sexy, endearing way. "No, that's not what I thought. It's…" He glanced down at her feet. "I guess I'm not used to seeing you without high heels."

Becky followed his gaze downward, feeling really dumpy, not to mention really short. She'd put on a pair of gym socks to buffer the cold coming up from the floor. "As much as I love my Manolos and Jimmy's, even I don't sleep in them—or wear them to breakfast in the house."

He moved to the refrigerator and opened the double doors. "Speaking of breakfast, what would you like?"

Staring at his sexy profile, Becky could come up with a whole menu of things she'd like—all of them X-rated. "I don't eat breakfast, but thanks. Coffee's fine for me… and maybe some juice if you have it."

Setting a carton of eggs and a stick of butter on the counter, he shook his head and clucked his tongue—the same tongue that had made her feel amazing things just forty-eight hours ago. "Haven't you heard breakfast is the most important meal of the day?"

Needing to put some distance between them, she walked around to the other side of the counter. "It depends on whose day you mean. Mine seems to unfold just fine without it. Personally I think the whole breakfast-as-the-most-important-meal movement is hype put out by the dairy industry."

He shook his head at her though she couldn't tell if he was annoyed or just amused. "You're full of theories, aren't you? Sit—I'll make the coffee. How do you take it?"

Elbows on the counter, she leaned in to watch him. Colleague or not, she found everything about him completely sexy, from the way he moved around in his kitchen, so confident and sure, to the way he gestured with his strong hands.

"Strong with plenty of cream, please, half-and-half, if you have it."

He seemed surprised. "No sugar?"

Becky couldn't resist. "I'm already sweet enough."

Looking up from scooping coffee into the cone filter, it was Max's turn to smile. "In that case, Miss Sweet Enough, take a load off. How do pancakes sound?"

She dragged out a stool and sat. "Like you're on a mission to make me fat."

Grinning, he turned away to the stove, sliced off a pat of butter from the stick and dropped it into the frying pan. Over the sizzle, he said, "I can't imagine you ever being fat. What are you, a size two?"

Becky was a size two petite actually, but the golden retriever ambling into the room saved her from saying so. Being born Angelina tall and curvy hadn't been in the cards—or genes—for her.

"Here, Scout." Max stopped what he was doing to pour dried kibble in the dog's bowl. "That's a good boy." Reaching down, he patted the animal's side. Looking back at Becky, he said, "He used to run with me when he was younger, but he's too old for that now. He has trouble with his hips."

She'd guessed as much from the dog's stiff movements and slow stride. "I'm sorry to hear that. Did you say you run?"

Straightening, he nodded and returned to making breakfast. "Yeah, only in the winter, that means the treadmill. I have a gym downstairs." She'd wondered how he stayed in such great shape. "You're welcome to use it while you're here."

"Thanks, maybe I will." If he kept feeding her as he had the previous night and promised to this morning, she'd better hit the gym, otherwise she wouldn't be a size two for much longer.

He poured coffee into two mugs, adding cream to hers. Watching him, she saw that he drank his black with a heaping spoonful of sugar. She'd licked and sucked and tasted nearly every part of him, but until now she'd had no idea how he took his coffee—how crazy was that?

Sipping her coffee, she offered, "I run, too." Her apartment building backed up to Rock Creek Park. Running through the park and then cutting through the National Zoo was a major benefit of her northwest Washington location. "I'm pretty much good to go until December. Once the really cold weather hits, I hibernate in aerobics class until the spring thaw."

Scout finished his food and headed for the family room, stopping by Becky for a petting. Watching her stroke Scout's ears, Max couldn't help remembering how good those soft, small hands had felt stroking his back and the rest of him. She had the gentlest touch of any woman he'd ever known. Thinking of the magic those tapered fingers and clean scrubbed nails had wrought, heat spread over his groin.

Whisking the lumps from the pancake batter, he cleared his throat. "It looks like you two have made up since last night."

Looking up from the dog's head in her lap, Becky nodded. "I'm a huge animal lover, in case you can't tell. I have a cat, Daisy Bud. She's a tiger-striped tabby. I found her as a kitten in the alley behind my apartment building, or she found me."

Wearing an oversized T-shirt, baggy sweatpants and with her pretty maple-colored curls tousled about her face, she looked soft and approachable, more like a teenager than a grown woman. Even with bed head and pillow face, she struck him as alluringly perfect and completely adorable. If there was a flaw, he'd so far failed to find it—and he was pretty sure he'd explored every square inch of her in New York. Picturing the tight, lithe and very womanly body lying beneath the shapeless clothes, he felt himself hardening.

It promised to be a long couple of months.

Once he'd gotten her settled in her room the night

before, he'd known he wouldn't be able to go to sleep right away, if at all. Instead he'd cleaned up the kitchen, made a fire and then settled in to read her book. By the end of the first chapter, he'd found himself really getting into the story. Although he still couldn't say he was a romance fiction fan—make that mystery erotica, whatever the hell that was—he had to admit she was a damned good writer.

He'd cracked open the book expecting purple prose and cardboard characters. Instead, Becky's writing was crisp and clean and stylish, her characters well-fleshed out even if he did find her protagonist, Angelina, less than sympathetic. Like him, she kept to a basic twenty-chapter structure, each chapter ending on a cliffhanger that propelled the plot forward. Who knew but this collaboration of theirs just might work out. Who could have predicted that his sexy one-night stand would be sitting in his kitchen in her stocking feet, about to eat pancakes and petting his dog? Real life really was stranger than fiction.

He carried the bowl of batter over to the stove and dropped large spoon-size globs onto the hot skillet. It had been a long time since he'd had someone other than his dog to talk to in the morning, let alone make breakfast for. He really should do a better job of keeping up the conversation.

Over the hiss of batter meeting scalding-hot butter, he called out, "I've had Scout since he was a puppy. We…I got him from a breed rescue group. Apparently his hind legs were too short and his eyes too wide-set to show him. He's been a great companion, though. Now that he's pushing eleven, the hip dysplasia is really starting to kick in. I'm not sure how much longer I can keep him going, but while he's still feeling pretty good, I don't mind making my vet a rich man."

He and Elaina had gone to look at the dogs together. Like Becky's cat, Scout had picked them, not the other way around. Max remembered watching the puppy trot up to Elaina without being called and settle onto her lap. It had been a happy day. Thinking of Scout's gray-muzzled head resting in Becky's lap a moment ago, Max felt a funny tightening in his throat.

The night before at dinner, he hadn't been prepared for the gut-wrenching feeling her tears had stirred in him. There was no denying he had a soft spot for the woman. Once she'd admitted her book contract had fallen through, turning her away was no longer an option. What the hell, maybe Harry was right. Maybe Drake could use a little softening and a lot of sex—and maybe he wasn't the only one.

Whoa, Max. She's your writing buddy, not your fuck buddy.

"I called my friend, Sharon, this morning to arrange cat care and she told me her dog just passed away. She's pretty broken up about it." Her big brown eyes were suspiciously bright.

"I'm sorry to hear that. I know from having Scout and other dogs before him that you get really attached."

He glanced at Becky and it occurred to him he was the one in danger of getting attached. Assuming they could figure out a way to work together, she still wasn't staying beyond the two months it took to finish the draft. If the collaboration was a bust, she'd be leaving in a week. And from everything she'd said since he'd met her, she wasn't looking for a relationship. Even if she had been, it was never a good idea to mix professional and personal affairs. Someone always ended up getting hurt and in this case neither of them could afford to let the work suffer. The book had to come first and it had to be good. Better than good, it had to be a blockbuster for both their sakes. They couldn't afford to walk around like hormone-blitzed teen-agers.

"Max?" Becky's voice called him back to the moment. Wrinkling her nose, she asked, "Is something maybe… burning?"

Max looked at the skillet and the blackened pancakes within. Damn, he'd zoned out and burned breakfast. That was a first—and a warning sign.

He carried the pan over to the trash can and upended it, the blackened circles sliding off his nonstick skillet. Other than feeling foolish, ruining breakfast was no big deal. He'd make another batch. There was plenty of batter.

Burned pancakes were no big deal. Getting burned by Becky, now that would be a real problem.

BECKY might not cook, but she was a crackerjack dish-washer and she insisted on doing the cleaning up. After polishing off the pancakes—she had been hungrier than she'd realized—she hopped down from the stool and started washing dishes and wiping down counters. Stealing glances at Max sitting at the breakfast bar reading the paper, she was struck by how natural it felt to hang out with him in his kitchen. She and Elliot had never shared such a cozy morning. He hadn't been a breakfast person, either and they'd eaten their other meals out. Looking back, his visits had been so brief and last-minute that they'd never really spent much time just hanging out. She and Max had done more talking in the past forty-eight hours than she and Elliot had in their entire six months of seeing each other. That was certainly a depressing statement.

They parted ways to shower and dress. Thirty minutes later, they met up in Max's office, one of the rooms at the back of the house. Stepping inside, Becky was struck by how quiet it was. Her northwest D.C. apartment looked out onto Connecticut Avenue, a busy thoroughfare. Writing without the backdrop of car alarms, ambulance sirens and honking horns was going to take some getting used to.

Max was already at his computer when she entered. Looking over his shoulder, he said, "I'm e-mailing Pat the details of our deal so she can put together the joint contract."

Becky nodded. "I'd like to look it over before you send it."

"Of course." He turned back to the monitor.

She hoped she hadn't offended him. She didn't think she had. He'd been in the business longer than she. Publishing contracts were legally binding documents, just like signing on the dotted line to purchase a car or a house, and she wanted to make sure he hadn't missed any of the points they'd discussed over breakfast. The provision that either party could break the contract and walk away at any time without being sued was key.

Until he finished, though, there was nothing for her to do. Restless, she roamed the room, focusing on getting her bearings—the location of office supplies, the flatbed scanner, the fax. Compared to the bare-bones setup she had at home—a laptop and flat-screen monitor—Max's office seemed opulent and a little daunting, if kind of dark.

She rounded his desk and pushed aside the curtains to let in the light—and caught her breath. The French doors opened out onto a panorama of snow-covered mountains and clear sky. A pond, obviously frozen, lay about a quarter mile from the house. Other than a gazebo and an ironwork bench, there were no structures, no houses and certainly no skyscrapers in sight.

Sensing eyes on her back, she turned around to find Max standing by the desk, an unreadable expression on his face. "What do you think?" He'd put on a soft blue pullover and stone-washed jeans. The sweater brought out the vibrant blue of his eyes, making them seem bluer still.

Becky felt as though she was on the brink of drowning yet again. To get her bearings, she turned away to look outside. "It's beautiful. I can see why you love it here. The view must be even more amazing come spring."

He joined her at the window, his hip accidentally brushing against hers—at least she assumed it was by accident. "Every season has its unique beauty, but autumn is the best. The mountains are an incredible panoply of color. I could show you photographs I've taken though no camera lens can quite capture what we see with the naked eye."

The innocent reference to *naked* had her thoughts swirling back to their time together in New York. She caught herself holding her breath and wondered why she was still so skittish around him—and so incredibly turned-on. The stranger sex mojo should be wearing off by now if not burned out altogether. Instead, the attraction felt stronger and hotter than ever.

"I'd love to see them sometime." Uncomfortable with him standing so close, she dropped the curtains and stepped away. She had started over to the computer to read over the e-mail when she spotted the leather-framed photograph on his desk.

Becky stopped in her tracks. A man didn't keep a woman's picture lying out in plain view on his desk unless he had strong feelings for her. She was sure Elliot hadn't bothered to set out even a snapshot of her.

Her and Max's amazing night was less than forty-eight hours old, the memory still fresh and achingly tender. She knew she should move on, but she couldn't resist picking up the picture for a closer look. "Your girlfriend's very striking. She reminds me of my heroine, Angelina."

It was true. The tall Mediterranean-looking woman in the picture would have made a good stand-in for Becky's British-born but half-Italian heroine. The biggest difference was that her waist-length black hair looked wavy instead of straight.

Max came up behind her, and Becky felt the heat of him penetrating all the way through her clothes. "Elaina was Greek-American. And she wasn't my girlfriend, she was my wife."

"Was?"

He hesitated and then nodded. "She died last year on New Year's Day." He reached around to take the picture from her.

So that explained his claim of having gone almost two years without sex. It also shed light on why he'd killed off Drake's wife, Isabel, in a previous book. The one she'd read had described her as a tall, dark-haired, dark-eyed cryptologist who'd died helping her bounty-hunting husband on a mission. Isabel must have been based on Elaina.

Surrendering the photo, Becky lifted her gaze to his face. "I'm so sorry."

Setting the frame down, he avoided her eyes. "She was sick for a long time—cancer. Toward the end, the pain got pretty bad."

"Is that why you checked out of the publishing scene and went underground, to take care of her?"

She'd meant it as a compliment, but Max didn't seem to be taking it so. His sexy mouth flat-lined and the light left his eyes, leaving them as vacant-looking as the windows of an emptied-out house on moving day. "I didn't go *underground* as that damned reporter insisted on writing. I didn't go anywhere at all. I stayed right here in this house, the house we built together, and Elaina and I did our thing. It wasn't like I'm some saint or martyr. I did exactly what I'd wanted to do since the day I met her, and that was to be with her. Her being sick just meant we had to figure out a new way to do that and still be us."

Becky looked at him, emotion thickening her throat. Adam Maxwell wasn't just sexy and charming and talented and successful. He was all of those things in abundance, but, even more, he was loyal and decent, trustworthy and true, a one-in-a-million good guy, the kind her friend, Sharon, would call a "keeper."

"Watching someone you love that much die must be so hard. I can't imagine how hard that must be."

"It was hard. It *is* hard. That year was the hardest one of my life, but it was also one of our best. We did a lot of crying but we did a lot of laughing, too—and remembering all the good times we were lucky enough to have shared. We spent just about every waking moment together and nothing got in the way of that, absolutely nothing, not even the book I was working on. I set my laptop up in our bedroom, and I wrote when I could and when it finally got too hard, when she needed me too much, I shut the damn thing down and forgot about it for months."

He'd sacrificed his career and put his life on hold for his wife and the best part was he hadn't done it grudgingly but gladly. To be loved like that, to be wanted like that— Becky couldn't even imagine it. It was horrible to admit, but she was almost envious of a dead woman.

Elliot had the hots for her in the beginning, but whatever he'd felt for her obviously hadn't run very deep. Love and passion, was it really possible to have both with one person outside the pages of a romance novel?

"I'm sorry," she said again and left it at that because really, what more was there to say?

She thought back to the interview he'd given the *New Yorker*. The issue would have come out around the time Max lost his wife or shortly afterward. He must have been raw with grief, devastated, perhaps even angry with the world. By the time she'd come to the housewife-porn quote, Becky had been too pissed off to read the rest. Until now, it had never occurred to her to give him the benefit of the doubt. She suspected there was a lesson in that.

He gestured to the computer. "Have a look at that e-mail I drafted. If it seems okay to you, then go ahead and hit Send. If not, we can talk about any changes you want when I get back." He turned and started toward the door.

Thinking of the beautiful, barren landscape at her back, Becky wondered where he meant to go. There must not be another house for miles.

She followed him to the door. "If you want some company or—"

His adamant headshake cut her off. "I'm going into town for supplies. I'm not sure when I'll be back."

He was obviously upset, and it was all her fault. If only she'd tamped down her writer's curiosity and let the picture pass without comment. Mentally kicking herself, she said, "Max, I'm so—"

He turned and left the room before she could get the word *sorry* out.

9

Shouldering his weapon, Drake looked over at Angelina. Kneeling on the cabin's dirt-packed floor, the beautiful Brit was still arming up. "Crikey, Angie, get a move on. We haven't got all bloody day."

Angelina looked up at him through glaring green eyes. "I always clean my gun and triple-check my taser before going out on a mission. It's my ritual."

Drake yanked off his broad-brimmed hat and scoured the sweat from his forehead before it rolled into his eyes. The blooming woman would be the death of him, and they hadn't yet cleared the cabin. "Is that so? Next you'll be telling me you knock your heels together three times, too."

"As a matter of fact, I do."

MAX AWOKE the next morning late but in a better frame of mind. As much as it had hurt him to talk about Elaina, now that he had, he felt as if something had been released inside him. He showered and dressed and came downstairs humming "New York State of Mind." The half-filled coffeepot confirmed Becky had come down already.

When he walked into his office, coffee mug in hand, he found her at his computer. "Good morning."

She finished typing her current sentence and looked up. "Good morning. I hope you don't mind me helping myself to your computer. My laptop screen is pretty small."

"Not a problem." He sat his coffee down and came to stand beside her, relieved she showed no signs of being pissed off at him for cutting out on what was supposed to have been their first day of work. Last night at dinner she'd been mighty quiet, but then so had he. Looking over her shoulder, he said, "On a roll, huh?"

She nodded, gaze drifting back to the screen. "I'm working on bio sketches for our main characters, including the antagonists. I'm almost finished with Angelina's. I figure you can get started on Drake's."

Max had lived with Drake through three books, longer if you counted the time the Aussie adventurer had first burst into his consciousness. He didn't need a "bio sketch," whatever the hell that was. He knew his character inside and out.

Hoping to avoid the topic of writing exercises, he said, "I finished your book last night."

That obviously got her attention. She swiveled away from the screen and looked up at him. "Dare I ask what you thought?"

"I liked it," he said without hesitation. "I didn't expect to but I did. I thought the Falco character was a little over the top but otherwise the story sailed right along."

"Over the top? How do you mean?" She turned to face him.

"Well, if Angelina is such a crackerjack spy, why would she fall for a guy like that? I mean, it's not like there weren't plenty of signs that he was not only a double agent but also a player."

Becky bit her bottom lip as though the remark struck

some kind of personal cord. "It happens. Smart, nice women fall for jerks all the time. Haven't you ever heard the saying that love is blind?"

He snorted. "In that case, Angelina needs a pair of night-vision goggles."

Becky rolled her eyes. "And this from the man who writes about a middle-aged Australian bounty hunter who's apparently filthy rich yet can't commit to building anything more substantial than a one-room shanty on his own property."

Middle-aged! Max felt his good mood slipping. "Drake doesn't need to flaunt his wealth. It's the land he loves, not material possessions."

And so began their first day of collaboration. It was clear working together wasn't going to be the cakewalk Pat and Harry had pitched it to be. Even agreeing on a writing schedule turned into a major negotiation. Sitting down to block out the book later that day, they quickly learned they had very different ways of working. Max was a fly-by-the-seat-of-his-pants writer who liked to start with a general idea and flesh it out as he went along. Becky was a meticulous plotter who lived and died by her outline. She blocked out each chapter scene-by-scene through to the end before she could even think of writing the book. Surprises made her crazy, while for Max the surprise, the adventure, was half the fun.

They also had completely opposite internal clocks. Max admitted that anything before ten was way too early for him. Working alone, he didn't usually get down to writing until after dinner. Once the story got cooking, though, he'd sometimes write straight through to dawn. That wasn't going to cut it for Becky. A morning person, she did her best work before midafternoon, preferably with an hour's exercise break at lunch. Unless she was on a roll or a deadline crunch, by the time dinnertime came around she was ready to shut down her computer for the night.

Even more challenging than meshing conflicting work habits and schedules was comingling the storylines from their previous books. It was a lot like sending your characters on a blind date with nowhere to go.

With the tension mounting on both sides, Max suggested they move to the family room where it would be easier to relax. He went into the kitchen to put on a fresh pot of coffee. When he came out again, a mug in either hand, Becky was settled onto the couch, Scout sprawled over her feet, a notepad in her lap.

The cozy domestic scene tugged at his heart. He couldn't help noticing how good she looked there in his family room, how right. He carried the coffee over to the low pine table. Setting the mugs down, he hesitated, eyeing the empty plaid cushion beside her. Too close for comfort, he decided—his, at any rate.

He glanced again at his new partner, head bent over the pad and writing meticulous notes in her neat, precise handwriting. Today's ensemble was a soft pink sweater and jeans—and gym socks. For whatever reason, the latter struck him as really cute.

The whole character-sketch exercise, on the other hand, struck him as a pure pain in the ass. Writing wasn't an "exercise" you practiced. It was something you just did. When he was in that magical state known as The Zone, the words gushed out of him like a mountain stream, sometimes rushing out faster than he could type. On those occasions, he put aside whatever else he was doing and just went with it. Still, this character-sketch thing was apparently part of Becky's process and judging from what he'd read so far of her book, it obviously worked for her.

Trying to get into the spirit of the thing, he settled into the nearby leather chair and asked, "By the way, how old is Angelina supposed to be?"

Pen stalling, Becky glanced up. "Excuse me?"

He was pretty sure she'd heard him, but he repeated himself anyway. "I asked how old she is."

She snapped up her chin. "What difference does it make?"

He held up his hands in the air. "Hey, you're the one who insisted on doing character sketches. I'm just trying to get a better feel for who she is."

"She's…thirtysomething."

"You haven't given her a definite age?" From a few feet away, he studied her, wondering why age seemed to be such a tender topic with her. She couldn't be much past thirty and these days thirty was the new twenty, or so the media claimed.

"No, as a matter of fact, I haven't. Why, is that some kind of writing faux pas? I mean, it's not like she's going to settle down and have Drake's baby."

He shrugged, wondering if perhaps he'd hit a nerve. Could it be her snappishness over all matters age-related had to do with her own biological clock ticking? Testing the waters, he said, "You never know, she might. If she's still in her thirties, it could happen. Women in their thirties have babies all the time."

Fuming brown eyes bored into him. "You make it sound so simple, so cut-and-dried, but it isn't. Did you know that once a woman hits the age of thirty-five, her chances of getting pregnant go down by fifty percent? And that after thirty-five, her fertility declines by a steady ten percent each year?"

Max hadn't known that, but then he hadn't made an indepth study of the subject as she obviously had. In the first half of their marriage, he and Elaina had been too busy with their careers and traveling and generally enjoying each other to think about adding kids to the mix. Like so many people, they'd figured they had time, maybe not all the time in the world but definitely a lot more than they'd got. They'd just started seriously talking about starting a family when she'd been diagnosed.

"Don't tell that to Susan Sarandon," he quipped. A fan, he knew the popular film actress had given birth twice in her midforties.

He could see he'd been wrong to make the joke. Becky stabbed her index finger into the air, but he thought her eyes looked glittery, as if she was holding back tears. "Be that as it may, if you think I'm going to stand by and let Drake knock up my heroine and then leave her high and dry while he rides off into the sunset for his next adventure, think again, mister. Anyway, the point is moot."

"How's that?"

"If you must know, Angelina is on the pill."

"You've given her a birth-control method but not an age?"

He felt a tickle at the corners of his mouth and struggled not to laugh. He was coming to see she took her character a lot more seriously than he did his, yet another difference between them.

"She's very…active." A tinge of pink swept into her cheeks.

"Active, huh?" Wondering just what kind of book

he'd signed up to cowrite, he asked, "You mean she sleeps around?"

She scowled. "If I said a male character was active, you'd say he was a stud, but if Angelina does the same, she's a slut. That's really fair—*not.*"

"I didn't call Angelina a slut, you did. And by the way, who are we really talking about here?"

Becky hesitated. Watching her nibble her bottom lip constantly reminded him of all the amazing things she'd used that full, sexy mouth to do to his body. Try as he might, and he had to admit so far he hadn't tried all that hard, he found himself semiaroused more often than not. The steamy scenes kept flashing through his mind like a triple-X-rated movie trailer. Seeing her every day—and every night—for the next two months wasn't going to help with that, either. The sexual chemistry that drew them together like magnets back in Manhattan hadn't gone away just because they'd become writing partners. Sitting across the room from her rather than beside her on the sofa, a deliberate choice, he could still feel the pull of her sensuality across the empty space.

Setting down her coffee mug, she said, "Angelina, of course."

Max wasn't so sure. "Look, for whatever it's worth, I really don't think you slept with me to get the book deal." Catching her skeptical stare, he added, "Okay, I did at first but you have to admit that was a pretty amazing set of coincidences that brought us together."

"That was a weird day," she admitted. "I'd just come from lunch with my editor—*our* editor—and she dropped the bomb on me about my book sales and then pitched teaming with you and, well, the bad news really threw me."

Hearing that the prospect of teaming with him counted as bad news on a par with a bombed book wasn't exactly flattering, but he held back from saying so. If this collaboration was going to have a hope of working, he needed to get into not only her head but the head of her character.

"Sounds serious."

She nodded. "I felt pretty low. After Pat left for her next meeting, I ordered a martini and then went on a thousand-dollar shoe binge at Saks."

"One pair of shoes cost you a grand!"

Growing up in a well-off family, he'd never wanted for anything, but frugality was one of the core values his parents had imparted. Dropping a grand on a pair of shoes wouldn't enter his mind. No wonder she'd been so upset when one went missing—and been so over the moon when he'd found it and brought it back to her. But considering the part those sexy red shoes had played in bringing them together, they were worth every penny.

"Two, actually, at least before tax. I got a second pair of pumps."

Max hesitated. The ice had been broken. There was an opening, if he dared take it. "Since it seems to be confession time, when I first saw you on my doorstep, I thought I must be dreaming or hallucinating. I'd just spent an entire day kicking myself for not waking you up before I left that morning and getting your phone number, not to mention your last name." He stopped, realizing he'd said a lot more than he'd meant to.

She lifted her wide brown eyes to his face. "You wanted to see me again?"

There was no going back now. He nodded. "I probably

shouldn't admit it, but yes, I did." He almost said "do," but caught himself in time.

Her gaze slid away. She fiddled with her pen. "I probably shouldn't admit this, either, but when I woke up in your room and found your note and the rose—that was really sweet of you, by the way—I wished I'd told you my name, my *real* name, so...so we could keep in touch. But I guess it really doesn't matter at this point." She lifted her slender shoulders in a shrug and the casualness of the gesture coupled with her matter-of-fact tone really got under his skin. "What we had in New York was a fling, a one-time deal. It's not like we have to worry about it happening again."

"Right, a one-time deal." Max sipped his coffee, just poured from the freshly made pot. He remembered stirring in his usual shovelful of sugar and yet the brew that had tasted so satisfyingly sweet moments ago suddenly tasted really bitter. "Now that we've squared real life away, do you think we can wrap up this character-sketch bull— business and get down to some actual writing?"

"Not quite. We're not finished. Actually we've barely started." She reached for the notepad.

Annoyed—okay, hurt—by her casual dismissal of their New York night, Max said, "I already know Drake through and through, and as for Angelina it's pretty obvious she's you in a black wig."

Becky's eyes flew open. "That is so untrue. If anything, we're almost polar opposites."

"Opposites, huh? If you believe that, then you not only write fiction, you must also live it."

She glared at him. "What's that supposed to mean?"

"You obviously love to shop. She always dresses in

couture clothing right down to the designer shoes. You're in great physical shape and she's always running or rap-peling or hanging out of something. She obviously enjoys sex and you…" He hesitated, sensing he was about to step over a line and asking himself whether or not he cared. "Well, if my recent memory serves me, you're very good in bed."

She shot him a piercing look, confirming the line had been crossed. "Is that all?"

"Not quite. She has your eyes, not the color obviously but the shape. Yours turn up at the corners just like hers do."

"They do?" Her shy gaze met his and Max could almost see the current of awareness pulsing between them.

"Yes, they do." Pressing his advantage, he said, "The one thing of yours she doesn't have is your heart."

She hesitated. "Having a heart can land you in all kinds of trouble."

Some jerk must have hurt her badly. Probing for what-ever reason—curiosity, concern or some mingling of the two, he said, "Well, she seems to take the whole British sangfroid thing to the extreme. When it comes down to it, she's pretty bloodless."

Her smile vanished and her eyes turned wintry. "Just because she's not always dissolving into a puddle of tears and standing by waiting for a man to rescue her doesn't make her bloodless. Next you'll be saying she's a bitch."

"Well, now that you mentioned it, she doesn't seem to care much about anyone other than herself."

"And I suppose Drake is a font of empathy?"

Max felt himself bristling. He tried to give her positive feedback and she responded by attacking him. "He's not supposed to be. He's a man."

"That's—that's sexism."

"That's reality. Look, all I'm saying is Angelina isn't every man's walking wet dream. Some of us like our women softer, warmer, more…"

"More what?"

"More like you."

The real-life Angelinas of the world were a dime a dozen. Women like Becky were rare as the prize opal he'd sent Drake out in search of in his second book.

"Like me? But Angelina always knows just what to do and say. She always has the perfect comeback line."

He lifted a brow and looked at her. "You don't do so badly yourself."

"She doesn't take shit from anyone."

He shook his head, amazed at how adept she was at selling herself short. "And this from the woman who left five messages on my cell and then tracked me down hundreds of miles on New Year's Day to show up at my door with luggage and a laptop."

"And she's a crack markswoman, a sharpshooter."

"Not a skill most of us have a need for in our daily lives."

"And she has this perfectly straight, perfectly shiny waist-length black hair. I can put her in a tropical rainforest or in a London fog, it doesn't matter. Her hair never frizzes."

"I've never been a fan of straight black hair. Reminds me too much of Cher. You have beautiful hair. I know women who'd kill to have curls like yours. And it's also very shiny and silky. I noticed it the other night."

The intensity of his gaze holding hers sent a warm shiver shooting through Becky. Self-conscious, she reached up and tucked a curl behind her ear. The heat hitting her face told her she must be blushing. After the no-holds-barred sex they'd shared in New York—the urgent, seeking hands, the warm, wet mouths and the sultry promises they'd whispered to each other in the dark—it was nothing short of ridiculous to be embarrassed over an innocuous compliment and yet...

Shifting in her seat, she said, "If this collaboration of ours is going to have a chance of working, we probably shouldn't keep bringing up New York."

"Who's talking about New York? I meant last night at dinner." He broke into a very broad, very wicked grin. "You must have sex on the brain, Becka. An occupational hazard of being a romance writer, I guess."

"What did you call me?"

"A romance writer."

"No, I mean before that. What name did you call me?"

"Becka. It suits you. Becky sounds like a little girl's name and Rebecca is too stiff, too formal. Becka suits you."

She folded her arms across her chest, alarmed by her heart's sudden fluttering. He'd come up with a special name for her. Nobody ever had before unless you counted Becky, but she'd pretty much given that name to herself. Like many middle children, she'd grown up feeling lost in the pack.

Becky cleared her throat. "Getting back to Angelina, she's tall. She could look you in the eye."

He lifted his shoulders in a shrug, reminding her of how amazing it had felt to anchor her hands to that solid shelf of flesh and bone. "You're plenty tall enough and besides, I didn't mind bending." He opened his mouth but stopped short of saying more. Suddenly he was all stiff-lipped New Englander and guarded gaze. "All I'm saying is don't you sell yourself short. You're beautiful and smart and talented."

"You think I'm talented?" Coming from bestselling author Adam Maxwell that constituted high praise indeed.

He nodded. "You're a damn good writer and you'd be a success in any genre you chose to write."

This time the compliment touched her. "Thank you."

"You're welcome." He took a sip of his coffee. Setting the mug back down, he said, "Now answer me this. If Angelina's so great, then why doesn't she have a significant other—until Drake, I mean?"

"That's the beauty of her—she doesn't need a man to validate her life. She comes and goes as she pleases, she answers to no one."

Suddenly it occurred to Becky that not only didn't Angelina have a steady boyfriend, the supersleuth didn't have so much as a pet or a potted plant waiting for her at home, either. Scratch that—she didn't have a home. Becky, on the other hand, had a lovely apartment, assuming she could still afford the rent, her precious Daisy Bud to greet her at the door every time she came back home, and people like Sharon and her family, all of whom loved and cared about her a lot. Angelina's "life" might be packed with adventure but there was nothing substantive in it, nothing more. It was just possible Max might have a point.

And yet who was he to criticize her? It was childish of her, she was a grown-up author with a book to get out after all, and yet with the sexual tension between them spiking by the hour if not the minute, she badly wanted to wipe that smug smile from his face. If she couldn't take him to bed, the very least she could do was take him down a peg—or two.

Taking a sip of her coffee, she asked, "What about our buff bounty hunter, Drake?"

Max supposed turnabout was fair play, but that didn't mean he had to like it. "What about him?"

"He's obviously you."

After yesterday, she expected him to rocket up from his seat and announce he needed a walk. Instead, he didn't seem fazed. "He's a composite of people I've met over a decade of travel."

It was her turn to express skepticism. "Oh, right. And I suppose it's pure coincidence you both just happen to be six foot three, blond and, er…built. You both have traveled all over the world. Thirty countries, didn't you say? You both have degrees in archeology." *You both lost your wife.* "Except for his Australian accent, you might as well be twins."

Max hesitated. Until now, he'd forgotten how much about himself he'd shared with her in New York. So much for anonymous sex; he'd apparently bored her with his life story straight out of the gate, right down to the deeply personal fact that until she'd come along he hadn't had sex in almost two years. Looking back, it seemed crazy to reveal that much about yourself to a stranger, even a stranger you were planning on sleeping with, but Becky then had been so very easy to talk to. He wished they could get past the crazy chemistry, and whatever else had them at each other's throats, and recapture some of that ease now.

Searching for a new subject, something unexpectedly nice struck him. "By the way, do you realize you just referred to Drake as *our* character?"

Becky hadn't. "I did, didn't I? Do you mind?"

He hesitated and she wondered if he might be mulling

over intellectual property rights and potential future lawsuits. Instead he smiled. "No, I don't mind. Actually it's kind of nice."

Yes, Becky silently agreed, *it kind of was.*

10

Fingers slipping on the splintered wood, Angelina looked up the collapsed mine shaft into the sliver of sunlight. Mere minutes ago she'd stood on solid earth. One misstep onto Falco's booby trap had sent her hurtling underground.

Drake's face appeared in the pinpoint of light. "Hold on, Angie. I'm coming."

A moment later, a thick climber's rope dropped down the hole, the tail swinging just above her. She grabbed hold, releasing her grip on the collapsing wall just as the last of the rotted boards and crumbled earth gave way. Gripping the hemp, she braced her feet on the tunnel wall and climbed as Drake pulled her to the top. As soon as she was within reach, he shoved a large hand through the hole and wrapped his strong fingers about her wrist.

Angelina had never been so happy to be captured in all her life. Feet once more on solid ground, she let go of the rope and wrapped her arms around Drake's muscle-corded neck, burying her face in the salty hollow of his broad shoulder. "Easy, love," he said, stroking the tangles from her damp face. "I've got you safe now." He swiped the smudge of dirt from her cheek with his callused thumb.

Embarrassed by her moment of weakness, she
stepped back from his embrace. Brushing dirt from
her legs she looked up and said, "Thank you, I think."

Blue eyes, meltingly tender, smiled down into
hers. "You're welcome, I think."

BECKY WOULDN'T have believed it those first rocky few
days, but by the second week, she and Max had settled into
a schedule, a complicated set of compromises that got
easier as the days passed. Bit by bit and day by day the
written pages were piling up.

Now that they'd started getting into a groove, she found
she was enjoying having another writer to bounce ideas
off. She was also just plain enjoying spending time with
Max. Not Max her nameless midtown Prince Charming,
or her sexy one-night stand or even the bestselling author,
but rather Max the man who liked dogs and cooking and
long walks in the snow.

She couldn't imagine anyone who less fit the stereotype
of a spoiled star author. He obviously had money, and yet
he was the most down-to-earth man she'd ever met. Other
than the sixtysomething housekeeper who came in once a
week to change the bed linens and vacuum and dust, he
didn't have servants. He didn't even have a secretary. He
chopped his own wood and cooked their meals and drove
into town to buy plumbing supplies from the hardware store
to fix the leaking faucet in her guest bathroom. Becky
couldn't help admiring his hands-on approach to living.
Drake's Code wasn't a set of stupid macho rules he'd made
up for his fictional character but a set of ethics Max lived by.

Except for the sexual tension that never seemed to go away between them, their arrangement was working out even better than Becky had supposed. Other than missing her cat and her friends, especially Sharon, she didn't feel all that homesick. D.C. had never really felt like home to her, and she had no desire to move back to Maryland where her parents and siblings still lived. Visiting her big, boisterous family always left her feeling like a fish out of water, whereas with Max she not only felt at home but comfortable in her own skin.

That afternoon they sat side by side at the computer, Becky manning the keyboard. The chapter they were working on was a love scene written from Angelina's viewpoint. Though Becky had written steamy scenes aplenty in the past, she'd never done so with a writing partner. That her collaborator happened to be a man she'd recently slept with, a man to whom she was still madly attracted, made the whole scenario that much more awkward. With the tension between her and Max mounting by the moment, no wonder the words on paper weren't working.

She drummed her nails atop the keyboard caddy, wishing there was some chocolate nearby. "Drake lifting Angelina's hair away from her neck and running his mouth alongside of her neck just doesn't work for me."

"Why not?" Max asked. He sounded grouchy but then again they had been working crazy hours. "It's an erogenous zone for most women, isn't it?"

Becky trained her gaze on the computer screen, hoping her warm face didn't translate into a vividly visible blush. Her own neck was a particularly sensitive area as Max well knew. Back in New York, he'd kissed and licked and nibbled her throat to their mutual hearts' content. At times such as this, she had to force herself to remember it was Angelina and Drake they were discussing.

"Well, er…I'm not saying it doesn't feel good to her. Of course it feels good—better than good. My point is it's not in her character to stand there passively while he puts the moves on her. She's more proactive than that."

"Okay, I'm wide open here. Let's walk through it step-by-step the way we did the action scenes."

Despite his matter-of-fact tone, Becky hesitated. "Are you sure that's a good idea?"

He shrugged but his gaze was anything but casual. "I'm game if you are. What would Angelina do if a man, Drake, was kissing her neck like…like this?" He angled his head and found the ultrasensitive spot just under Becky's ear with his mouth.

Gooseflesh broke out all over her. She sucked in her breath. "She'd uh…" Damn, but it was just about impossible to think rationally, to think at all, with Max doing… well, *that*. "She'd touch him back, definitely."

He slid his lips down the side of her throat, pressing open-mouthed kisses along the way. "Now we're getting somewhere. How would she touch him…or should I say where?"

He lifted his head, dark blue gaze holding hers, daring her to look away, his fingers toying with the sensitive area of her clavicle exposed by her sweater, raising a thrumming ache inside her pressed-together thighs.

Becky swallowed hard. Though she'd been sipping from a bottle of water throughout the day, she suddenly felt as though cobwebs had sprouted inside her mouth and throat. "Angelina is very straightforward about what she wants, and in this case, she wants Drake. Even though she knows she shouldn't, that it's not in the best interest of the mission to continue sleeping with her partner, she can't seem to stop thinking about him."

Max's hand slid to her shoulder. "That's her motivation but what would she do?" He leaned closer, drawing her toward him, his warm breath striking the side of her face. "Where would she touch him? How would she touch him? She must know he's waiting for her to give him some sign, any sign, that it's okay to break their no-lovers rule."

Rules of any sort suddenly seemed very far away to Becky. Pounding heat pooled inside her panties, her breasts felt heavy and hypersensitive, and her racing heart felt as though it might break through the wall of her chest at any time. Out of the corner of her eye, she caught a flicker of motion from outside the window. Turning to look, she saw it was snowing.

She swung her head back to Max and like an idiot announced, "It's snowing."

Scowling, he dropped his hand and drew back. "It's New Hampshire. That happens a lot here."

"But this looks like a really good snow, a Christmas snow. Let's take a walk."

One dark blond eyebrow edged upward. "I thought you hated cold weather?"

"Just a short walk. The fresh air will do us both good."

Becky couldn't speak for Max but for herself, her next activity was going to be either a cold walk or a cold shower. Either way, she needed to get her temperature back down and her perspective back in line before she did something really stupid, like begging him to go to bed with her.

"Okay. But just remember that tonight when we have to stay up finishing this scene, that this time you were the one who called break, not me."

He pushed back his chair and stood. The position put her on eye-level with his waist and for a fleeting few seconds she imagined herself reaching out to cup him, slowly rolling down his pants fly, and then drawing him into her mouth. Remembering how amazing he'd tasted, how she hadn't been able to get enough, she felt her face flush even hotter—and the pulse between her legs strike even deeper—more evidence of just how much she needed that walk.

"Let's go then." He reached down a hand to help her up. Reminded of their meeting in New York when he'd picked her up off the sidewalk—and peeked at her underwear—Becky let him lift her up, glad he couldn't possibly guess how wet the crotch of her panties must be by now.

He ran his gaze over her, his blue eyes looking as hot as she felt. "We need to bundle you up. That low-necked sweater needs a scarf at least." He glanced down to her feet. "And those fancy boots of yours aren't going to cut it, either."

She followed his gaze down to her high heeled Manolos. "They're the only ones I have."

He hesitated, a funny look rolling over his face, and she wondered if he might be considering bagging the walk and getting back to work after all. The thought brought about a bizarre sense of letdown. "I might have something that'll work." He turned and started out into the hallway.

Becky hesitated and then followed him out. As much as she needed to escape the close confines of the house, no way could she wear Max's boots. His feet were huge compared to hers. If she tried, she'd only end up falling, something she'd done way too much since meeting him.

She found him buried head and shoulders inside the coat closet. He backed out and turned to her, holding out a dusty pair of knee-high black snow boots. "These might work."

Becky glanced down at the shoes. Clunky and without a gram of style, they were too small to be his. Reaching out to take them, she almost said so when it hit her. Shit, they must have belonged to his wife.

Avoiding her eyes, he picked up the second boot and dusted it off. "Your feet are a lot smaller than hers were—you're a lot smaller period—but I figure you can stuff some cotton or tissues in the toes if you need to. It's a walk, not a run. I'll hold your hand if you want. I promise I won't let you fall." He lifted his face and looked up at her, and the raw vulnerability in his blue eyes had her forgetting all about how much she hated the cold.

"These are good. I can work with these." She took the boots from him, hugging them against her chest. "Give me a couple minutes to pile on those layers, and I'll meet you back down here, okay?"

"Okay."

She started toward the stairs. At the bottom, she turned back. "Max."

He lifted his bowed head to look at her. "Yeah?"

"I won't let you fall, either."

THEY WALKED side-by-side, theirs the first footprints in the otherwise pristine snow. Scout pranced ahead, more puppy than old dog. The fast-falling flakes were so big and soft-looking Becky could almost imagine the white sky above was one big exploded feather pillow. What had started as a quick way to bring about a short-term sexual cool-down had turned into more, much more. Looking ahead to snow-covered mountains and sparkling ice-crystal-covered trees, Becky felt as if she and Max were the only two people in a magical winter world.

She turned to Max. Reaching out, she squeezed his gloved hand. "Thank you."

He tucked her arm in his and looked over at her, his eyes intensely blue amidst all the winter white. "For what?"

"For—I don't know, taking a walk with me. This is really nice. It's beautiful out here."

He fixed solemn eyes on her face. "There really aren't words to do justice to a New England snow, not even for a writer. You have to see for yourself. And I can tell you really get it. Not everyone does, but you do."

More than the perfect snow or the dramatic mountain backdrop, it was sharing this with Max, the feel of his big hand holding hers, the echo of his boots crunching a twin trail next to hers that made the moment so very special. Even if she was walking in another woman's shoes—literally— she knew in her heart this walk counted among the most special of her life, one of those precious picture-perfect moments when the magic washes over you, and you feel connected to something greater and grander than yourself.

She smiled, her face frozen but the rest of her body toasty warm beneath the layers. "I may rethink always sending Angelina to tropical climates."

Fireside evenings, steaming mugs of hot chocolate or warm apple cider, even walks in the snow—certain life-style aspects of the New England climate were not without their charm. Or maybe it was just that she liked sharing those things with Max. It was a startling and disconcert-ing discovery and one she set aside to consider later— much later.

Their walk, and Becky's reprieve, ended far too soon. Even though her toes felt frozen solid inside the too-big boots, she was sorry to see the house come back into view.

Thinking of the still-to-be written love scene and the very real, very unresolved sexual tension mounting between her and her sexy writing partner, she hated to think about going back in.

They trudged up the gravel drive to the front porch. Protected by the hipped roof, they stood at the door shaking off snow. Standing on tiptoe, Becky finished dusting the flakes from Max's broad shoulders.

He glanced back at her. "Am I done?"

"Yes." Settling back on her soles, Becky felt as though she was the one who was done—done for.

For two weeks now, she'd fought her desire for Max as they'd shared intimate dinners and cozy fireside chats and one-on-one work sessions that lasted late into the night. Ironically it had taken a bracing winter walk to push her over the brink, to make her see that whatever there was between them, it wasn't going to burn out or fade away on its own. Much like Drake and Angelina, the outcome was predetermined, even scripted. She wanted Max even more than she had in New York. Fighting her feelings in the name of professionalism wasn't getting her anywhere. If anything, self-denial was wreaking havoc with her concentration, blocking her creativity and generally muddling her mind.

Max turned around. His gaze dropped to hers. This time she didn't look away as she had earlier in his office. Instead, she reached for her Angelina-like bravery and met his eyes steadily. Remembering his mention of Drake needing some sign, she stood on her toes and rested her hands on his shoulders and brushed her mouth over his, a silent offering.

His arms went around her, anchoring her to his chest. "Christ, Becka, what are you doing to me?"

Mouth hovering over his, she said, "I'm not sure. I just really need you to kiss me. You can consider this a sign if you want to."

He let out a groan. "Oh, I want to all right, I more than want to."

His mouth covered hers, and he slid his gloved hands into her hair, knocking off her knitted hat and pulling her even harder against him. She opened for him and he deepened the kiss, his tongue teasing the sensitive seam on the roof of her mouth before joining with hers.

He stopped to run his leather-sheathed thumb over her bottom lip, drawing a shiver that had nothing to do with the cold air. "Don't be sorry. I'm not."

To show how very not-sorry she was, she pressed closer, rubbing her breasts against him through the layers, finding a warmed patch of exposed skin on his neck with her lips and tongue, losing herself in the wonder of him, drowning not only in his eyes but in all of him. It was like being back at the Serena Lounge when they'd first come together like magnets, without conscious thought, words or even real names. Only, despite cold noses and bundled clothing, this was even better because it wasn't a stranger she was kissing. It was Max.

Breathless, Becky broke off the kiss and settled her flat-soled feet back onto the porch planks, second-guessing herself. She always felt so much taller, stronger and braver—so much more Angelina-like—wearing her heels.

"Max, this is crazy. What are we doing? What *is* this?"

He shook his head, his blue eyes melting her with their warmth and tenderness. "Damned if I know. If you figure it out, be sure and tell me. On second thought, don't, not now anyway. For now, let's just go with it. It worked pretty well back in New York."

"That was different. We didn't know each other then, not even our names."

He lifted one dark blond eyebrow and stared at her, looking sexier than any man had a right to look. "Are you saying only strangers can have good sex?"

She shook her head. "No, of course not, but coauthoring a book together changes everything. We're writing partners. Adding a sexual component to the mix is adding yet another unknown. We don't know how it will affect the work. It might be disastrous."

"It might be pretty damned wonderful, too. We'll never know unless we give it a shot." He slid his gloved hand beneath her chin, lifting her face to his. "Come to bed with me, Becka. Come to bed with me and let me make love to you."

In the midst of feeling more turned-on than ever before in her life, Becky felt purely, powerfully afraid, and not only because of the potential impact sex might have on their writing. Before, in New York, they'd been strangers. Beyond the pleasure of the moment, a one-night stand wasn't supposed to mean anything. If she made love to Max now, though, it would mean something, to her at least. For his part, it was obvious he was still crazy about his dead wife. Regardless, if she slept with him again, leaving at the end of the two months wouldn't just be hard—it would be brutal. It had taken her a full year to get over Elliot, and he was no Max. Could she really risk pain on that par again?

Max's seductive whisper interrupted her agonizing debate. "Come to bed with me, Becka. Before we write any more lovemaking scenes for Drake and Angelina, we need to create some for you and I."

MAX SAT on the side of his maple four-poster bed, Becky standing in the space between his thighs, his hands resting on her slender hips, hers anchored to his shoulders. They'd scripted nearly the same posture for Drake and Angelina's first time together in the outback hotel room, only Becky's petite, tightly packaged body was a thousand times sexier than Max could imagine her fictional heroine's ever being.

He reached up and started on the row of dainty pearl buttons fronting her angora sweater. Unlike Angelina, who frequently sported unisex designer biker gear, Becky was all woman right down to the pretty, feminine things she wore. Even her winter sweaters were soft and warm and delicate.

"So beautiful…"

He slid the sweater off her slender shoulders and reached for the zipper of her jeans. A glimpse of peach-colored silk greeted him, bringing him back to their first meeting on the New York sidewalk, the image of her spread white thighs burned into his brain for all time.

He felt a trickle of come slide down his penis and swallowed hard, determined to hold back for as long as he possibly could. "I need to get these damned jeans off you."

Feeling as though he was unwrapping a week-old Christmas present just discovered beneath the tree, he tugged her jeans down over her tight little behind and shapely legs. Becky stepped out of the pants and then lifted one slender foot to slide the pile aside.

She turned back to him and Max caught his breath. She was even prettier than he remembered, and he remembered her as being very pretty indeed. Wearing only her silky peach-colored bra and panties, she reminded him of a pocket-size Venus, all soft curls, warm brown eyes and alabaster skin.

Before Becky, petite women weren't what he'd thought

of as his type. Elaina had been built much like Becky's fictional heroine, almost six feet tall and, before she'd gotten sick, generously curved. In comparison, Becky was tiny, and yet her body was perfectly proportioned, tight and toned; her breasts small but lovely, the areolas dusky pink, the nipples pronounced and, if his memory served him, ultrasensitive.

Determined to take his time, he reached up and traced the outline of her bra with a single finger, drawing a shiver. He buried his face in her cleavage and inhaled her rosemary-mint fragrance in one intoxicating breath. "God, I'd almost forgotten how good you smell, how beautiful you are."

She skimmed her soft fingers over his jaw. "You make me feel beautiful. You have ever since I met you."

He lifted his head and met her shining eyes and knew she was remembering their sexy night in New York, as he was. That night was many things in his mind, one of them a hell of a lot to live up to. His hands, warm a minute ago though they'd only just come inside, suddenly chilled to ice.

Becky must have noticed because she reached down and took his hand between her two tiny ones. "We don't have to do this, you know. If you're having second thoughts, if you don't want me—"

He cut her off with a shake of his head. "Not want you? Are you crazy? I can't stop wanting you—and don't act like that comes as some kind of big surprise, either."

Since she'd pushed her way inside his front door and back into his life, he hadn't been able to concentrate on much beyond wanting her. Coauthoring the sexy book day in and day out without being able to touch her was nothing short of torture. If he had to write one more bedroom scene for their fictional protagonists while being denied the very real pleasure of Becky's body, he'd implode.

And yet he was nervous, which at first didn't make sense. They'd had sex before, in New York, not once but several times. Between the dim lights and the drinks and the overall anonymity, the experience hadn't felt entirely real, which had made it easier for him to give himself up to the sexy, surreal moment. This time was different. This time he knew her name, the way her mind worked, and something of her heart. She wasn't a stranger anymore or an empty fantasy, either. His sexy Cinderella had become much more to him than a one-night stand and going to bed with her was going to mean something.

As if reading his mind, she said, "Things were a lot simpler when we were strangers."

"Simpler doesn't always mean better."

Rather than say more and risk breaking the mood, he unhooked the clasp at the front of her bra. Her breasts swung free, her dusky-rose-colored nipples already hard for him, which was only fair. God knew he was hard for her. He bent his head and drew one firm bud into his mouth, loving the trusting way she leaned in to him, how readily she peaked against his tongue.

She let out a low moan, one hand leaving his shoulder to slide into his hair. "Oh, God, Max, you're torturing me but don't stop. Not yet, anyway."

"Don't worry, baby. Stopping isn't anywhere on my mind. I'm just getting started." To prove it, he bent and tongued her other breast while his thumb played with the nipple that was already warm and wet and hard from the ministrations of his mouth.

Becky gasped and ran frantic fingers through his hair. "God, Max, it feels so good. *You* feel so good."

He looked up at her. "Not as good as you feel. Sometimes I catch myself staring at you and remembering how wet and tight you felt around me, and I think I'm going to explode."

"I know," she said, her pretty face flushing. "Writing those love scenes, there were times I could hardly keep myself from mounting you there in the office." She bit her lip. "I can hardly wait to take you inside me now."

They'd been stupid, stubborn fools to waste these past weeks. Determined not to waste a moment more, he slid two fingers between her parted thighs and stroked her slit through the moist silk, then bent his head and laved kisses over her mound. Inhaling her musk and heat, remembering the salty taste of her, his mouth watered and his swelling cock thrummed.

He angled his face to look up at her and slid his fingers inside her panties. "You're going to have to, for a while at least."

She was very wet and very warm, almost scalding. His digits glided inside her, her tight channel closing around him like a fist.

She gasped and ground her hips into his hand, her curls streaming over her pretty face. "Oh, God, that feels so good, so amazing."

"It's supposed to."

Buried deep inside her, he worked his fingers scissors-style, slowly at first and then increasing the tempo. Becky rocked against him, her hips matching his rhythm, her other hand cuffing the back of his neck and urging his greedy mouth to make love to her breasts.

Like a bowstring drawn tight to the point of breaking,

suddenly she snapped back, her body going rigid. "Oh, Max!" She shuddered, her release rolling through her, her tender inner flesh quivering against his cream-coated fingers.

She pulled back to look at him from beneath heavy lids. "That was so good. I can't tell you how good."

He tucked a silky brown curl behind her ear. "You don't have to tell me, baby. This isn't a scene we're writing. It's real life. And the best part is I'm nowhere near finished with you."

"You're not?" Her mocha eyes scoured his face.

"Not by a long shot. Think of this as a really fancy banquet, and we're still on the appetizer course."

Laying his hands on her slender waist, he stood and swung her around, changing places to seat her on the side of the bed. She was such a little thing, so small and light. He'd noticed that the night in New York when he'd lifted her and carried her over to the piano. Sometimes it was hard to fathom that such a tiny woman could have such force of will, such unyieldingly opinions, but over the past weeks he'd come to appreciate that about her, too.

"Oh, Max." She rested her forearms on the mattress, slipped off her panties and opened her legs for him.

Standing over her, he took a moment to appreciate the view. She was drenched, her labia rosy-pink and glistening, wetness leaking from her slit from where she'd come moments before.

He shucked off his sweater and the T-shirt beneath and then dragged over a pillow and slid it beneath her head. "You can watch me if you like. I want you to watch me." The thought of her watching while he tongued her brought on a sharp tug of desire.

Holding her gaze, he went down on his knees on the

side of the bed. He buried his head in the sweet spot between her slender white thighs and lapped the cream from her labia, then used his fingers to spread it over her clit.

Becky moaned. She lifted her head from the mattress. "Max, please, don't make me wait any longer." She sat up, then reached for his jeans' zipper and rolled it down.

He wasn't wearing briefs and his swollen cock sprang free, harder and thicker than he'd ever known it to be. When she took him in her hand, he knew he couldn't wait any longer. He reached over to pull open the night table's bottom drawer and brought out the box of condoms, one of several "supplies" he'd picked up on his last trip into town. At the time, he hadn't been sure he'd get the opportunity to break the seal on the box, but he was very glad he would.

He rolled on the prophylactic and positioned himself over her slit, sliding the sheathed tip up and down, a slow, salacious tease. She moaned, "Please," and arched up to meet him, her hands anchoring her to his hips, her nails grazing him in her eagerness.

Max didn't mind. "What do you want, baby?"

She shifted her head on the pillow and looked up at him with feral eyes. "You know what I want."

"Say it, then." His voice came out as a hoarse command.

She hesitated. "I want you...I want you inside me. I can't wait. I don't want to wait. Oh, please..."

Max didn't need to be asked again. He entered her in one smooth, clean thrust, burying himself to the root. Becky cinched her strong runner's legs around his waist and the pressure of her straining to meet him almost pushed him over the edge.

Almost. Keeping his distance, keeping his control, he

pulled out of her and entered her again, slightly harder this time. She wriggled on her bottom and begged for more, and he got a dark pleasure in going still and making her wait, making them both wait, until they were so crazy for it they wouldn't be able to get enough.

"Please, Max." Her seeking hands slipped from his hips to his backside, her soft fingers kneading his buttocks and then trailing the seam between.

He arched back and hooked her slender ankles over his shoulders, increasing the angle, the pressure, the pleasure that was almost pain. "Is this what you want, sweetheart?"

"Oh, God, yes, yes!"

He pulled out of her and sank hard fingers deeply inside her, searching out the spot he knew would drive her wild. Her sudden soft shriek told him he'd found it. Moisture slid over his fingers and rolled to the inside of his wrist. Taking away his hand, he sank his cock into her once more, her inner flesh so searing he felt sure it would melt the condom.

"Oh, God, Max!"

He knew the instant the orgasm hit her, her inner muscles milking him like a small, silk-gloved fist. Max couldn't take it anymore. He reared back and drove into her, hard and fast, full and deep, her spasms shooting them both over the edge and beyond.

"Becka!"

"YOU HAVE some crazy ideas, you know that?" Max said sometime later. They were lying in bed, and Becky had just whispered her next salacious suggestion into his ear.

It was dark outside and, book deadline or not, they'd been too lazy to get up and switch on a light. She couldn't make out his face in the shadows beyond the whites of his eyes and the gleam of his grin, but the husky timbre of his voice assured her that in this case *crazy* constituted a good thing—a *very* good thing.

She stroked a hand down the side of his lean jaw and wished to God she didn't want him quite so much. Never before had she lost such complete control of her body in bed. Could her heart be far behind? "You bring it out in me. No one ever has before."

As much as she'd steeled herself to be like Angelina and have sex like a man, with no thought for the future, no emotional investment beyond the moment, putting that plan into play was proving to be a lot harder than she'd expected. The more time she spent with Max, the more she found herself feeling.

And yet the wound from Elliot's betrayal was still more scab than fully healed scar. When she entered her next real relationship with a man, she wanted to do so as a whole, healthy, totally together person. She just wasn't there yet and, until she was, "friends with benefits" was about all she could handle. On second thought, better make that "colleagues" with benefits.

Determined to switch her busy brain back off and savor the moment as Angelina would, she turned her head to the side and laid her cheek against his broad breastbone, the taut skin at once very warm and amazingly smooth. "You're six foot three and I'm five foot one. That's more than a full foot's difference and yet we fit together, don't we?" From the photograph, his wife had looked to be a tall woman, close to Max's height.

He lifted his head from the pillow and looked down at her. "I hadn't thought much about it, but you're right. We do fit. I'd say we fit damn near perfectly. We're good together. Not just this but…well, everything."

Uh-oh. Becky held back from answering. She knew Max liked her, certainly he lusted after her, but friendship and sexual attraction didn't add up to love. And how could he love her or anyone else when he was so obviously still passionately in love with his dead wife? Not only did he keep Elaina's photograph out on his desk but he kept her snow boots in his hall closet. Who knew how many other mementos were lying about? Even if she were in the market for a committed relationship, she didn't want to settle for being somebody's rebound. She'd already spent one afternoon walking in Elaina's shoes. She didn't want a future living in the dead woman's shadow.

Her dark thoughts must have found their way to her face because he lifted his head from the pillow and asked, "Becky, what is it? What's wrong?"

So much for shutting down my mind and living in the moment. She studied the sheet in her hand, avoiding meeting his eyes. "I just don't want either of us to get too used to this, that's all."

The mattress shifted as Max sat up in bed. "So what are you saying?"

She edged her eyes up to his. Why the hell did being a grown-up have to be so hard? "Whatever this is, whatever we are right now, it's a plot twist, and a wonderful one, but the basic outline stays the same."

"Casual lovers like we were in New York, you mean? No strings, no…feelings."

Holding on to the sheet, she sat up and looked over at him. With his hair mussed and the sheet riding his waist, he looked rumpled and sexy and yes, good enough to eat.

The only thing spoiling the picture was the wounded look in his eyes.

Hating that she'd hurt his feelings, or at least his pride, she reached out and laid her hand on his bicep. "Just be my lover, Max, that's all I ask. That way when the book's finished we can go back to our lives without any hard feelings on either side. No strings, regrets and above all, no sappy goodbyes, okay?"

Glancing down at her hand banding his bicep, Max almost laughed aloud at the irony of his situation. It was shaping up to look as if Becky really wasn't that different from her character after all. Had he really survived the past year of hell and come back to life only to fall for the female equivalent of a player?

Hiding his disappointment, he reached down and covered her hand with his. "If that's the way you want it, Miss St. Claire, then once again we have a deal."

11

Angelina sat cross-legged before the campfire, naked beneath the heavy quilt. Staring into the purple and orange flames, she felt dreamy and sated and altogether unlike herself. After her near miss at the mine shaft, she and Drake had come back and made camp for the night—and love for hours. Her typical postcoital reaction after such a vigorous sexual session was to mount her motorcycle and ride off into the sunset. Instead she didn't want to move so much as a muscle.

Drake came up beside her and handed her the bottle of whiskey. "Here, love, have a drink of this. It'll warm you."

She smiled up at him. "You've already done that but thanks." Taking the bottle, she sensed something was amiss. "What is it?"

He ran a hand through his short blond hair. "Scotland Yard just rang on the mobile. The two weeks we had to track down Falco and the plans for building the next-generation missile system have been winnowed to one."

MAX AND Becky sat side-by-side on the family-room floor, toes stuck out toward the dancing flames of the fire, the printout of the first ten chapters of their book stacked on the floor between them. Red pen in hand, Becky had decided to give her eyes a rest and make the markups on the hard copy. Max sat next to her, head bent over the portable computer resting on his lap, typing out the next chapter draft. They were both trying hard to be good and work—just not quite hard enough.

Max set the laptop aside on the floor and turned to her. "Hungry?"

She nodded. "Always."

He'd left a pot of lamb stew simmering on the stove, the delicious aroma floating down to tickle Becky's nostrils, a far cry from the frozen dinners she was used to eating back home. Since she'd shown up on Max's doorstep, he'd spoiled her with his dinners and his back-rub breaks and yes, his lovemaking. She was going to miss all of it once she went back home but mostly she was going to miss him. Her boyfriends before Elliot had, for the most part, been nice enough guys but there'd either been a sexual spark with little in common, or a lot in common with next to no spark. With Max, there was an abundance of both. It was really too bad she'd met him sooner rather than later. Once she was ready for a real relationship, she couldn't imagine finding a man to match him.

Reaching over, he took her chin between his thumb and finger and turned her face toward him. "Me, too, though not for stew."

He traced the outline of her bottom lip with the pad of his thumb, making her shiver. Running it along the seam of her lips, he teased them apart.

Torn between needing to be good and wanting to be bad, she shook her head, feeling as if a tiny devil was perched on her one shoulder and an equally tiny angel on the other. "You're determined to distract me, aren't you?"

"Uh-huh." He slid the edge of his thumb inside. "How am I doing, by the way?"

"Pretty good." Better than good. The devil was definitely winning the upper hand.

"Just pretty good?"

"Okay, very good. But you should stop."

Blue eyes brushed over her face. "It doesn't feel good?"

She started to answer, and he seized the chance to slide the tip of his thumb inside her mouth and then out. "Because—because we're supposed to be working."

He smiled his warm smile, gaze riveted on her mouth. "In that case, think of it as research."

"Research, huh?" Giving up, she set the papers aside and reached for him, her hands sliding atop his shoulders, loving the strong, solid feel of him beneath her fingertips. "I usually rely on Internet search engines and books for that."

He grinned. "See, that's another area where we differ. Me, I'm into experiential learning. You might even say I'm a hands-on kind of guy."

He leaned in and kissed her. His warm tongue tasted spicy from the mulled cider they'd drunk earlier. He slid it between her lips as he had his thumb. "Sorry." Pulling back, he looked anything but. "There I go kissing you again, but how can I help it? You're very kissable."

"I am, am I?" She met his teasing smile with one of her own.

"Uh-huh. And you taste amazing." The wicked look in his eye hinted he wasn't only talking about her mouth.

A moment later he confirmed that by sliding a hand between them and palming her through her jeans. Becky sucked in her breath. At this point, the angel was out of the picture—completely.

"Three guesses where I'm thinking of kissing you next." His hand's slow, kneading strokes seared through the denim, bringing moisture pooling into her panties.

"Is it lower than my mouth?"

"Uh-huh."

"My breasts, then?" she asked, warming to the game.

He lifted his other hand and cupped her with a slight squeeze. "You do have beautiful breasts. I want to kiss them, too, but in this case I'm thinking even lower."

"Lower?"

His fingers went to the zipper of her jeans. Holding her gaze, he tugged the zipper down. "I want to kiss you there, right there. In fact, I could lick and tongue you all night, starting right now."

She leaned back against the side of the sofa, opening her legs. "We don't have all night. We have a book to write, remember?"

"I remember. But you know what they say about all work and no play." He slid two fingers inside her open jeans and slid them along her damp, lace-covered crotch.

Becky's breath hitched. She tilted back her head, a hairbreadth from coming. "Let me guess. It makes Becky a dull girl?"

"Uh-huh. And it makes Max a very frustrated boy."

The office phone rang like a siren. Looking at each other, they shared a collective groan. Max rolled to his knees, resting back on his heels. "I should pick up. Not too many people have that number. It must be important." He glanced at the manuscript she'd set aside. "Keep working so we can play when I get back."

"Sounds like a deal," she said though she seriously doubted she could focus now.

Watching his sexy, jeans-clad butt walking away, she held in a sigh. Distractions aside, in another few weeks the book would be done and there would be no real reason for her to stay on. Having a built-in relationship expiration date rendered every second of every minute they spent together infinitely precious. Instead of wondering where their relationship was headed and fretting over the future as she always had before, she could let down her guard and live in the moment.

Sexually she'd never been able to let go like this before, not even with Elliot. Her ex had kept her on such an emotional roller coaster straight from the start that it hadn't been easy to relax with him in or out of bed. Lately she'd caught herself thinking that what Max and she shared might be the real deal, not just a fling. But then, blurring the line between fantasy and reality was an occupational hazard of fiction writing that had cost her big-time. She'd spent months deluding herself into believing Elliot loved her back, not to mention dealing with the financial fallout of having quit her job. Max seemed as different from her ex as day was from night, but having made such a huge mistake in judgment once—and not all that long ago—how could she trust herself to know for sure?

Max's return brought her out of her musing. "That was Pat. She says they need the book a month earlier."

Still struggling with her dilemma, Becky took a moment

to absorb the news. Once she did, the jolt hit hard. "That's crazy, maybe even impossible."

Max heaved a sigh. "Not impossible, but I agree, crazy."

"Why the rush?"

"She found out through the publishing grapevine that a project being touted as the next big action-adventure blockbuster book is coming out around the same time as ours. Even though the mystery and erotica components set our story somewhat apart, she doesn't want us to have to face that kind of stiff competition for the lists. If we can get this in by the end of next week, we might have a decent shot at beating them to the shelves—and the top ten."

"She really thinks our book has bestseller potential?"

"She knows it does, and so do I. Don't you?"

Becky hesitated. Like any other writer, she'd had her share of bestseller fantasies but before now, she'd been content simply to be able to support herself with her writing. Since teaming with Max, she'd found herself reaching for the stars on a daily basis. It was scary to build up her hopes that high, but it was exciting, too—an adventure.

"What did you tell her?"

She was almost afraid to hear his answer. Of course they'd do their utmost to make the new deadline. With so much riding on this project, what choice did they have? Still, if he'd signed them up for what promised to be two weeks of hell, two weeks of too much coffee and too little sleep, without talking to her first, she was going to be really, really pissed.

"I told her I'd talk it over with you, and we'd get back to her in the morning."

We. She liked the sound of that. "Thank you."

He sent her a questioning look. "For what?"

Smiling, she held his gaze for a long moment. "For being my partner."

MAX SAT at the computer, putting the final spit and polish on chapter fifteen of the novel's twenty chapters. They were down to the wire, with just another few days to go, but fortunately the manuscript was close to complete. There was the one fight scene yet to rework with a secondary character added in, but overall the manuscript was in good shape. He calculated they were another day from finishing. If they kept the momentum up, they might even wrap things up later that night. If so, not only would they have met the Deadline from Hell but beaten it by a day.

Even in its current form, the book was the best thing he'd ever written. He knew the cause, of course. Becky. The chemistry between them was coming out in their two main characters in a major way. The sex scenes between Drake and Angelina sizzled, but so did the rest of the manuscript. Reading over the working draft, he found himself agreeing with Pat. The book had movie deal written all over it. The downside was that the sooner they finished, the sooner Becky would be leaving. It was crazy but these last few days he'd caught himself coming up with distractions to draw the writing out.

Max ran a hand through his hair. It felt slightly greasy but then he hadn't showered since the morning of the day before. His legs were stiff and the small of his back pounded as if someone was hitting it with a hammer. He thought of the all-nighters he'd pulled back in college and grad school and then those a few years back when he'd sat up with Elaina and shook his head. If he'd gone looking for a custom-made reminder he wasn't a kid anymore, this was it.

"Okay, let me try this out on you. What do you think about Angelina…"

He stopped when she didn't immediately answer. By now he knew she wasn't shy about jumping in. It wasn't like her not to have an opinion, especially where her fictional creation was concerned.

"Becka?" He turned to look at her over his shoulder.

She was asleep. Curled up on her side on his leather office couch, her delicate hands tucked beneath her head, she looked serene and lovely and innocent, the throw blanket slipping off her shoulder. This was his golden opportunity to shape the book without consultation or compromise, and yet at some point over the past few weeks he'd gotten used to doing both. It wasn't that he didn't trust his talent or his writer's instincts—he did. The thing was, he'd grown comfortable working as part of a team. More than comfortable, he'd grown to like it—a lot.

He crossed the room and went down on one knee beside the couch. Laying a light hand on her shoulder, he said, "Hey, sleepyhead, rise-and-shine time. We have a book to get out."

She cracked open an eye and looked up at him. "I guess I fell asleep, huh?"

"Yeah I guess so, and I need to pick that plotting brain of yours. Our characters are trapped in that collapsed mine shaft and time and air are running out. There's a crawl space at the top. The air will last longer if there's only one of them there."

She pulled herself up on her forearms, caramel-colored curls streaming her face. "Okay, give me a sec to wake up, and then I'm on it."

"You got it." He kissed the tip of her nose.

Feeling as stiff-legged as Scout, he got up and crossed over to the computer. Once she got up from the couch, he might trade places with her. He could use a power nap himself. In the interim, he reached for the remote and switched on the TV. One of the drawbacks of a tight deadline was that complete immersion in the work meant cutting oneself off from the outside world. He hadn't read a newspaper or watched television in days. For all he knew, North Korea could have conquered the world.

He found a cable news program in progress and stopped surfing. Hoping to gather the highlights, he settled back in his desk chair to watch. The anchor was asking his guest, a good-looking gray-haired man in a dark suit, to weigh in on the issue du jour, something to do with subway safety in the context of the latest terrorism threat. The camera panned over to the guest commentator for a close-up. The guy's lean, youngish face, deep-set dark eyes and broad shoulders filled the TV's flat screen. Max couldn't think of his name, but he'd seen him from time to time on similar programs as a consultant or special guest. Whoever he was, he was an authority in his field—some kind of counterterrorism work. For whatever reason, he'd always struck Max as a little too sure of himself, a little too smooth.

Staring straight at the camera, he addressed the host. "As I was saying to Katie Couric over coffee just the other day, since 9/11 the Feds and law enforcement have made enormous strides in ensuring that transportation security is tighter, and the public is safer than ever before. That's *ever*, Doug. But in a free society such as ours, there's always going to be some level of threat…"

Jesus, what a name dropper. Max would bet anything that off camera he was a first-class prick. He picked up the remote to switch channels but before he could, Becky shoved the quilt aside and marched across the room.

She punched the off button on the set and swung around to face him, eyes glittering in her very flushed face. "Is it possible to have some peace and quiet to work in around here or is that asking too much?"

Max looked over at her, wondering what her problem was. Ordinarily she preferred writing with the television or music playing in the background. "You must have woken up on the wrong side of the couch. What was that about?"

She shook her head, gaze sliding away. "I'm just worried about finishing on time, that's all. Sorry."

He got up to stand beside her. Touching her arm, he realized she was shaking. "Why is it I don't think that is all?"

She shrugged and fixed her gaze on the computer behind him. And suddenly it struck him. Gray hair. Lean face. Dark, deep-set eyes. All-black wardrobe. Explosives expert.

He shot his gaze to her face. "That guy on the TV is Falco, isn't he?"

Her eyes flashed open. She bit her bottom lip. "Don't be ridiculous. Falco is a composite character. I'm a fiction writer. I make up stuff all the time. That's what we do, remember?"

"Sorry, Becka, but I'm not buying." He shook his head, wishing he could get himself to the studio in New York where the program was being broadcast from in time to plow his fist into the cocky bastard's face. "Ever since I first met you, I've had a gut sense that some jerk must have burned you pretty badly and then reading your last book confirmed it. Angelina is obsessed with Falco."

"She is not." She shook her head, though she still

couldn't look at him. "You're letting your imagination run away with you."

Max hesitated. They should be having this conversation with both of them fully awake and fully functioning, not buzzing on caffeine and adrenaline and the effects of sleep deprivation. And yet, who knew when he'd get another shot? Right now she was still sticking to her plan to leave in another week. This might be his one chance—make that his dazzling opportunity—to break through to her. Once he did, maybe he could change her mind about leaving. It was worth a try. Whoever this former G-man jerk was, it was obvious he'd hurt her badly. To react so strongly, she must still have feelings for him.

Pushing jealousy to the back of his mind for now, he said, "Come on, Becka, let it out. You'll feel a hell of a lot better afterward. Trust me, I know."

She looked at him, the raw misery in her eyes tugging at his heart. "I don't know what you're talking about. There's nothing to let out."

He blew out a breath. She was a tough nut to crack, that was for damned sure. "Lying to me is bad enough but lying to yourself is a whole lot worse."

"I'm not lying to anybody."

"In that case, look me in the eye." When she still wouldn't, he grabbed hold of her shoulders. He brought his face down and rested his forehead against hers, willing her to see how much she meant to him, how much he…loved her.

Christ, he loved her, he really did. When they'd first met, he'd lusted after her and in the course of the past weeks of writing he'd grown to like her a lot, so much so that he'd admitted he wanted her in his life and not just as a writing partner. But love, well, that was a hell of a big deal. After Elaina, he hadn't been able to imagine himself ever loving another woman again. Loving somebody made you vulnerable, it made you raw. Practically speaking, loving a woman still so obviously hung up on her ex wasn't the brightest of moves and yet here he stood with his heart on his sleeve, head-over-heels smitten. Over the past weeks, his sexy Cinderella had gotten under his skin—and penetrated straight to his heart.

Pulling back to look down at her, he prayed he wouldn't do or say anything to wreck his already slender chances. "I love you, Becka. I don't know what that jerk did to make you this way, but I'm going to find a way to break down that goddamned wall you've built up around yourself if it's the last thing I do."

She lifted haunted eyes to his face. "I can't let myself love you or anybody right now. I'm sorry but I just can't. Somebody did hurt me, really badly, and I can't risk letting that happen again. I want to believe that you're different, that we're different, but I just don't know how to tell for sure."

Max pulled her closer, willing her to melt into him. "This is the real thing. I know it. I can *feel* it. All you have to do is let go and let yourself love me back. Let go, Becka. I'll be here to catch you, I promise."

Holding her flush against his chest, he could feel the tension in every rigid muscle. To hell with the book. If need be, he'd set aside the day and make love to her until she not only saw how much he loved her but felt it, too.

Mouth pressed to her ear, he said, "I'm not going to hurt you, Becka, and I'm not going to walk away, no matter how hard you push me. Let me love you, Becka. Give me a shot at least. If I screw up, at least it's my screwup and not payback for some other guy's mistakes."

"I'm sorry, I can't." She shoved against his chest with both hands.

He dropped his arms to his sides. "Becka, wait."

Shaking her head, she backed away toward the door. Reaching it, she turned and tore out of the room. It took all Max's force of will not to go after her. In the back of his mind, he remembered an old saying, a favorite of Elaina's.

If you love something set it free. If it comes back, it's yours. If it doesn't, it never was.

Standing in the middle of the study, he asked himself how something as beautiful and basic to human nature as loving someone could be so complicated, so hard.

RENTAL-CAR keys in hand, Becky got as far as the gravel lot before the episode in the study sank in. She swung around to look back up at the house—Max's house. Over the past weeks it had become more of a home to her than she'd ever had before, and not because she liked big, sprawling rooms with timbered ceilings and pine paneling.

Max loved her. He'd said so, not only with his mouth but with his beautiful blue eyes—tender, earnest, loving. Max loved her. And, she saw with thunderbolt clarity, she loved him back. Loving him wasn't something she had to work on. It wasn't something she had to try harder to do. She loved him, she just did, and every error in judgment she'd ever made in the past, Elliot included, paled in comparison to the blazing brilliance of that beautifully simple fact. Her sexy Prince Charming from midtown hadn't just captured her heart. He'd made her trust in love again, and beyond that, in herself.

Retracing her steps up the path, she wondered what he must think of her—emotional basket case, high-maintenance lay or psycho girlfriend? Given the way she'd run for the hills, she wouldn't blame him if he told her to just forget it. There was only one way to find out.

Inside the house, she didn't bother with hanging up her coat. Walking into the study, she stopped in the doorway, one foot inside, the other still in the hallway, a fitting metaphor for how she'd approached their relationship until now.

Max sat on the side of the sofa. He looked up, his eyes holding a silent question.

Hands shoved in her coat pockets, Becky hesitated. She'd never been good with talking about her emotions and since the Elliot episode she'd bottled up her feelings even tighter. But looking into the twin pools of Max's weary blue eyes, she told herself that this time, with this man, it was okay—safe—to let go and fall in.

"I love you, too."

His eyes widened and then brightened. "Wow, you romance writers don't waste time with lead-ins or segues, do you?" He got up and started toward her.

Becky reached out a hand to hold him off. "Before you say anything more, you need to know what you're getting into."

He halted in midstep, expression turning wary. "All right. It's not going to change a damned thing, at least not on my end, but go on."

She bowed her head, unsure of where to begin, or even how. "His name is Elliot Marsh."

Becky stopped to swallow back the lump building in her throat. This was hard, so hard, but not because she was still in love with Elliot. She wasn't, she knew now. But looking into Max's face and seeing the honest love shining forth from his clear blue eyes, it hurt to think she'd once been willing, make that *desperate* enough, to settle for so very much less.

Clearing her throat, she continued, "I met him through a friend at the consulting firm in D.C. where I worked. He's a media consultant for a major television network now, but he used to work for the Feds. He comes into Washington once or twice a month, or at least he used to. There was a spark between us and he was, well, very complimentary." Now that she'd taken the lid off her personal Pandora's Box, she couldn't seem to stop the bottled-up feelings from spilling out. "We had this amazing weekend—well, more like an amazing thirty-six hours—and I thought, 'This is it, what I've been searching for all my adult life, romance like I'd dreamed about ever since I read my first Gothic novel in middle school.'"

He kept his distance, but his gaze held hers. "He played you, led you on." It wasn't a question.

She hesitated. "Looking back, it was more like *I* led me on."

Wow, another revelation. Until now, she'd chalked the episode up to poor judgment. Now she saw that her need to feel loved, to feel special rather than lost in the crowd, had been a big part of it, too.

"There were plenty of signs from the beginning. I just didn't want to see them. He asked me to move out to L.A. with him and said I should start thinking about what kind of engagement ring I wanted and whether to get married on the east coast or the west. I even let him talk me into quitting my consulting job. He said if I wanted to make it as a writer, I had to really focus on my craft. He certainly acted like he was willing to support us both."

He stood and crossed the carpet toward her. "What happened?"

"He dumped me. No Dear Jane e-mail or phone call or any explanation. One day he just showed up in D.C. at what had been our favorite restaurant with a twentysomething blonde on his arm. I guess he decided it was time to trade up."

"Not up but down." He took a step toward her and reached for her hands. "You're a knockout, Becka. Any man with half a brain would be proud to be with you. I know I am. You're also funny and smart and talented and kind. Anyone who can't see that must have blinders on— and that includes you. As for Elliot, I don't know what his problem was. Personally, I've always had a thing for grown-up women. I'm just weird that way." He lifted her chin with the edge of his hand.

"I like that you're weird that way. I more than like it. I meant what I said. I really love you, Max."

Now that she'd put herself out there and said it, *really* said it, the sense of relief was enormous. Tears filled her eyes and spilled over to trickle down her cheeks.

Gaze tender, Max swiped the pad of his thumb over the wetness. "After Elaina died, I thought I could never love someone again."

"And now?"

He didn't hesitate. "Elaina will always hold a very special place in my memory and my heart, but my time with her is in the past. My present and my future are with you."

Becky felt as though she'd stepped inside a romance novel or better yet, a fairy tale, only the love in Max's eyes when he looked into hers was one-hundred-percent real. She launched herself into his arms, wrapping hers about him as tightly as she could. "Oh, Max, I've loved you ever since I fell head over heels for you on that sidewalk in midtown—even before you rescued my shoe. I just didn't trust myself to believe it before. I was so afraid of messing up again and getting hurt."

"What about now?"

She lifted her head from his chest and looked up at him. Her gaze met his and she steeled herself to take that age-old leap of faith, trusting that he would be waiting on the other side to catch her. "It's taken me a while to get there, but I can finally trust myself to know a good thing, and a good man, when I see him—and I'm looking at him right now."

"In that case, Cinderella, shut up and kiss me."

Max leaned in and covered her mouth with his. His lips, soft and gentle, brushed over hers, his tongue sliding between her parted lips to touch hers. Though they'd kissed countless times before, somehow this felt like the very first.

Holding her face between his hands, he ended the kiss. Smiling down at her, he asked, "You know what I want to do right now?"

Feeling breathless and light-headed as any storybook princess kissed awake by her Prince Charming after a centuries-long sleep, Becky shook her head. "I could probably guess, but tell me."

His smile broadened into a grin. "I want to take you upstairs and take your clothes off piece by piece and make love to you as slowly and as sweetly as either of us can stand. How does that sound to you?"

"Like a sexy fairy tale come true." She glanced over to the computer, their current chapter filling the monitor. "But can we spare the time? We did leave Drake and Angelina in kind of a bind."

"Let them figure it out for themselves. They need to learn to be more independent, anyway." Taking her face between his hands, he leaned in. "Right now, I'm all about the muse."

12

Drake swung one leg over the side of the camp bed. He had one foot on the dirt-packed floor when Angelina called him back. "Lie here and be still with me."

They'd been on a near death march for days now, stopping only long enough to snatch a few hours of sleep before dawn broke again. The success of their mission depended on their reaching Toro Toro in the next twenty-four hours, recovering the stolen plans, and getting the hell out of there.

Thinking he must have misheard her, Drake looked over his shoulder and asked, "Come again?"

Angelina swallowed hard, the ripple traveling along the elegant column of her bare throat. "We can carry on with the business of conquering evil and reclaiming the stolen missile plans and saving the free world in another moment or so. For now, though, just lie here and be still with me."

FACING EACH OTHER in Max's bed, Max carried Becky's hand to his mouth and pressed a kiss to the sensitive spot inside her wrist, smiling when she shivered. She had more erogenous zones than any woman he'd ever known—and he didn't think he'd ever get tired of hunting for more.

But unfortunately they had a book to finish. With regret, he reached to pull the covers down and get up. "We should probably get back to our characters. Time's running out for them and us."

Throwing a shapely leg possessively over him to keep him there, she slid her hand slowly down his chest to his stomach and then beneath the sheet. "I think you should stay right here and make love to me again. I vote for that." She wrapped her small hand about his shaft and slid it slowly up and down.

Throbbing against her palm, Max blew out a breath, about a minute away from losing his willpower and his work ethic. "Unfortunately, we have a manuscript to finish." With regret, he eased her hand away. Looking down at his erection tenting the sheet, he said, "We'll save this for later. Think of it as our motivation to churn out those final chapters. You get some rest. I'll come wake you up when it's your shift."

She slid a hand to the side of his jaw. Brushing her mouth over his, she said, "Write fast, Max. Write really fast."

SHRUGGING into his shirt, Max opened the door and stepped out into the hallway. Given the breakneck schedule they'd been on, he couldn't resist letting Becky sleep for a few more hours. Since the call from Pat, they'd been working crazy hours and earlier he'd seen her pressing a hand to her lower back as though it hurt. Back pain was an occupational hazard of writing. She needed the sleep more than he did. While she rested, he'd get to work on the scenes they'd agreed in advance he would take the first crack at writing. By the time she got up, he'd be able to turn them over to her for editing and catch some shut-eye himself. Once they'd gotten into tag-team mode, the writing had gone a lot faster. He'd been so sure when it came to his work that he was a solo act, but writing was turning out to be a pretty good metaphor for life overall.

It was easier to get through with a partner.

Before Becky, he always thought the next woman in his life, assuming there was one, would be a facsimile of Elaina. Another tall, big-boned girl with soulful dark eyes and a messy mane of dark hair. Becky was petite, blond, and about as all-American as they came. Elaina had favored oversized sweaters, no-nonsense jeans, and sensible shoes. Becky was into couture clothing and designer footwear. Elaina's temperament had been placid as a midsummer sky. Becky's was more like that summer sky once it had split with the first thunderbolt of an unexpected storm. Elaina had accepted him for who he was.

Becky challenged him to become all the things he'd yet to be.

THEY FINISHED the manuscript around noon the next day. Seated at the keyboard, Max hesitated, the cursor hovering above the send button that, once struck, would catapult their manuscript into cyberspace and land it in Pat's e-mail in-box in a matter of moments.

He turned to his pretty coauthor. Even running on empty, she was a sight for sore—*really* sore—eyes. "You should do the honors."

Becky stood behind him, hands clenching the computer chair, a lump in her throat. Funny how she was experiencing none of the adrenaline rush that always came with completing a manuscript. If anything she felt oddly reluctant to let the book go, a first for her. Though Max had said he loved her, and she loved him, she wasn't yet sure what that meant. They were two very different people who'd carved out distinct lives for themselves. How those lives would mesh once the book collaboration was out of the picture remained to be seen.

She stepped back from the computer, willing herself to shake the negative thoughts from her head. If nothing else, the past few weeks of fresh starts and dazzling opportunities should have taught her to trust in the universe—and herself.

"No, thanks. You go ahead."

Max twisted his head around to look back at her over the shelf of one muscular shoulder. "You're sure?"

After making love earlier, he'd collapsed on the office couch for some much-needed sleep. The side of his face still bore creases from the imprint of the couch pillow and the back of his hair stood up in a cowlick worthy of Dennis the Menace. Becky thought he looked amazing.

Becky nodded. "Yes, I'm sure."

Max clicked Send. Seconds later Drake and Angelina and Falco and all the rest were hurtling into cyberspace. Exchanging first high fives and then congratulatory kisses, their creators went back to bed.

BECKY WAS still sleeping the next morning when Pat called to say she'd read the book in one four-hour marathon sitting and had loved it. There'd be a few minor editorial changes coming, mostly fluff stuff, but otherwise it was as pristinely perfect a manuscript draft as she'd ever seen. In fact, she'd already passed it to the bigwigs upstairs and the in-house buzz was building at breakneck pace. It seemed the powers that be were willing to front list the book, which meant putting major promo dollars behind it.

The second call came an hour later from Harry on the home line. Max ran to answer it, hoping to intercept the phone before it woke Becky. Harry might be an A-list agent, but he couldn't seem to hire a decent receptionist to save his life. Whoever he sat out front always managed to mix Max's office and home numbers up.

Busy picking up several days' worth of collected clutter, he switched the call to speakerphone. "Hey, Harry, what's up?"

"I have great news, Maxie. I just got a call from my coagent out in L.A. I sent him a copy of your manuscript." Harry's voice was jubilant.

"You mean Rebecca's and mine," Max corrected.

"Whatever. I can't say much, we're at a very preliminary stage of the negotiation, but you should know that a major Hollywood production company is considering optioning it for a motion picture film. We're talking bigscreen, Max, and that means big bucks."

This was just the break Becky's career needed. More thrilled for her than himself, Max answered, "That's fabulous. Becky's sleeping right now, but this definitely merits a wake-up call."

"Not so fast. For the moment, let sleeping dogs—or in this case, coauthors—lie. If the deal goes through, and it will, the producers want you to write the screenplay solo."

Max hesitated. Dialogue was more Becky's strength than his. "I'm a novelist, not a screenplay writer."

"So you'll learn. They'll assign you a cowriter behind the scenes to show you the ropes."

"What about Becky?"

"Do not fret, my friend. Rebecca St. Claire is history. We couldn't do anything about the coauthorship on the novel, that's a done deal, but you have my personal guarantee you will never have to coauthor anything, including the Drake and Angelina screenplay, with that woman ever again."

Max snatched up the receiver. "Are you saying you've found a way to cut Becky out of the screenplay deal?"

Harry hesitated. "She will be compensated for creative translation of her character to film, of course, but that's the tip of the iceberg, a small piece of the pie. You won't have to worry about her ever again. You don't have to thank me, Maxie, it's the least I can do."

Max held the phone away from his ear, feeling sick inside. The very last thing he'd wanted his agent to do was cut out Becky.

"Why am I not hearing champagne corks popping, huh? I thought you would be pleased."

"I'll have to call you back. In the meantime, you should know that unless the screenplay deal is revised to include Becky as coauthor, there is no deal. Got it?"

"But Maxie—"

Max hung up. A month ago Harry's news would have shot him clear over the moon but not so now. He would refuse, of course. In the interim, he didn't want Becky to find out. She'd really pushed the envelope on her writing these past weeks, not to mention taught him a thing or two. She felt deservedly good about the book they'd sent in, and he didn't want anything to wreck that for her. He'd fix things behind the scenes so that when the screenplay deal came around, she'd be a full partner. A Hollywood screenplay would open up a world of new contacts for them both.

Another coauthorship would, of course, require they continue to spend time together. So far, neither of them had broached the sticky subject of when Becky was leaving—

or when she might be coming back. He wasn't really interested in living in D.C. but he remembered her mentioning her family was in Maryland. He didn't yet know how important it was for her to stay near her relatives and friends. On the positive side, she no longer had her consulting career tying her to the area, but she still wasn't crazy about cold weather or the countryside. Who knew? Maybe they'd split the difference and get an apartment in Manhattan? He could hold on to his house in New Hampshire as a weekend and holiday retreat. The dog would miss running off leash outside but then again the old guy didn't move so fast or so far anymore. Becky had a cat, and Max wasn't thrilled about that but he wasn't allergic. Somehow they'd all learn to adjust.

Max stopped himself when he realized he was picking out honeymoon locations and naming their two point five children. Before he planned any further, he should probably consult his sexy partner. The new year had brought a bounty of fresh starts and dazzling opportunities, not just for Becky but for them both. It was like coming downstairs on Christmas morning as a kid and having so many presents under the tree to unwrap you didn't know where to start. Having too many wonderful choices was the sort of "problem" Max was happy to have.

BECKY HUNG UP the phone in her bedroom, Max's betrayal ringing in her ears. After hearing him say "Are you saying you've found a way to cut Becky out of the screenplay deal?" she'd quietly replaced the cordless in its cradle. She didn't need to hear any more to know that Max had sold her out.

A few weeks ago, she wouldn't have been all that shocked. He was the bestselling author, after all, and as an up-and-comer she'd heard the horror stories. It wasn't unheard of for a big-name author to steal work from someone lesser known.

But that was before they'd made love and it had meant something, before she'd poured her heart out to him about her failed relationship and stupid mistakes, before he'd wiped away her tears and kissed her lips and told her how much he loved her. If she hadn't just heard him say the damning words with her own ears, she never would have believed it.

Hearing footsteps coming up the stairs, she snatched up a book and moved away from the phone to the rocking chair by the window. He entered her darkened bedroom a few minutes later. "I'm sorry if that phone call woke you up."

Closing the book she was pretending to read, she said, "That's okay. I was awake anyway. Who was it?" Out of the corner of her eye, she kept close watch on his face.

"No one really."

"No one?"

She turned to look at him, her heart turning over at the slick ease with which he lied to her just like…Elliot. Her former lover, she felt sure, wouldn't hesitate to steal someone's glory. It seemed that once again her judgment had failed her. Though they looked and behaved very differently, both men were cut from the same cloth.

He shrugged, but she didn't miss how he couldn't look her in the eye. "You know telemarketers. There's no getting off the phone with them. It's probably just better to hang up."

"Yeah, I guess so."

"I'm going to drive into town for groceries. We're down

to our last egg and Scout's kibble bag is scraping bottom.
You want to come? Lunch at the truck stop, all the blue
plate specials you can eat on me. Surely you can't resist
an offer like that." Max winked at her, and Becky felt as
though an invisible razor were slashing at her heart.

"No, thanks. I think I'll hang out here and take a bath."

He stopped in his tracks and turned around. "You
okay?"

"Sure, why?"

"You don't seem like yourself."

Look who was talking. "I guess these late nights are
finally catching up with me."

He crossed the room to her, stopping behind her chair.
"Okay, you rest up. I'll be back in a couple of hours and
then we'll celebrate—really celebrate—okay?" He leaned
in to kiss her, but she turned away at the last minute. His
lips met her cheek instead.

Pulling back, he looked down on her and asked again,
"You sure you're okay?"

"Positive."

This was worse than her restaurant run-in with Elliot.
She'd realized now she'd only been infatuated with him.
She'd fallen in love with Max. And once again she'd placed
her trust—and her heart—in the hands of the wrong man.
Would she never learn?

The crunch of Max's car tires on the gravel drive had
her adrenaline kicking in. She jumped out of the chair and
rushed to the window in time to see him back out of the
drive, leaving her own snow-covered car behind. Thank
God she'd held on to her rental, otherwise she'd be stuck.
Heart thudding, she turned her attention to packing. Fortunately she didn't have much beyond the outfits she'd

brought for her overnight New York stay and the few essentials she'd picked up over the past month, an extra pair of jeans and some toiletry products. The fancy shoes from Saks, including her Cinderella slippers, took up most of the space in her suitcase. Picking out one of the pair, she zipped up her suitcase and headed downstairs to Max's study.

He'd left his notepad by the computer. Tears welling, she bent over to write her farewell note.

Max,
Congratulations on the screenplay deal. Just so you know, you don't have to bother getting your agent to work any behind-the-scenes deals to cut me out. I'm cutting myself out. I never want to work with you again. I never want to see you again—period.
    If the shoe fits…
Becky

Becky backed out of the room, leaving the note and the high-heeled red slipper on Max's chair.

13

Angelina strapped on her helmet and zipped the front of her Belstaff jacket before mounting her bike—a 1974 Ducati Imola 750 she'd picked up the day before. The vintage bike was her reward for another mission accomplished. It hadn't been easy but she and Drake had reclaimed the rocket plans and gotten out of Toro Toro amidst heavy enemy fire and copious explosions. The papers now resided in a vault in an undisclosed and highly secure government location.

She swung her leg over the side of the bike and revved the engine. It roared to life and seconds later she was zipping through the winding Venetian streets, long black hair lashing the arid Italian air like a dragon's tail. Only, instead of contemplating her next erotic encounter and mystery-solving adventure, she found herself wondering about Drake. Where was he? Did he ever think of her?

Was he…happy?

WRONG, wrong, wrong!

Becky stared at her laptop screen through bleary eyes. She'd rewritten the first fifty pages of her new book so many times over the past month, she felt as if she'd come full circle. No matter which version of the manuscript she picked up, the prose was the pits. Falling in love had softened Angelina so that she'd lost her edge. Instead of planning her next solo adventure, she was preoccupied with missing Drake. It was pathetic.

Exhausted as she was, Becky had to get out of the apartment, if only for a little while. Maybe a jolt of caffeine would help. "I'm out of here," she said to no one in particular.

"Well, if you're going to mope, then good riddance."

She swung around to find Angelina perched on the edge of her kitchen counter, long legs tucked beneath her. Wearing an oversized cashmere sweater with Diesel Super Slim stretch jeans, she was her usual fashion-forward self down to her Manolo leopard-print pumps. Still, something seemed different…missing.

"Who's moping? I was just going out for a walk." Even though she had one foot out the door, she slipped back into her computer chair. They hadn't had a creator-character heart-to-heart in a very long time. Judging from her muse's pout, Becky had been neglecting her, among other things. "How have you been, by the way?"

Angelina put on her game face and smiled. "I'm brilliant, absolutely brilliant. Where are you sending me on my next adventure, by the way?"

"Honestly I have no idea," Becky answered.

The pisser was she really didn't. She was burned out on planning exotic adventures for fictional characters. "Any place in particular you'd like to go?"

Angelina let out a sigh. "I'm bored to death of Italy, France and England, and the Greek Isles have been done to death. I used to have a fancy for Malta but...I don't bloody care, Rebecca. You decide."

Uh-oh. Angelina not having an opinion was a huge red flag that something must be really wrong. Becky gave her creation the once-over, struck by how much Angelina had altered in one month. Her upswept eyes looked more muddy than jade, there were dark, puffy circles beneath, and her waist-length hair lacked its usual luster. Becky recognized this as the face of a woman who'd come out on the wrong side of love.

"If you'll pardon my saying so, you don't look so good. You're missing Drake, aren't you?"

Angelina snapped up her head, but this once her curtain of hair failed to fall back perfectly around her shoulders. "Don't be absurd, Rebecca. You're the one who's pining, not me."

"Is that so? There's no point in trying to pull the wool over my eyes. I created you, remember?" If you couldn't have a frank talk with your own fictional creation, what was the world coming to?

The corners of Angelina's sensuous mouth dipped down. "Why did you do it, Rebecca?"

"Why did I do what?"

"Ruin everything by giving me a soul." Angelina tossed Becky an exasperated look. "Bugger! Things were good for us before Drake and Max came on the scene. We were free to come and go as we pleased, we could shop until we dropped, come in at any hour of the day or night, sleep with anyone we fancied—well, *I* could, at least. But no, you had to tinker with perfection. You had to open Pandora's bloody Box and introduce soul mates into our lives, and now look what we've come to."

Becky hesitated. "Do you really think Max and Drake are our soul mates?"

Angelina lifted one perfectly-plucked eyebrow and regarded her. "You ought to know the answer to that, Rebecca. After all, you wrote the book."

I WROTE the book, I wrote the book, I wrote...

The butting against the top of her head brought Becky out of the dream. It took several seconds before she realized she must have fallen asleep at her computer. She lifted her head from her folded arms and looked straight into Daisy Bud's amber-colored eyes. From her perch atop Becky's computer cart, the cat leaned in and nuzzled her neck.

Becky reached out and scratched the cute little white spot beneath Daisy's chin. "Sometimes I wish you could talk—people talk, I mean. The whole spaying incident aside, I bet you'd be a pretty damn good relationship advisor. You always manage to get exactly what you want out of me while giving back so much more."

Back in D.C. and with Sharon gone home to Fredericksburg, Becky ought to be a lean mean *writing* machine. Instead she'd found it really hard to focus. She couldn't seem to get Max out of her mind. The other day, she'd had the radio on when the DJ had played Billy Joel's "New York State of Mind." She'd thrown it into the nearest wall and cried for a solid hour.

From a career standpoint, though, everything seemed to be working out for the best. Thrilled with the coauthored book, Pat had offered her a contract for a spin-off series on far better terms than anything she'd had previously. Provided she could meet the demanding deadline schedule—and without Max in her life, what else did she have to do but write?—Becky would be a guaranteed best-seller in her own right. She wouldn't need Adam Maxwell any more than he apparently needed her.

The problem was she'd liked having a partner, or rather, having Max for a partner. Working on the next Angelina book without him and his character was turning out to be hell on wheels. No matter how hard she tried coming up with a new love interest for her heroine, she simply couldn't create one who was Drake's equal. No matter whether the hero in her book was blond or dark haired or blue eyed or brown, in her mind's eye he was always Drake in disguise—and that meant he was *always* Max.

Padding into the kitchen, she poured kibble into Daisy's bowl and considered fueling up, too, starting with coffee. Her Starbucks fix was obviously overdue.

She went into her bedroom, changed into better clothes and tidied her hair. Still thinking about the dream, she stuck twenty dollars and her key in her jeans pocket and headed out into the hallway. In the past she'd used Angelina as a means to experience life at arm's length without having to dive in and really live it. She'd let her creation have all the adventures, all the fun that she was too chicken to go after. Maybe it was high time she cast herself as the leading lady, the heroine, of her very real life.

One of the first things she'd done after coming back from New Hampshire was to dig out her Christmas wish list: Become bestselling author. Take trip to Ireland. Go on motorcycle ride. Go to animal shelter and find feline friend for cat. Save up down payment for house. Meet man of dreams and fall in love…"

She supposed she could cross the last one off her list.

She'd met and fallen in love with Max. Too bad she'd forgotten to stipulate that he be trustworthy. She couldn't do much about that, but she had made some progress on the other items on her list. The other day she'd set up a meeting with a travel agent to book a trip to Ireland for June. She'd started saving in earnest, including putting herself on a shoe diet. Not that she regretted splurging on her red satin "Cinderella slippers" for even a minute. The shoe she'd kept resided in its Saks box at the back of her closet. She wondered what Max had done with the one she'd left behind. Thrown it out, she supposed. The thought not only depressed her, it made her heart hurt.

Becky took the hall elevator down to the lobby and exited through the double glass doors of the main entrance. The first person she saw when she stepped outside was the college kid who delivered her Thai food on Friday nights. Since she'd seen him last, he'd toned down his dyed ink-black hair to a more natural nut-brown and pared his body piercing ensemble to a single safety pin stuck through his left eyebrow. Goth-style aside, he'd always struck her as a decent, hardworking kid. He stood on the apartment pull-up next to a parked motorcycle talking to a pretty blonde. They each wore thick, black leather biker jackets and had helmets tucked beneath one arm. Judging from the silly smile on his face, he liked this girl a lot. Becky bet she could slip by without him even seeing her.

She started walking when the glimmer of sunlight striking chrome stopped her in her tracks. *Go on motorcycle ride.* The hulking Harley seemed like her modern-day equivalent of a knight in shining armor's white horse.

Becky had never been on a motorcycle in her life, not the vintage Italian one Angelina favored or the kid's

Harley. Like her knowledge of foreign countries, the little she knew about bikes came from the Internet or books, not firsthand experience. Maybe, just maybe, it was time to change that.

Chalking up her courage, she turned back and walked up to the edge of the sidewalk. The couple stopped talking and stared at her as though she was a creature newly landed from outer space, which was about how she felt—odd, out of step, and yes, old.

"You probably don't remember me, but I live here in apartment 812." She jerked a hand to indicate the highrise behind her. "You deliver my Thai food."

The kid pulled his gaze away from his girlfriend. "Sure I remember you—shrimp pad thai and a side of tod mun."

God, I am so predictable. Her delivery order struck her as a metaphor for everything wrong with her life.

"Yeah, right, that's me." She really ought to move on, but she couldn't, not yet anyway. "Is that bike yours?"

As conversation starters went, hers was pretty poor. Obviously the bike belonged to him. Why else would he be standing next to it wearing full gear? Duh!

"Yeah, I just bought it. I've been saving for a couple of years now."

So that's where her five-dollar tips had gone. Well, at least he'd had a goal and the determination to make it happen. Good for him.

She looked from the kid to the bike and back at him, her heartbeat kicked up to a rapid fire pace. "I know this may come off as a weird request, but what would you say to giving me a ride on the back of your bike?"

His eyes widened. "Seriously?"

She answered with a jerky nod. "Seriously." She'd apparently already lost her mind, but she hoped he'd say yes before she lost her nerve, too.

He exchanged glances with the girl and then turned back to Becky, expression sheepish. "I don't know. We're supposed to catch the matinee of *Lawrence of Arabia* at the Uptown."

The girlfriend chimed in with, "The actual one with Peter O'Toole—back when he was really hot," she added.

In the midst of her nervousness, Becky felt the corners of her mouth kick up. As far as she knew, there'd been no remake of the classic 1962 epic film. Impressive, though, that they even knew who Peter O'Toole was, let alone were setting aside a Saturday to hang out at a refurbished Art Deco movie theater. She was liking these kids more by the minute.

Remembering the twenty she'd stuck in her pocket to pay for coffee, she said, "What would you say to twenty bucks for one ride around the block?"

The boy's eyes popped. "Are you serious?"

"Totally."

He looked over at his girlfriend and asked, "Mind?"

She shrugged her narrow shoulders. "It's no big deal. We can always catch the last show."

He swung his head back to Becky. "You're on."

He introduced himself as Nathan and the blonde as Lisa. Lisa let her borrow her helmet and gave her a few pointers about balancing on the bike. "When he turns the corner, lean in, don't jerk back. He won't go fast but you should borrow my jacket, too, just in case. You never know what kind of shit—I mean stuff—will fly up from the road."

Heart racing, Becky slid her arms through the sun-warmed leather and strapped the helmet onto her head. Stepping back, she divided her gaze between them and asked, "How do I look?"

Strokes of Midnight

It was a stupid question with an obvious answer. Thinking back to when she'd been their age, she remembered how anyone over thirty had qualified as, if not exactly ancient, certainly solidly middle-aged. So much for thirty being the new twenty....

Nathan surprised her by giving her a thumbs-up. "You look really good, Miss Stone."

"Hot," his girlfriend added, and Becky suddenly felt a warm, confident feeling override her nervousness.

"In that case, let's rock 'n' roll." She mounted the bike behind him, swinging her leg over the seat in one fluid motion that would have done even Angelina proud.

"Hold on tight, Miss Stone."

She wrapped her arms around the kid's slender waist and leaned ever so slightly in. He revved the engine and they took off, Springsteen's "Born to Run" rocking inside Becky's head.

A HALF HOUR later, Becky walked back inside her apartment with windblown hair and chapped cheeks. The motorcycle ride around the block had been so exhilarating she'd cajoled Nathan into taking her around a second time. She doubted she was in danger of becoming a biker babe anytime soon—glancing into the bathroom mirror, she decided the whole helmet-head scenario was probably a deal buster—but daring to try something she'd always secretly wanted to do felt like a step in the right direction. Even if it was only a baby step, it was a step forward all the same.

She was pulling her hair back into a ponytail when the phone rang. Ordinarily she screened her daytime calls so as not to break her train of thought when she was writing, but she hadn't gotten back to work yet. Still buzzing from her recent adventure, she hoped the caller was Sharon. Her friend had decided to stay in Fredericksburg for the time being, a development Becky suspected had to do with an upswing in her romance with a certain sexy detective.

Instead of Sharon on the phone it was Pat. Becky felt her glow fading. She hadn't spoken to Pat since she'd overheard the phone conversation between Max and his agent. Ordinarily her editor preferred communicating any editorial changes by e-mail unless there was something substantive to discuss.

"Becky, it's Pat. I have some fabulous news for you."

Well, at least this time a phone call really did mean something positive. Relaxing, Becky said, "That's great. What is it?" She held her breath, half hoping Pat's "fabulous news" had something to do with Max.

Indeed it did. "I just got the call from Harry Goldblatt. His coagent out in L.A., the one who handles film rights, called to say that Spielberg picked up a three-year option on your and Max's book. We're not talking a TV movie of the week but a major motion picture. The news is all very hush-hush for now, though, so don't tell anyone, not even your mother. We want to make the announcement at the book launch party."

Having overheard Max on the phone with his agent, the news didn't come as a complete surprise. Still, Becky felt overwhelmed. "Back up and tell me what book launch party?"

"It's two weeks from today. Publicity's booked the Rainbow Room at Rockefeller Center. Everything's going to be first-class all the way. Everyone who's anyone in publishing will be there, including the media."

Becky hesitated. "That sounds great but I...I don't think I can make it."

"Why the hell not?"

She seized on the one excuse every editor should respect. "I have a deadline, remember?"

"Consider yourself granted a week's extension—two weeks if you need it."

"My, er...pet sitter is going to be out of town. I don't have anyone I can trust to take care of Daisy Bud."

That wasn't exactly true. Daisy would be fine at the boarding kennel at the vet's as long as the stay didn't extend beyond a few days. But hard-bitten New York editor that she was, Pat was also a huge animal lover. She had a pair of standard poodles, a cockatoo and a tank of tropical fish all crammed into her midtown west one-bedroom.

"So board her or ask a neighbor to look in on her. We're talking one day away, two days tops. She'll be okay."

Back to the proverbial wall, she fished, "I guess Max will be there?"

Pathetic, Becky, really bad. Pat worked for a publishing house, not a dating service. Manuscripts were her business, not matching lonely hearts.

"Now we're getting down to it."

She'd wondered how much Pat knew about her and Max's personal relationship, and her editor's tone alone answered that question. She must know everything more or less.

"What has he said to you? I mean it, Pat, I want to know."

"To me, he hasn't said a word. Other than e-mail, I haven't spoken to him in a month. He's apparently back in hermit mode, though Harry's sworn on a stack of Bibles that he'll be there for the party."

Max. How could she possibly face him, let alone face him in front of a roomful of members of the publishing elite, reviewers and camera-popping paparazzi? Even after a month apart, the memory of the very Elliot-like way he'd betrayed her still really hurt.

Pat wasn't taking no for an answer. She spent the next few minutes doing her usual sales job, citing all the good publicity Becky going to the party would bring and finally making it clear Becky didn't have a choice—again.

"Cheer up, kid. This is your big break. The kind of break most writers only ever dream about. You've worked too long and too hard to blow it now because some macho male writer made you cry."

As much as she hated to admit it, Pat was right. She was acting like an infant. If anyone should feel embarrassed about showing his face, it was Max, not her. She hadn't done anything wrong. She had no reason to hide.

And yet, when she clicked off the cordless and replaced it in the phone cradle, the irony of her situation hit her like a pie in the face. Her big break had finally come around— and wouldn't you know it, the only thing she felt breaking was her heart.

14

"Mind you don't move so much as a muscle, Falco, or I'll blow your bloody head off."

With her nemesis caught in her rifle's crosshairs, Angelina found herself missing Drake, not only his weapon backing her up but his warm blue eyes and sexy smile. Even when you were an internationally sought-after sleuth turned secret government agent, life worked better with a partner.

Hands in the air, Falco advanced, more than six feet of trained-killer male sheathed in a black Ducati leather jacket and matching chaps. It had been almost a year since she'd lured him back to her hotel room, seduced him and tied him up, all to get him to give up the whereabouts of the stolen missile plans. Now that she and Drake had recovered them, she was free to act on her own behalf. Encountering him out of the blue in a pub in London's Haymarket theater district was a dazzling opportunity she didn't mean to waste.

Smile cocky, Falco dropped his hands and edged menacingly closer. "Angelina, love, you're bluffing—again. You wouldn't harm me, not after that amazing night we spent in Chelsea."

"Is that so?" Angelina pulled back on the trigger—
and blew the bastard to kingdom come.

BECKY CAUGHT an early train from Washington's Union
Station to New York on the morning of the party. Once
there, she treated herself to a nice lunch, a strictly neces-
sary pilgrimage to Saks for a kick-ass dress and finally a
soothing massage in the hotel day spa.

The Chelsea was booked when she called to make her
reservation, which was probably for the best. As much as
she loved the place, she wasn't sure she was ready to go
back just yet. Besides, Max was probably staying there in
his usual suite. It was hard enough knowing she'd be
seeing him later that night. Bumping into him in the lobby
or, worse still, the lounge, didn't feel like something she
wanted to sign up for just now.

Instead she booked a single room in the Hilton on
Avenue of the Americas. Though she generally didn't like
big hotels, she couldn't fault the location. The hotel was
within easy walking distance of Rockefeller Center where
that night's book launch gala would be held.

She had a few hours to kill before she needed to get
ready and as badly as she wanted a pre-event glass of wine
to calm her nerves, she also wanted a walk. It was spring
and springtime in New York wasn't to be missed. And yet
when she stepped out the front of her hotel, she couldn't
bring herself to start down Avenue of the Americas where
she'd literally run into Max. She thought his agent had an
office somewhere close by. Either way, she didn't think she
could handle any more "coincidental" meetings. So far her
horoscope predictions from January had both come true.
She had indeed gotten more than her share of "fresh starts"

and "dazzling opportunities." What she hadn't gotten was a happy ending, at least not when it came to love.

So she headed around the corner and cut down to Seventh Avenue on the outskirts of the Theater District. Rosie O'Grady's was a steak and seafood house in the tradition of the venerable turn-of-the-century New York saloons. On weekdays the street-level bar was a popular watering hole, drawing patrons from the after-work office crowd, as well as tourists from the nearby hotels. If she were lucky maybe she could snag a table to herself and get not only a glass of wine but a snack, too.

She walked inside and bypassed the hostess stand for the bar—and found herself staring straight ahead at the tall silver-haired man who'd once broken her heart. Elliot. What the hell was he doing in an Irish bar in midtown Manhattan? Sure, he came to New York from time to time, but the trendier bars in the Village or Alphabet City were more his style. Hoping he hadn't seen her, or that if he had he would stick to treating her as though she was invisible, she whipped around and headed for the door.

"Becky. Becky Stone!"

The slightly husky voice she remembered all too well stopped her in her tracks. Bracing herself to face him, Becky turned around.

He left his buddies at the bar and sauntered over to her. "Becky, I thought that was you. You look…you look amazing."

He slid his gaze slowly over her, taking in every detail, missing nothing. If she had any thoughts his remark might be empty flattery, the open admiration in his deep-set dark eyes confirmed it. She must look pretty damn good—make that *amazing*.

The last time she'd been alone with him, he'd left her wrapped in a bath towel, a sex flush and a cocoon of false hope. But then the universe had a funny way of seeing that loose ends were tied up, or so it suddenly seemed. She'd imagined this moment so many times, prayed for it even, and now that it had materialized, instead of facing him weak-kneed and stammering, she was able to lift her chin and meet his gaze head-on.

"Thanks, Elliot. You look good, too."

Tall, broad-shouldered and prematurely gray, he was more or less his same handsome self. Staring up at him, all macho self-confidence and cool, practiced smile, she realized he didn't have nearly the effect on her he'd once had. Instead she found herself studying him with a critical eye. The bridge of his nose was wide, really wide. Funny how she'd never noticed before. It was such a prominent feature. And the lines on his forehead were more deeply chiseled than she remembered, or maybe they'd always been that deep and she'd overlooked them until now. And how was it possible that she could have missed the cruel curve to his mouth or the soulless vacancy to his deep-set brown eyes? A year ago that tall, broad-shouldered body had driven her crazy, but now he struck her as too thin, borderline gaunt. And she remembered that he waxed his chest. When they'd been together, she'd written off the practice as an L.A. thing, but now it struck her as really vain.

"I was just having a drink with some friends from the studio." He gestured over his shoulder to the handful of men who, like him, wore designer dark suits and silk ties. Turning back to her, he said, "Why don't you join us? I'll introduce you to some people."

Amazing how he hadn't bothered to speak to her the last time he'd seen her in public but now that they'd met again by chance and he happened to be dateless he seemed to have all the time in the world.

She shook her head. "I can't. I have to get ready for an event—a launch party for my new book, actually."

Rather than congratulate her or ask what she was working on these days, he said, "That's too bad. We could have had dinner and relived old times."

Even at the height of her hormone haze, she'd recognized he had a supersized ego, but now she sensed his behavior bordered on narcissism. Still, she couldn't really regret the six months she'd spent under his spell. Yes, he'd hurt her, deeply and profoundly, deliberately and cruelly, but looking at him now she suddenly understood that his hurting her was part of the gift. It had freed her to love someone else, the *right* someone else. Because of him, she'd been free to love Max.

Max. Finding herself face-to-face with Elliot brought the contrast between the two men into even sharper relief. Whereas Elliot was all about himself, Max was more interested in hearing about other people. Unlike so many writers at his level, he rarely if ever let his ego get in the way of the work. He was so low-key about publicity, he'd gotten a reputation in the publishing world as a hermit, whereas Elliot loved the camera entirely too much.

The more she thought of it, the harder it was to believe Max had betrayed her. Thinking back to the phone conversation she'd overheard, she tried telling herself she was only making excuses for a man's bad behavior once again but something just didn't...well, it just didn't *feel* right. Now that she'd started trusting her intuition again, she couldn't dismiss the sense of unease. Even with the damning dialogue echoing in her ears, running off had been a big mistake. Until she confronted him, she'd never have closure. Fortunately, tonight's book launch party would provide her with the chance to get to the heart of the matter once and for all. It was time for Cinderella to stand tall and dig in her heels rather than run away.

Elliot's lowered voice pulled her back to the present. "I feel really badly about how things ended between us." Leaning closer, he confided, "I must have written you a dozen e-mails I never sent."

Uh-huh. Sure you did. She must have honed her judgment over the past year because her ex struck her as transparent as glass. Were she to meet him as a stranger again, she didn't think she'd be so easily taken in.

She shrugged, sensing a huge weight had been lifted from her shoulders. "Don't worry about it, Elliot. Looking back, I figure you did me a favor."

He'd never made her happy, not really, and now he'd lost the power to make her miserable ever again. Looking up at him with eyes wide open, she saw him for what he was, just another player with a fake smile and a smooth pickup line—and a hollow heart.

If she hadn't seen him with the twentysomething in D.C., she might still be on the hook waiting for him to call, making plans she knew in her heart he wouldn't keep, darting gazes around a party wondering if he hadn't found someone younger or prettier or both to sneak off with. That was no way to live. It wasn't living at all. Remembering how much of her energy that relationship had drained, she could appreciate her time with Max. With Max, she'd always felt energized and upbeat and good about herself on all levels.

His tense look relaxed, and he flashed his signature smile, the one she'd once found so irresistibly sexy but which now struck her as smarmy. "I'm coming into D.C. later this month. Maybe we could get together for dinner or…something."

Becky wasn't even tempted. "Thanks, Elliot, but no thanks. You take care of yourself, though." She reached out and patted his arm as though he were a puppy.

Leaving him staring after her, she turned and walked out of the restaurant, a spring in her step. The smile breaking over her face barely waited for her to clear the threshold. Grinning from ear to ear, or at least that's what it felt like, she walked back up Seventh toward her hotel. She did indeed have a publishing party to attend—and unfinished business with Max to settle once and for all.

FEELING LIKE a reluctant Cinderella, Becky stepped off the elevator to the Rainbow Room later that night, her new hair and evening gown props to set the scene and cover her nervousness. She'd chosen the floor-length chocolate taffeta halter dress with care and, she realized, Max in mind. Looking into the Saks dressing-room mirror earlier that day, she'd thought the rich shade worked well with her hair and eyes. Usually she shied away from wearing long dresses, feeling that they made her look even shorter, but in this case the straight skirt with its flared hem flattered her petite figure by giving her a longer, leaner line while the deep V-neckline and knotted front made the most of her small breasts. And of course, she had on a killer pair of satin-covered Manolos and carried a beaded Kate Spade evening bag to set the whole thing off.

She surrendered her wrap to the girl working coat check and then followed piano music down the corridor to the event room. The pianist wouldn't be Max this time, but regardless she hoped he wouldn't play "New York State of Mind."

Located on the sixty-fifth floor of 30 Rockefeller Plaza, the landmark restaurant and nightclub had been the premier venue for posh Manhattan social functions since the 1930s. But it wasn't the crystal-cut Art Deco chandelier crowning the high ceiling, the revolving dance floor or the spectacular multicolored lighting engineered to produce a rainbow effect that had Becky catching her breath. It was the view. Floor-to-ceiling windows provided a peerless panorama of the Manhattan skyline. A quick look around was all it took for her to spot several landmarks—the distinctive spire of the Met Life building, the Empire State building, the large green patch that was Central Park—and Max.

Backlit by the setting sun, he stood beside one of several easels bearing a poster-size blowup of their book cover, looking more like a model for *GQ* magazine than an author, even a bestselling one. His black tuxedo fit his broad shoulders and tall, lean body as though it was painted on, and he'd let his dark gold hair grow to brush the back of his collar.

The telltale flicker of his brow confirmed she'd caught his eye, too. His gaze met hers and Becky found herself drowning once more in that deep blue soulful sea. There was no looking away, no moving out of his field of vision. Suddenly it was as if they were the only two people in the room, the world, and she realized she wouldn't have it any other way.

He shifted his attention back to his conversation companion, a pretty twentysomething redhead in a tulle-skirted black cocktail dress that Becky recognized as a Vera Wang, and her heart dropped to the floor like Universal Studio's Tower of Terror amusement park ride.

God, I am such a fool. On second thought, better make that twice a fool.

Running into Elliot that afternoon had shown her how many times stronger her feelings were for Max. Elliot hadn't broken her heart so much as bruised her pride. Seeing him from the perspective of more than a year apart, she realized she hadn't loved him any more than he'd loved her. Sure, she'd been infatuated with him, but never once in the short time she'd spent with him had she felt so much as a flicker of the flaming passion and soul-deep connection she'd known with Max.

But you could only hold on for so long. She ventured another glance across the room to Max, yet another relationship she needed to release if she wanted to move forward with her life.

Pat hailed her from halfway across the room. "Becky, there you are." Wearing a beaded, black, long-sleeved top and skirt, the older woman sallied up beside her and opened her arms for a hug. "I was beginning to wonder if maybe you weren't coming."

Becky returned the greeting, relieved she wouldn't have to walk in alone after all. Stepping back, she shot her editor a wink. "What? And ignore a direct order from my commander-in-chief?"

For the first time in their five-year association, Becky saw the older woman blush. "Well, it wasn't an order, not exactly. More like a strongly worded suggestion."

"So said Mussolini." Becky accepted a glass of champagne from one of the circulating servers. "At any rate, I'm here now. And by the way, I absolutely love the cover. The folks in the art department went all-out again."

"Everyone got the word from on high that this project

was to be first-class all the way." Pat hesitated, biting her bottom lip. "Max was pleased, as well."

"Was he?" One eye on her coauthor, Becky couldn't resist asking, "Who is the red-haired woman he's talking to?"

Pat glanced their way. "That's Lydia Evans, the in-house publicist assigned to this project. She planned this fabulous event, and she'll be working closely with you and Max on the post-launch promo."

So the redhead wasn't Max's date. That was a weight off her mind but hearing Pat speak of her and Max as though they were partners still brought a stab of pain. She didn't want to be just his writing partner or for that matter, his casual lover for one night or one month. She wanted him for keeps. And yet knowing how he'd sold her out, how could she possibly trust him with her heart?

"I see. Well, she's done a great job."

Pat swept a satisfied look over the packed room. "We're counting on tonight to really build the industry buzz. Once the book hits the shelves, there are several publicity spikes planned, including a national book tour."

Becky choked on the sip of champagne she'd just taken. "You're sending me and Max on tour together?"

As if taking her gratitude for granted, Pat beamed. "It was supposed to be a surprise, but, well, I hate surprises, especially when it means I'm the one who has to hold back the secret. Yes, there's a month-long tour in the works but don't thank me. Thank Lydia. She set the whole thing up. Ten major U.S. cities with book signings and cable television and radio spots and well…why don't I just introduce you and let her go over it all?"

Becky panicked. Meeting Lydia meant coming face-to-face with Max, and for that she needed to work up her courage. "That's okay. They're obviously in the middle of a conversation. I'll meet her later."

Pat took hold of her by the elbow. "Don't be silly. Any conversation they're having might as well include you. It'll save Lydia from having to repeat all the plans to you later."

Becky started to protest but Pat was already steering her through the packed room toward Max. For someone who claimed she was allergic to working out, the older woman's grip was like iron.

She didn't let go until she delivered Becky to them. "Sorry to interrupt, kids, but look who I found."

Max shifted his gaze from the publicist to Becky. "Who, indeed."

Praying her voice would hold steady, she said, "Hi, Max."

He nodded. "Becky."

Their eyes met, melded. Memories flooded her—the scent of his skin, which always reminded her of the beach, the warmth of his hand shaping her hip as though he were smoothing away her every care in the world, the deep, low groan he gave just before he came.

Though it had only been a month since she'd seen him last, she found herself marking slight but noticeable changes. He certainly didn't look like a man gloating over cutting his partner out of a major contract deal. He looked thinner than she remembered. It wasn't a dramatic difference, but she suspected he'd dropped a good five to seven pounds. For a fleeting moment, she dared hope the weight loss meant he was missing her, but that was crazy. Even if he did miss her, a pretty big if, men didn't pine the way women did. She, on the other hand, had dropped a dress size, a fact discovered when she'd been trying on evening gowns in the dressing room of Saks earlier that day. That first week back in D.C., she'd barely been able to choke down a frozen entrée.

Becky held out her hand, alarmed to see it shaking ever so slightly. "Lydia, it's very nice to meet you. You've done a wonderful job with the event. Everything is lovely." She gestured toward the ice sculptures meant to represent Drake and Angelina, the cloth-covered food stations, the waitstaff butlering champagne and canapés.

"Thank you, Miss Stone. I am so incredibly thrilled to be working on this project. My mom is a huge fan of yours. She must own every one of your paperback Regencies, even the out-of-print copies."

Catching the flicker of amusement in Max's eyes, the first warmth she'd felt from him since she walked up, Becky bit her lip. "That's…very flattering."

Small talk, mostly centered on the upcoming events, made the circle. A tuxedo-clad server stopped by with a tray of champagne glasses and even though she suspected alcohol was the last thing she needed at the moment, Becky exchanged her half-empty glass for a fresh one.

Pat laid a light hand on Lydia's arm. "If you'll excuse us, there are some people I'd like Lydia to meet."

"Of course," Max said, and even though Becky knew she had no claim on him, never had and never would, she couldn't help feeling gratified that he didn't seem to give the redhead so much as a goodbye glance.

Left alone with Becky for the moment, Max raked his gaze over her. "Good dress."

His frank appreciation had her blushing from scalp to collarbone, but for the sake of her pride, she wouldn't allow herself to look down or away—not even to follow his eyes, which seemed to be devouring her.

"Thank you."

"You're welcome." His gaze came back to her face. He sent her a long, lingering look. "When you first walked in, it took me a moment to recognize you—and once I did, you took my breath away. You cut your hair."

"Just this afternoon." Self-conscious, she reached back and touched the back, which came just below her nape. "I'm still getting used to it."

The stylist had cut it in graduated layers, leaving the front longer to frame her face. Walking back to the hotel after running into Elliot, she'd realized that not only was she over him but she had been for some time. Since she'd met Max, she'd thought of Elliot rarely, if at all. Such a momentous epiphany deserved some sort of celebration, or at least an outward sign to commemorate the change.

"You look beautiful, but then you always do." Before she could step away, he touched the side of his hand to her cheek.

The caress was Becky's undoing. "Don't." She backed up a step, nearly knocking into an older gentleman she recognized as a book reviewer for *Publishers Weekly*. "Pardon me." Turning back to Max, she shook her head, tears welling. "Damn you, Max. I thought I could do this, but I can't." She turned to go.

Strong fingers banded her wrist, the warm hold she remembered all too well anchoring her in place. "Becka, don't. Don't disappear on me, not again, not before we've had a chance to talk."

Having him call her by the special name he'd given her was nearly her undoing. She felt the press of tears at the backs of her eyes and a telltale lump lodging in her throat.

This wasn't fair, this wasn't right. How could he stand there staring at her with wounded eyes as though she were hurting him when he was the one who'd done all the hurting?

She wrenched away. "I didn't disappear. I left you a note, remember?"

He snorted but his expression was pained. "A short note saying I'd sold you out, I couldn't be trusted and you never wanted to see me again? You call that closure?"

"Well, you can't be trusted—can you?"

"There's only one way to find out. Let's get the hell out of here." He took hold of her hand again, lacing his fingers through hers, and this time she didn't think he'd be letting go so easily.

Before she could answer, a pale-faced young man stepped forward and introduced himself as a photographer with the *New York Times*. "I want to get a photo of the two of you for the book section. Can you stand by the cover poster?" Lifting the camera dangling from the strap around his neck, he gestured them over to the blowup on the easel.

The dreaded publicity photo op had reared its ugly head. It seemed there was no escaping. Could this evening get any harder? Becky had no choice but to take her place at Max's side and smile for the camera.

The photographer took several shots, promised them each copies and then faded into the crowd. Max swung around to Becky. "We need to talk, but first I'm getting you the hell out of here."

Plate piled high with canapés, Pat pounced on them. "Did I hear you say you were leaving?"

Max answered for them both. "Yes."

"But you're coming back, right? I mean, you're just stepping out for a cigarette or…or something."

Max shot their editor a bland look belied by the fire in his eyes. "I quit smoking years ago."

It was Becky's turn to speak up. "I'm afraid we're calling it a night. At least I am."

Pat divided her horrified gaze between them. "But you can't leave. You just got here. You're the guests of honor!"

Becky spoke up, "And it's been a lovely party. Please tell Lydia again how much we appreciate all the trouble she's gone to. We'll be in touch."

His palm pressed to the small of her back, Max steered Becky through the crowd toward the exit. Several guests stepped into their path to offer congratulations but beyond an obligatory smile and a handshake, Max kept them on course. Out in the hallway, he tipped the attendant to retrieve Becky's wrap, slipped it around her shoulders and headed for the bank of exit elevators.

The elevator opened at once, no common occurrence in a building that boasted sixty-seven stories. Max let go of her hand and stepped back. "After you."

She hesitated and then stepped inside. Max walked on behind her. The elevator doors closed, cutting them off from the world beyond. Fixing her gaze on the display above their heads, she watched the numbers fall, reminded of that magical night at the Chelsea when they'd stood arm in arm in the hotel elevator, impatient to reach Max's rooftop suite so they could continue making love.

Turning to Max, Becky swallowed hard. "You'd better talk fast. We just passed thirty-two."

Yanking his bowtie loose, he said, "Sounds like a lucky number to me." He reached across her to the control panel and hit the emergency button. The elevator jolted to a stop.

Unable to believe what she'd just seen, Becky whirled

on him. "Have you lost your mind? The security guards will think terrorists have taken over the building."

He shrugged. "If spending the night in a police lockup is the only way I can get you to listen to me, then I'll make the sacrifice."

She shook her head, suddenly weary of everything that should be easy turning out to be so very hard. "If you're not crazy, then you must be drunk."

His clear-eyed gaze met hers, and she saw he wasn't intoxicated, just determined. "I'm not drunk. I only had one Scotch, half of which I just left behind. As for the crazy part, you bet I'm crazy—crazy about you."

She fisted her hands on her hips, dug in her high heels, and glared up at him. "Were you so crazy about me when you sold me out for the script-writing deal? Don't bother denying it. I heard you talking on the phone to your agent."

Max stared at her for a long moment, and then he tossed back his head and laughed.

"What's so funny?"

Swiping the back of his hand across watery eyes, he shook his head. "Didn't your mother ever warn you that people who eavesdrop never hear any good?"

Leave it to a man to put you on the defensive when he was the one in the wrong. "I wasn't eavesdropping. The phone rang right beside my bed and I reached for it. I wasn't sure you were even in the house until I heard your voice on the line. It was dumb luck that I heard you congratulating your agent on cutting me out of the screenplay deal."

"Too bad you didn't stick around to hear the rest of it."

"The rest of what?" A sinking sensation that had nothing to do with the elevator ride hit her full force.

"The part where I told him that unless the deal was rewritten to include you as coauthor, there was no deal."

Becky shook her head, which spun as though she'd downed a whole bottle of champagne instead of a few measly sips. "Is that the truth?"

Max moved closer. "The whole truth and nothing but."

As much as she ached to throw herself against him, to lock lips with him and feel his strong arms wrap around her, she held her ground and kept her distance. The physical chemistry they shared was nothing short of amazing, but this was too important an issue to be swept aside because of surging hormones. She needed more from a partner and more from herself than great sex alone. She also needed mutual trust and understanding and respect—and above all, true love.

For once in her life, this once, she wasn't willing to settle.

She took a small backward step, eyes looking up into his. "How can I be sure you're not just telling me what you think I want to hear? When I asked who'd called, you lied and told me it was a telemarketer."

"I was trying to protect you. I didn't want your feelings to get hurt or for you to start doubting your talent." Max laid his hands atop her shoulders. "That was wrong of me, I see that now, but what I said about the screenplay stands. I'll call Harry in the morning and have him send you a copy of the contract so you can read it for yourself. You'll be getting one anyway. For the deal to go through, two signatures are required—yours and mine."

"W-why would you do that?"

He shook his head, his gaze melting. "Drake really misses Angelina."

"He does?"

"Uh-huh. He's been living on microwave dinners and self-pity for a solid month now, and it's getting really old. What about you?"

"Angelina's miserable, too. She hasn't cleaned her revolver in a month and the last time she dropped in, her shoes were looking really scuffed."

"That does sound serious. Do you think there's any chance of those two ever getting back together?"

"I think there might be if…"

"If?" His eyes pierced hers.

"If Angelina thought Drake really loved her, I think she'd come around pretty quickly."

"He does love her, Becka. He loves her with his whole heart. In fact, she's the only woman in the world for him." Smile gentle, Max lifted her chin with the edge of his hand. "I've come to a similar conclusion myself."

"You have?" She felt a tear splash her cheek, a happy one this time, and didn't bother to wipe it away.

"Uh-huh." He caught the tear on the pad of his thumb. "Both my writing and my life work a lot better with a partner—as long as she's you."

Just a month ago that declaration would have been more than enough—she would have made it be enough—but a lot had changed in the past four weeks and most of the changes had happened inside her. She felt as though she'd climbed to the top of the mountain, faced down every demon she'd ever had and then climbed down again, stronger and more clear-eyed than she ever would have believed she could be. She didn't want to be Max's casual lover or his writing partner or some contemporary combination of the two. She wanted to be his partner in every way—his lover, his colleague, his best friend and, yes, his wife.

"Are you through?"

"Not hardly." He swallowed hard. "I thought that after losing Elaina, nothing, absolutely nothing, would have the power to scare me ever again, but I was wrong. Living without you this past month has been scary as hell for me. I miss you, Becka. I more than miss you—I love you and the thought of living the rest of my life without you in it scares the hell out of me. Say you'll marry me, Becka, and I promise I'll spend the rest of my life coming up with new adventures and new ways to make you happy."

"I don't need new adventures. All I want is a fresh start and the dazzling opportunity to be happy—with you."

"In that case, we'd better get to work. The clock on the screenplay is ticking, and I'm going to need some serious inspiration, in the form of you naked in my bed. I have that suite at the Chelsea through the weekend. You remember it, don't you?" He slanted her a sexy half smile.

Happy tears welling, Becky nodded. "But I'm not sure I can wait to get there. We just might have to make do with the backseat of a taxi—or perhaps a stalled elevator."

Max's arms went around her. "I like the way you think, Miss St. Claire." He pulled her against him and angled his face to hers.

"Just try to keep up, Mr. Maxwell." Locking her arms about his neck, Becky leaned into his kiss, feeling as though she'd finally come home.

Reaching for her gown's side zipper, Max whispered into her ear, "Think of this as the first chapter of the first book in a brand-new series."

Drowning in his deep blue gaze, she asked, "Will it be erotic romance, mystery or action-adventure?"

Max rolled down her zipper and slid a warm hand inside her gown. "Knowing us, I'd say all of the above."

Epilogue

SEATED ACROSS from one another at the linen-draped table, Angelina and Drake clinked champagne glasses. "Good thing we finally got that lot together, eh, Angie?"

Angelina nodded. "Your idea to stage that book launch party was bloody brilliant. It really saved the day—and the plot—from sinking. Without it, I don't know how we would have budged Becky out of D.C. or Max out of New Hampshire. They're both so bloody stubborn." She held out her glass. "Is there any more champers?"

He pulled the bottle of Cristal from the ice bucket and topped off both their glasses. "And no more brilliant than your notion of bringing the Elliot bloke on stage as a secondary character in the final chapters. Seeing him in that New York pub really sharpened the story arc, not to mention opened Becky's eyes to how much Max meant to her."

"Quite." Feeling a kindred spirit with her creator, Angelina smiled back. The dark passion she'd felt for Falco paled in comparison to the rich kaleidoscope of love, partnership and, yes, lust she shared with Drake, her unlikely leading man. The diamond-in-the-rough Aussie adventurer had stolen her heart—no small feat given that until recently she'd existed without one.

He captured her hand and pressed a kiss into her palm. "I venture to say our two creators are going to live happily ever after."

New soul aside, Angelina shook her head, her curtain of glossy black hair falling back into perfect place around her bare shoulders. "*Happily ever after* is the closing line for fairy tales, not mystery-erotica novels."

He lifted a dark blond eyebrow. "You mean *action-adventure* mystery-erotica novels, don't you?"

Rather than argue, she let out a sigh. He really was the most impossible fictional male creation—impossible to resist, that was. "The best a novel in any genre can manage is to end hopefully. These days a happy ending is never guaranteed."

"Is that so?" He took the champagne glass from her and reached for her hand. "There are bloody few guarantees in fiction or in life," he admitted, pressing her palm to the left side of his chest where his own newly issued heart announced his love for her with every fierce beat. "But when it comes to love, we can pledge to do our very best to love our partners with all our hearts and minds and bodies have to give. Surely we can manage that much at least?"

Smiling into Drake's earnest eyes, Angelina nodded. "Yes, love, that much we can manage—and perhaps a good deal more."

* * * * *

Turn the page for a sneak preview
of the first book in the new miniseries
DIAMONDS DOWN UNDER
from Silhouette Desire®,
VOWS & A VENGEFUL GROOM
by Bronwyn Jameson

Available January 2008
(SD #1843)

Silhouette Desire®
Always Powerful, Passionate and Provocative

Kimberley Blackstone didn't notice the waiting horde of media until it was too late. Flashbulbs exploded around her like a New Year's light show. She skidded to a halt, so abruptly her trailing suitcase all but overtook her.

This had to be a case of mistaken identity. Surely. Kimberley hadn't been on the paparazzi hit list for close to a decade, not since she'd estranged herself from her billionaire father and his headline-hungry diamond business.

But no, it was *her* name they called. *Her* face was the focus of a swarm of lenses that circled her like avid hornets. Her heart started to pound with fear-fueled adrenaline.

What did they want?

What was going on?

With a rising sense of bewilderment she scanned the crowd for a clue, and her gaze fastened on a tall, leonine figure forcing his way to the front. A tall, familiar figure.

Her head came up in stunned recognition, and their gazes collided across the sea of heads before the cameras erupted with another barrage of flashes, this time right in her exposed face.

Blinded by the flashbulbs—and by the shock of that momentary eye-meet—Kimberley didn't realize his intent until he'd forged his way to her side, possibly by the sheer strength of his personality. She felt his arm wrap around her shoulder, pulling her into the protective shelter of his body, allowing her no time to object. No chance to lift her hands to ward him off.

In the space of a hastily drawn breath, she found herself plastered knee-to-nose against six feet two inches of hard-bodied male.

Ric Perrini.

Her lover for ten torrid weeks, her husband for ten tumultuous days.

Her ex for ten tranquil years.

After all this time, he should not have felt so familiar but, oh dear, he did. She knew the scent of that body and its lean, muscular strength. She knew its heat and its slick power and every response it could draw from hers.

She also recognized the ease with which he'd taken control of the moment and the decisiveness of his deep voice when it rumbled close to her ear. "I have a car waiting outside. Is this your only luggage?"

Kimberley nodded. "I assume you will tell me," she said tightly, "what this welcome party is all about."

"Not while the welcome party is within earshot. No."

Barking a request for the cameramen to stand aside, Perrini took her hand and pulled her into step with his ground-eating stride. Kimberley let him, because he was right, damn his arrogant, Italian-suited hide. Despite the speed with which he whisked her across the airport terminal, she could almost feel the hot breath of the pursuing media on her back.

This was neither the time nor the place for explanations. Inside his car, however, she would get answers.

Now that the initial shock had been blown away—by the haste of their retreat, by the heat of her gathering indignation, by the rush of adrenaline fired by Perrini's presence and the looming verbal battle—her brain was starting to tick over. This had to be her father's doing. And if it was a Howard Blackstone publicity ploy, then it had to be about Blackstone Diamonds, the company that ruled his life.

The knowledge made her chest tighten with a familiar ache of disillusionment.

She'd known her father would be flying in from Sydney for today's opening of the newest in his chain of exclusive, high-end jewelry boutiques. The opulent shopfront sat adjacent to the rival business where Kimberley worked. No coincidence, she thought bitterly, just as it was no coincidence that Ric Perrini was here in Auckland ushering her to his car.

Perrini was Howard Blackstone's right-hand man, second in command at Blackstone Diamonds, a legacy of his short-lived marriage to the boss's daughter. No doubt her father had sent him to fetch her; the question was *why?*

* * * * *

*Get swept away down under with the glitz
and glamour of the Blackstone empire as
Kimberley tries to determine the real reason
behind her "reunion" with Ric....*

Look for
VOWS & A VENGEFUL GROOM
by Bronwyn Jameson,
in stores January 2008.

Silhouette®
Desire

When Kimberley Blackstone's father is
presumed dead, Kimberley is required to take
over the helm of Blackstone Diamonds. She
has to work closely with her ex, Ric Perrini, to
battle not only the press, but also the fierce
attraction still sizzling between them. Does Ric
feel the same...or is it the power her share of
Blackstone Diamonds will provide him as he
battles for boardroom supremacy.

Look for

VOWS &
A VENGEFUL GROOM
by

BRONWYN
JAMESON

Available January wherever you buy books

Visit Silhouette Books at www.eHarlequin.com   SD76843

nocturne™

Jachin Black always knew he was an outcast.
Not only was he a vampire, he was a vampire
banished from the Sanguinas society. Jachin, forced
to survive among mortals, is determined to buy
his way back into the clan one day.

Ariel Swanson, debut author of a vampire novel, could
be the ticket he needs to get revenge and take his
rightful place among the Sanguinas again. However,
the unsuspecting mortal woman has no idea of the
dark and sensual path she will be forced to travel.

Look for

RESURRECTION: THE BEGINNING

by

PATRICE MICHELLE

Available January 2008 wherever you buy books.

REQUEST YOUR FREE BOOKS!

2 FREE NOVELS PLUS 2 FREE GIFTS!

HARLEQUIN®

Blaze®

Red-hot reads!

To fulfill his father's dying wish,
Greek tycoon Christos Niarchos must
marry Ava Monroe, a woman who
betrayed him years ago. But his soon-to-
be-wife has a secret that could rock
more than his passion for her.

Look for

THE GREEK TYCOON'S SECRET HEIR

by

KATHERINE GARBERA

Available January wherever you buy books

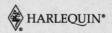

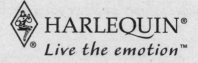

COMING NEXT MONTH

#369 ONE WILD WEDDING NIGHT Leslie Kelly
Blaze Encounters—One blazing book, five sizzling stories
Girls just want to have fun.... And for five bridesmaids, their friend's wedding night is the perfect time for the rest of them to let loose. After all, love is in the air. And so, they soon discover, is great sex...

#370 MY GUILTY PLEASURE Jamie Denton
The Martini Dares, Bk. 3
The trial is supposed to come first for the legal-eagle duo of Josephine Winfield and Sebastian Stanhope. But the long hours—and sizzling attraction—are taking their toll. Is it a simple case of lust in the first degree? Or dare she think there's more?

#371 BARE NECESSITIES Marie Donovan
A sexy striptease ignites an intense affair between longtime friends Adam Hale, a play-by-the-rules financial trader, and Bridget Weiss, a break-all-the-rules lingerie designer. But what will happen to their friendship now that their secret lust for each other is no longer a secret?

#372 DOES SHE DARE? Tawny Weber
Blush
When no-nonsense Isabel Santos decides to make a "man plan," she never dreams she'll have a chance to try it out with the guy who inspired it—her high school crush, hottie Dante Luciano. He's still everything she's ever wanted. And she'll make sure she's everything he'll *never* forget....

#373 AT YOUR COMMAND Julie Miller
Marry in haste? Eighteen months ago Captain Zachariah Clark loved, married, then left Becky Clark. Now Zach's back home, and he's suddenly realized he knows nothing about his wife except her erogenous zones. Then again, great sex isn't such a bad place to start....

#374 THE TAO OF SEX Jade Lee
Extreme
Landlord Tracy Williams wants to sell her building, almost as much as she wants her tenant, sexy Nathan Gao. But when Nathan puts a sale at risk by giving Tantric classes, Tracy has to bring a stop to them. That is, until he offers her some private *hands-on* instruction...

www.eHarlequin.com

HBCNM1207